QUARTER PAST MIDNIGHT

Jan Prestopnik

Best Wishes!
Jan Prestopnik

QUARTER PAST MIDNIGHT

A Novel
A Ghost Story
A Tale of Forgiveness

This book is a work of fiction. Events, names, incidents, and locales are products of the author's imagination or are used fictitiously. Any resemblance to actual events, locales, or persons, living or dead, is entirely coincidental.

To Rich,
my husband and very best friend,
with love.

"Fear not that sound
  like wind in the trees:
It is only their call
  that comes on the breeze;
Fear not the shudder
  that seems to pass:
It is only the tread of their feet
  on the grass;
Fear not the drip of the bough
  as you stoop:
It is only the touch
  of their hands that grope —"

Edith Wharton

Chapter 1

THERE IT WAS AGAIN.

Aaron Latimer stared through the drizzle, across the black lake at the mountain on the opposite shore. He knew he'd seen the twinkling light last night, hadn't imagined it, and here it was again. He pulled the heavy old quilt tighter around his shoulders and grasped his mug of hot tea more firmly to keep from spilling it. He was determined to keep his eyes on that light.

Yes, it was definitely moving now, to his left, down the opposite shore, in front of the only other cabin on Spruce Lake. The light hovered briefly, then slowly returned. It stopped, rose a foot or so, became still for several minutes, and then vanished. Aaron kept his eyes wide open, forcing himself not to blink. When his eyes began to water, he closed them briefly, then opened them again. The light was gone now, but it didn't matter; he knew he had seen it.

The chill air seemed still at first, but Aaron was attuned to the night noises surrounding his old family camp, the rustlings in the dead leaves around the porch, the sudden whine of a mosquito near his ear. And something else, a sound that didn't fit.

He slapped at his cheek, connected, and rubbed the dead bug from his face. The far off lonely moan of a loon interrupted the night, and the leaves overhead whispered quietly, maybe with the wind, maybe from the quick beating wings of an owl. A stealthy stirring in the underbrush suggested a fox or raccoon searching for food as the rain dripped from the eaves in staccato points, splattering the rocks below. Still he stood on the long porch, listening, peering at the dense black across the water.

He could almost make out his SUV in the parking area below, jammed in crookedly, the result of his irritation when he'd arrived the day before. Connie had no right to disrupt their lives this way just because he'd accepted this photo assignment. Aaron grimaced, remembering his hasty rush to leave their Syracuse house. Connie had already gone, so there was no-one to appreciate his wrath, which just compounded it. He recalled his impotent rage, throwing his belongings into the SUV and backing out of the driveway with a squeal of tires, a nice show for the neighbors on their quiet, dignified street.

He had calmed somewhat before he'd gone very far; there was no point having a smash-up just to prove his anger. But when he thought about her leaving him for the summer, his hurt had surfaced all over again. Stepping on the gas, laying on the horn when that idiot in the pickup truck had tried to pass him on a curve – he admitted he'd vented his annoyance childishly. He had burst into the parking area at camp, slammed the cargo door shut after grabbing his clothes and gear, and stormed up the long path to the cabin. Even here at the quiet, still lake, it had taken some time for his blood to cool.

The rain dripped steadily, plunking on the heavy wooden railing, puddling up in small black bubbles, splashing back onto his boots. Connie wasn't here; no one was here, and it wasn't going to prove anything to stay upset with her. He breathed in deeply, glad now that he had remained calm when Connie left for Saratoga, grateful that she hadn't witnessed his temper tantrum. The display had been unlike him, and he was smart enough to recognize its ineffectiveness. They would ride this out. She would be back.

He missed her more than he was angry at her now. And he was hurt and resentful that she wasn't standing here beside him.

The porch he stood on stretched fifty feet along the entire front of the cabin. Solid log beams had supported the massive porch roof through a hundred brutal Adirondack winters and still kept sturdy guard. The camp itself, poised importantly on the steep, rocky mountainside, overlooked the water below. In daylight, the view would open to a vista of Spruce Lake, taking in the north and south shores on either side and Spruce Mountain towering on the opposite eastern shore.

Now, in the night, all was black.

The rain had picked up; Aaron could hear its steady beat tapping persistently against the porch roof over his head. The wind's low moaning chased through the high treetops and blew through the latticework apron under the porch. Even with the quilt wrapped snugly over his warmest jacket, the chill crept through him. But Aaron remained there, huddled under the layers, and stared at the sky. The pinpricks of starlight that usually seemed bigger and closer out here in the wilderness were invisible tonight, hidden by black clouds in a black, stormy sky.

A log in the camp fireplace burst, cracked, and fell, bringing him inside. It was warmer before the fire, and he shrugged off the quilt, letting it drop onto a well-worn armchair. The electric clock said twelve fifteen, just a little past midnight, the start of a new day, time to be in bed. But Aaron wasn't tired.

The welcome smell of the burning fire mixed with the chemical scents of the cleaning agents he had used the day before. He had spent the better part of an afternoon sweeping the floors, washing and setting aside the dishes he would use and cleaning off furniture, banishing a winter's worth of stale dust. He had opened all the windows and doors, shaken out a couple of blankets and sponged out the kitchen cabinets in preparation for his two month stay. It had been therapeutic, a way to order his environment, to force his body into useful work, and a cleansing for his mind and heart, as well.

The cabin looked clean now and felt comfortable, and he was ready to enjoy his summer holed up here doing what he liked best, writing and taking pictures. When Connie changed her mind and came to the lake after all, he would welcome her without rancor. At least he would try.

He picked up a straight, sturdy birch log, as big around as his wrist and as long as his forearm, and poked at the fire, stirring up ashes and coaxing flame from the sooty bed of charred wood. He would let the fire burn until it died a natural death and see if he could get back to the writing.

He just didn't understand Connie lately. If she had come along, the whole retreat would have been perfect, but she loathed the wilderness and found no joy in stalking a deer through the forest or wading among tiny fish that nibbled and tickled at her toes. He wished he could call her, but of course it was too late at night for that. Anyway, he knew her cell phone was off, the only number at which he could reach her and their six- year-old daughter, Egan. When they needed to talk, Connie had said, she would call him. And he could always leave a message if he wanted to.

Aaron swallowed tense anger and gazed up at a row of trophies greasy with dust on a shelf above a bookcase. He had won them in school – football, track, others. He'd been a three season athlete and was proud of those trophies. He exhaled a breath and poked the slow-burning fire again. Damn Connie. Nothing meant anything without her. He was used to calling the shots himself, and it irked him that she wanted to force a separation when they saw so little of each other already. Well, he had to go along with it. He loved his wife, so he would acquiesce. This time, it would all be played by Connie's rules.

His typewriter sat on a big oak library table near the fireplace, an electric floor lamp plugged in next to it. At home in Syracuse, he would have used the computer and enjoyed all the tools and toys of modern life - the Internet for research, clean, crisp sheets of white copy paper for his drafts, emailed submissions for the publisher.

He would have used a digital camera, too, for at least some of his photographs, and downloaded the photos. Reframing was easier that way, and any imperfections could be corrected easily, but he preferred to create this article without technology, the old-fashioned way.

After publication, he anticipated a series of lectures, at least that's what the publisher had promised. So harkening back to the 1930's would keep things authentic. The idea of 'roughing it' was in keeping with the theme of his article in progress. The clanky old typewriter and thirty-five mm. camera amused him. He enjoyed creating the persona of the eccentric backwoods writer. Even though this made Connie smile, he knew she was proud of his success. They both liked the fact that he could afford to be eccentric.

He had brought plenty of paper and a good supply of correction fluid, pencils, erasers, and even the new typewriter ribbon he had sought in three stores before a surprised shopkeeper had finally managed to order him one. He was short on the small, handy notebooks he used for field research, but felt sure he could pick up something similar at the lake store. The musty camp Colliers' Encyclopedia, his Peterson guide books, and three years' worth of Adirondack wilderness magazines were stacked on the bookshelf nearby. And he had his camera, tripod, and plenty of film. The woods themselves, his imagination, and a driving interest in completing the photo essay rounded out his necessary gear. All the tools of the trade were in place.

As the fire died slowly, Aaron sat in the hard-backed chair typing quickly. The data he had gathered that day, while he tromped around in the woods behind the camp, provided plenty of fuel for the introduction of his article on edible wild plants, and he felt confident, too, that the photographs he had taken so far would show well in print. The photo essay, although only in its beginning stages, was already taking form.

A glance at the clock on his table showed Aaron that one o'clock had come and gone. He stretched his arms and yawned loudly. The fire was a spent pile of glowing ash, and a chill was creeping into the old timbers of the camp. He roused himself and went to the kitchen, checked the stove burners, and turned off the light. He poked at the fireplace embers, spreading them to cool, and stepped out onto the porch for a last breath of cold, clean mountain air.

Across the lake, Spruce Mountain loomed high and wide, black as pitch, the little camp at its base dwarfed and invisible in the murky dark. He wondered again about the light he had seen, two nights running now, and both times at around a quarter past midnight. He would canoe over the next day to see if there were signs of life at the other camp, an unexpected resident maybe, or teen-agers straying onto the Posted property, camping out on the adjacent land owned by the state of New York.

Aaron locked the kitchen door behind him, secured the living room door, and went up to bed, burying himself in a pile of old olive army blankets and faded handmade quilts. His last thought before sleep was of Connie, the way he wished she were, strolling with him through the woods, laughing playfully at the antics of a chipmunk, holding a red eft in her hand while it tried to squirm away.

In his dreams.

He rolled over and waited for sleep to come.

Chapter 2

THERE WAS LITTLE POINT in carrying his cell phone here at camp - there was no signal - so Aaron hadn't even bothered to remove it from his car. But the squat, black rotary phone on top of the bookcase in the cabin was connected, and Connie had the number. It would do for the summer.

Aaron almost hated to be away from the building; the writing was the part he really enjoyed, and it would not accomplish itself. Plus, he might miss Connie's call, and as he tracked a doe in the afternoon shadows or walked further into the woods to find a specimen of white trillium or bunchberry, he always wondered in the back of his mind if she had chosen that moment to phone.

He hadn't brought an answering machine; it wouldn't be true to the image he was creating here at the lake, but he admitted there had been a few times when he'd wondered if that was a mistake. Why hadn't Connie called yet? He had left enough messages on her voicemail.

The morning sun had dried the night's rain on the dock and splashed gold rays over its weathered gray boards. Aaron stood watching a school of minnows flick beneath the surface of the water, then looked up and across at the cottage on the opposite shore.

Spruce Lake was small, about four miles in circumference, less than a mile from end to end, and a quarter of a mile straight across from the Latimer cabin to the only other camp on the lake.

Only three parties could claim ownership to the shores of the lake. One was the Latimer family, of which Aaron's little Egan was the youngest. The other two were New York State, with its 'Forever Wild' designation, and the Dunns, who had once owned the camp across the way. Aaron knew that the Dunn camp bordered state land on one side and met up with his own parcel on the other. Likewise, his own land bordered the Dunns' on the left and the state's on the right. If the property lines were to extend into the middle of the lake, it would create a neat, tri-cut pie, each of the three landowners getting a rough third of the whole.

He was curious about the flickering light he'd seen the past two midnights, so putting thoughts of Connie aside, he climbed the dirt path from the dock to the parking area, hoisted his canoe from the top of his vehicle, carried it down to the lake's edge, and slid it into the water. The early sun crinkled the still surface with tiny glittering points. Aaron looked at his own pristine waterfront and then again at the small brown cottage across the lake, visible now in daylight.

Kids must be camping in the state forest and trespassing onto the Dunn property. As far as he knew, no one had stayed in that camp for years; he felt a responsibility to be neighborly, to check on things for the absent owners.

Aaron's paddle dipped quietly, and good, clean air filled his lungs. In minutes, he was floating alongside the state land that stretched nearly a mile down one shore.

Aaron had never bothered to listen to his father's reminiscences about their sole neighbor on Spruce Lake. He remembered hearing that the family never stayed here anymore, and he recalled a vague story about a death. A young person, a teenage boy or girl, had drowned, he thought. After that, the whole clan had fled Spruce Lake. He wasn't even sure if they still owned the deserted cottage.

As a small boy, he'd been brought to the lake for the occasional Fourth of July picnic. His brother Chris had always begged to bring a friend along. While Aaron had tramped through the woods and swum in the icy, breath-snatching waters, Chris and his friend would remain on the sidelines, reading comic books, maybe rowing the little wooden rowboat down to the channel, sitting around. Aaron couldn't stand to just sit around.

Chris was a year older, but Aaron had always been able to outlift, outjump, and outdistance his only brother. Chris's natural talent for crunching numbers had been impressive at a young age, but Aaron had been the athlete, always the admired, the winner. In their early teens, a rift had developed and they now made no effort to see each other.

Why was he thinking about Chris now? Aaron shrugged the distasteful memories away and glanced back at the family camp that he and Chris now owned jointly. Had Chris even been here in the last few years? Aaron didn't know.

And he certainly didn't care.

The Latimer camp was picturesque, but it harbored memories that Aaron preferred to forget. He had dreaded being here during his high school years, and in his later teens had flatly refused to come. He had managed to construct a nice life for himself, and if it weren't for the hefty fee for his photo essay, would he be admiring the primitive accommodations nearly as much? He knew he wouldn't be. He wouldn't even be here.

But staying at the camp was free, comfortable, and familiar. The woods were handy and he knew the terrain. A long commute from Syracuse - or even Saratoga - might have been possible, but why bother when he could step outside each morning and begin work immediately?

No one said he had to love it here.

Aaron pushed the introspections aside and canoed closer to shore. He was not a man who belabored his feelings. He had reached his mid-thirties acknowledging them and then letting them go, and he was successful, wasn't he?

Yes, as a writer and photographer. He enjoyed the attention when someone occasionally recognized his byline, and he had no shortage of good contract offers for his nature articles.

It was only his personal life that had hit a snag. He grumbled his irritation with Connie and forged ahead, dipping his paddle deeply, hugging the shoreline.

The Dunn camp, he could see now, was definitely abandoned. Painted brown years before, it had succumbed to neglect. Animals had clearly made it a shelter from the weather; ripped screens and gnawed siding confirmed that the inhabitants were, these days, four-footed, and even from his boat, Aaron detected the acrid smell of nesting rodents. As he glided past, he could make out the rough wooden sign hanging by one nail above the peeling door: Dunn.

He remembered that the family had some children. He recalled rowing by as a teenager, dragged reluctantly to the lake to vacation with his family. He had seen kids splashing in the shallow water while toddlers played on the beach and adults sat on the now disintegrating dock. Perhaps those people had been the Dunn family. He hadn't set eyes on them, if that's who they were, in something like twenty years.

Drifting, Aaron glanced over the shape of the Dunn cabin -

squat, two low stories, a porch overlooking the lake, of course. A corner of the structure had caved in under the weight of a fallen beech tree, knocking out part of one wall below it. The other walls still stood, but were bowed and ramshackle. The crooked fireplace chimney looked on the verge of collapse, and bricks were scattered on the weedy grass. Along the waterfront, ferns and thornbushes fought for territory, and the wooden dock sections, pulled up haphazardly, rotted among vegetation. The green water curled up softly onto a scattering of rocks; wet sand suggested a neglected natural beach.

Aaron pulled his boat in closer. He was sure the light the night before had shone from right about here, but there was no sign of the waterfront having been disturbed, no footprints in the weedy sand, no depressed grasses where feet had trod. He looked again at the Dunn camp. The irony of dilapidated Posted signs made him grimace. Surely no person could venture into that hovel. Just the hint of rancidness in the air would be enough to keep one from trespassing.

He dipped his paddle into the clear water and turned the canoe, starting back. He would watch again tonight. If light flickered a third time, maybe he would investigate further.

Paddling back across the lake, Aaron examined his own camp with a critical eye. Sprawling, built high on the mammoth rocks that defined the property, the camp settled majestically on the side of Colson Mountain. Ferns and tiger lilies danced on the hillside below it.

The camp with its long, welcoming porch and the woodshed nearby were authentic Adirondack, of wooden construction, as cold as the outdoors in winter, a cool retreat in summer. And behind the camp, Colson Mountain soared up and away, bristling with beech trees and firs, stately maples, wide-trunked oaks, and pines and spruces that towered over the dark forest, majestic arrows pointing toward the sky.

His father's family had owned the land for over a hundred years; the date of construction was carved over the kitchen door. The rustic property had a certain value, he knew, but the knowledge did nothing to lift Aaron's spirits. What flaw in him, he wondered, made him avoid facing a past that was over and done with? Ironically, the single event that had shaped him into the person he'd become was also the one memory of Spruce Lake that he would never talk about.

He exhaled loudly, urging the canoe back to his own shore.

Aaron prided himself on his ability to complete one day at a time, to plan each step in his carefully arranged life. In his ordered existence, there was no slot for inner turmoil, for the tensions that rode just below the surface. Today, though, here at Spruce Lake, those tensions seemed about ready to erupt.

And Connie had left him; that was the worst thing. She had left him, and she said it was his own fault. And she had made it pretty clear that it just might possibly be for good.

Aaron squelched an unexpected sadness and reassured himself that Connie was wrong. Of course she was wrong. Before the summer was out, she would realize that.

Chapter 3

HE HAD MET HER at a book signing, on a beautiful, sunny, fall day when he'd been trapped for three hours behind a table in a godforsaken downtown Syracuse bookstore. He had been to Syracuse once or twice before, found it a dirty, unkempt city, and hadn't particularly looked forward to this signing. But it was necessary. And - now that his name was becoming more familiar to readers and lovers of nature writing - he was curious to see if he would be recognized. That, he admitted, would make the tedious drive from Hyde Park, up and over on the New York State Thruway, bearable.

The line had not snaked throughout the store lobby and on down the street, as his agent had joked that it might. But there had been enough people so that Aaron felt successful. His copies were stacked on the table before him; more were nestled in a carton behind the table, just in case. Happily, 'just in case' had turned into 'definitely,' and Connie had been one of those later visitors, coming across his table when he was alone and unsought. She was pretty, with light brown hair and a sophisticated way of dressing. Her flat shoes were practical, and her gray pants and ivory sweater made her look wholesome and smart.

She was alone, balancing packages from her afternoon of shopping. He watched her approach; there were few people about, and he felt pleased when she wandered over to the table. She placed her packages on the floor beside her for a moment while she picked up a copy of *Heart of the River*, his treatise on the Hudson and its history. She leafed through, landing on the back blurb and his picture. He saw her sneaking a peek at him, then back at the picture to see if the photo had captured him accurately.

She looked at it so long that he finally felt uncomfortable.

"Well?" he said, chuckling self-consciously.

She looked up from the photograph and into his eyes with her own startling blue ones. "You're better in person," she grinned, "plus I think I like the jacket and tie better than the flannel shirt." He had laughed, accepting her subtle criticism of his intentionally casual publicity photo.

She replaced the book on the stack and looked at him frankly. "Now, tell me three good reasons why I would want to buy this book," she said.

He had risen to the challenge and given her four. "One, it's a great price. There are so many things you *can't* get for twenty-six ninety-five."

"A decent bottle of wine. A ticket to the Syracuse game. A wind chime for my porch." She ticked the items off on her fingers.

"Two, everybody likes autographed copies, and this autograph could be worth something someday."

She glanced at him, nodding, agreeing . . . maybe.

"Three, the author is an expert in his field. And four," he continued before she could rebut, "you can look at my appealing likeness any time you want. Plaid flannel shirt notwithstanding."

She considered briefly, then smiled at him. "You may be an expert in the field, but honestly, it's not a field that interests me particularly."

He was surprised and felt slightly deflated; books on natural habitats, animals, plants, ecology, usually drew a very specific, even devoted buyer. Why had she stopped then?

She grinned again, and her cheek dimpled. "But a friend of mine loves this kind of thing. I guess I could sneak this out of his bookcase and see that appealing likeness whenever I need a fix." She handed him the same top copy from the stack and dug in her handbag for her wallet.

He opened the book to the title page. "What would you like me to write?"

"To Connie," she said. "C-o-n-n-i-e." He inscribed it obediently while she counted out bills.

"What's his name, Conrad? Connor?"

"His name's Blaine. I'm Connie."

"So you're buying two copies?" He pulled a second volume from the pile and opened it to the title page, pen poised for signing. A challenge.

"Don't press your luck," she laughed. "Blaine can borrow

mine if he wants to."

"I appreciate the purchase," Aaron said, "but why buy when you're not even interested in the topic?"

She flipped the book open to his picture and held it before him. The professional shot of his own head and shoulders stared back, broad shoulders and longish, wavy brown hair, a not bad-looking, confident face with a good nose and clear, intelligent eyes. She was right. The nonchalance of the plaid shirt was a bit much. He couldn't even say that someone had talked him into it. It had been his own foolish idea. He wondered if she saw him as pretentious.

He laughed again, meeting her eyes. "I'm pretty sure that picture's not worth twenty-six ninety-five. I'm afraid you've made a bad bargain."

She smiled, thanked him, picked up her bags, and turned away. The bookstore was still thrumming with people, but he had only a half dozen copies left. He made a split-second decision, and called after her. "Connie?"

She turned.

"I was just about to take a break. Maybe get a cup of coffee. Would you . . . ."

She was clearly surprised. Then: "It'll take a lot of coffee to reimburse me," she said dryly, "but I accept."

The cup of coffee had stretched into a sandwich and dessert, and then a stroll around Armory Square, where they peered into storefronts and poked through a secondhand shop. Back outside, the autumn breeze puffed Connie's shoulder length hair out along her collar, and he saw that she had small ears, flat and perfectly shaped. He would never forget the moment he had noticed that detail about her, the sun splattering around her, glinting off street signs and store windows. They discussed rivers and books, his work and hers, and the purchases she had made that day.

"I have a friend's wedding coming up," she had said, and she set her bags down near a lamppost and pulled out a sturdy cardboard jeweler's box, opened it carefully, and took out a stemmed crystal goblet. He could see its mate inside the box. "It's her pattern," Connie said. "Isn't it gorgeous?" The glassware glistened in the sun, bright, flashing stabs sparkling off the polished rims. She held it up to the light and looked at it. He saw sunny highlights glowing in her light brown hair. He agreed it was beautiful.

13

They stopped in a coffee shop for a soda and lingered while he told her about his work, places he had seen in his travels, people he had met.

She was a middle school math teacher in the city, had been at it for four years, and loved her job and her students.

He decided to ask her about her friend Blaine and felt sheepish when she immediately saw through him. "Yes, we're pretty close," she said with a grin.

He looked at her, waiting. She laughed at him, and her blue eyes sparkled. "I'm not seeing him exclusively, if that's what you want to know."

She had accompanied him back to the bookstore, he carrying her bags, and she had watched him load the last of his unsold books into his car. He had taken her phone number and, two hours later, had called her from his hotel, feeling foolish, unable to wait any longer. He was happy to find her home and receptive. She admitted her reasons for buying the book. He had looked so eager, and she wanted to help.

Aaron was surprised his Syracuse signing had resulted in meeting a woman that he liked so much, and even more surprised that his feelings for her deepened so quickly. She was smart, sensible, and kind. He admired her calm control of her own life and saw reflected there a sweeter, more pleasing version of his own need to organize and manipulate.

He wanted to be with her every day, and when his work took him out of state for days or weeks, he was impatient to get back to Hyde Park, impatient for the four hour drive to Syracuse so he could see her. He was twenty-six, and so was she, and he hadn't met anyone before that he cared much about. He had been very careful with relationships since his one horribly botched high school romance. But Connie Beckett was different; he fell in love with her quickly and pursued her with the one track mind with which he pursued all things he wanted.

He told his parents he had met the girl he intended to marry, packed up his Hyde Park apartment, and took a flat in Syracuse, a ten minute drive from her apartment. It didn't matter where he lived; he could write most anywhere. He talked her into showing him the city and discovered that there were things about Syracuse that he liked after all. And he claimed her, followed her, refused to be put off.

Somehow, in the days and weeks and months following that fateful book signing, Blaine had faded into obscurity, and Connie had become the most important influence in Aaron's life.

And now this. She had taken Egan and fled to Saratoga, leaving him no forwarding address. He needed to be at Spruce Lake to complete research for the article, but he hadn't planned on two months of solitude.

"You're never here, Aaron," she had said to him, throwing clothes into a suitcase while he sat forlornly on their bed, watching her pack. "You leave whenever you feel like it."

"It's my work, Con."

"I know it's your work. And I've tried to be understanding of that, but it isn't any good. You're here for a few days, then gone again. A week in Colorado, a week and a half in Boston, three days somewhere else. Now you're off to the lake."

"I asked you to come with me," he said.

"We agreed to take Egan to Saratoga this summer. She can't stop talking about going to the ballet."

"We could probably take a day and go to Saratoga. It's not that far from camp."

"No, we're not *taking a day*," she said. She gritted her teeth. "We have a beautiful apartment reserved for the summer. And anyway, I detest the lake." She folded a pair of linen pants into the suitcase and looked at him in exasperation. "I detest what our life has become, and it's terrible for Egan. You keep missing things, her soccer games, her concert at school. You never even met her kindergarten teacher last year."

"Yes, I did. Didn't I?" He wracked his brain. A fuzzy image of a slightly overweight woman with a blonde bob crept into Aaron's mind. But maybe that was the music teacher. Maybe he hadn't met the kindergarten teacher. But did that really matter? Egan was an excellent student. "Those are little things, Connie," he'd said.

"No, Aaron, they aren't. To her they're big things. They're the biggest things in her life, and her own father isn't interested in hanging around long enough-"

"That's not true." He was irritated. "You make it sound like it's intentional. I can't help where my work sends me or when."

"I think you should help it, Aaron." She zipped the suitcase and placed it by the bedroom door. "You made the official commitment to be married, and you have a daughter. Now you need to make the emotional jump to stick around a little more." Her eyes flashed. "No, make that a lot more. Egan and I have to be first, not a sideline. It bothers me a lot that you're off again

15

doing what you feel like doing, without thinking of us, even after we made summer plans together. Things have to change if it's going to work, Aaron." She flounced out of the room and went to Egan's room to help her pack.

Two hours later they were gone. Destination: Saratoga. Address: Unknown. Oblivious to his needs, she'd gone ahead and moved into the place they'd sublet for two months. He didn't know the address, of course. He hadn't paid attention when she'd made the reservations in the first place.

It annoyed him. Who did she think was funding this vacation apartment of hers anyway?

He stopped those thoughts. That wasn't fair. She was a professional in her own right, even if the teacher's salary she had earned before Egan was a fourth of what he earned in a year. Everything they had belonged to both of them. He didn't begrudge her the apartment or the ballet tickets or anything else she might decide to spend money on this summer, but he felt like some kind of a convicted criminal that she couldn't even trust him with her new address. And she refused to get a phone line because she was sure he'd try to trace her.

Well, of course he would.

"How am I supposed to reach you in an emergency?" he had asked, exasperated.

"Call my cell phone."

"That's ridiculous, Connie. You never have it on."

"No, but you can always leave a message if it's important."

"This is crazy," he told her. "You are really overreacting to a few little business trips."

She turned on him, flinging aside the stack of shirts she had been about to toss into her bag. "Overreacting! How dare you! *You* see what it's like to be the one left behind! Let me know how you like trying to get in touch with me and finding out that I don't bother with phone messages until three days later."

"That happened maybe once."

"That happens nearly every time you leave!"

"If I find out where you are I'm going to come after you, Connie," he said.

"Which is exactly why I won't tell you, Aaron. If you want to know where we're staying, come with us." Her voice softened and she sat down beside him on the bed. "Look, a summer apart might be good for all of us. We need to do some serious thinking about where we stand." She would call him, she said; he would certainly want to stay in touch with Egan, at least she hoped so. At the end of the summer, they would see how they both felt.

Well, he was three days into his summer of solitude, he hadn't even heard yet from Connie, and he already knew exactly how he felt. Soul searching was new to him, and emotional gymnastics gave him a headache, but he was very sure of one thing. He missed his wife and he missed his child, and he wanted them back. Maybe Connie needed two months to be sure, but he didn't. He loved them, and he wanted them to know.

It sure would be great if Connie could bother to pick up the phone and call, so he could tell her that.

Chapter 4

AARON HAD DETERMINED that the light was visible each night at a little after midnight and never at any other time. When he stood on the porch and peered across the lake during the day or in the early evening, he was disappointed. Sometimes he ate dinner sitting in one of the old painted rockers that lined the porch, watching the opposite shore with wonder, but seeing nothing. When he canoed near the Dunn camp during the day, there were never signs of life. It was only at a little after midnight that the light would appear, and he would watch for a while from his porch, entranced, until it moved and then flickered out, and all was pitch again. It had to be kids, teenagers camping, fooling around over there on the opposite shore. But at the same time each night? And wouldn't kids make noise if they were partying?

He stood on the porch on the fifth night. It was twelve ten. His eyes were bleary from writing, his body aching from climbing over rocks in the damp, slippery woods, searching for the elusive roseroot that he hoped would comprise the next section of the article. He knew it was unusual to find roseroot this far north, but he had read recently that someone had discovered it growing in the lower Adirondacks. If he could find and identify it with certainty, it would be a kudos for his article.

Unfortunately, he hadn't found roseroot, but he had managed to slip on a mossy rock and wrench his knee. He wondered now, as he felt the dull throbbing, if he would need to take something for the pain after all. He shifted his weight to the other foot, defying the ache that pulsed in his leg.

When he heard the crying begin, he felt his shoulder muscles relax and realized he hadn't even known he was tensing them. Yes, he'd expected it - the slow, childlike whimper, an unsteady moan that caught his attention and mimicked the wind in the trees. He knew, though, that it wasn't the wind. He had heard the cry before, even on still, silent nights, and it had chilled him.

Finally, he could make out the light across the lake flickering, moving up the beach. He could predict the movements.

He had told himself that if he saw it again, he would investigate, and he already held his jacket and a flashlight he'd found in the kitchen closet. His boat was ready, beached near the dock below. Favoring his right knee, he hobbled down the path and launched his canoe into the deep, black water.

He glided silently across the lake, the slight breeze rippling the water's surface and pushing him swiftly toward the opposite shore. He could see the light moving up the waterfront, then stopping for several minutes, just as it had on previous nights. The high, unearthly trill of a loon startled him, and he let out a breath. It was important to be quiet, although he wasn't sure why. To hide his movements, he paddled silently toward the state land adjacent to the Dunn property. He angled his boat in and, half hidden beneath overhanging pine branches, moved the canoe silently up the shoreline toward the light.

The light moved in the darkness, coming back toward him. He focused on it. Was it a flashlight? A flame? As he stared through the inky night, a form took shape slowly. A body, human, erect, not tall. Okay, then, teenagers trespassing. He watched as the figure, a girl with long hair, raised a lantern, a box of gleaming glass panels separated by strips of polished metal. The flame inside flickered brightly, casting ghostly shadows on the trees along the water's edge.

She was wearing a pale gown of some sort and walking toward him. As he hovered beneath the overhanging boughs, Aaron shivered in his lightweight jacket and pulled it closer around him. He could see her shadowed face. By the light of the lantern, she looked very young. But where were her friends? Where was the rest of the party?

When her face became more visible in the lantern's light, Aaron was surprised at the pain etched there. Her eyes were squeezed shut in crying, and as he listened, a low sound escaped her throat. The breeze lifted her long hair slightly, playing with it in the darkness. She turned her head, looking out toward the lake, and then stepped into the water.

Aaron gasped. He rose slightly from the caned seat of his canoe, meaning to rescue her if she should fall on the scattered rocks or stumble into the cold water. Pain wrenched his injured knee. The girl stopped and looked in his direction, gazing past him toward the channel at the far end of the lake. He seated himself again quietly, his little boat rocking slightly; he grabbed a tree limb for support.

The black water swished around the hem of her skirt, billowing it up around her ankles, frothing it on the surface of the water. After a moment, she lowered her lantern and turned back toward the desolate camp, stepping through the tangled growth on the water's edge.

He watched her go through the trees and up the rickety steps of the cabin. Before she reached the door, her light was extinguished.

Night sounds encroached, and Aaron rubbed his eyes. Had he imagined it? Was the glowing lantern real or a figment of his strong imagination? Was *she* real? It wasn't possible that a young girl was hiding out in this abandoned camp with its smell of decay, its broken roof and bulging walls. Why was she out here night after night, all alone, always at the same time, making the same movements? Crying the same eerie cry.

He sat for extended moments - he would not have been able to say how long - waiting for another sound, another movement. The Dunn camp remained black and silent. The state forest behind him was still. He pushed off in the canoe, gliding out, heading across the lake. The wind picked up a bit, and he fought against it, paddling harder. He reached his own waterfront, and among his own familiar beaching sounds - fiberglass on gravel, splashes in the water - he heard another familiar sound from across the lake - a whimper, a cry caught on the wind, then smothered in a long, exhaling sigh. And then silence.

Aaron turned quickly, but the abandoned camp was dark. No sight or sound disturbed the lake. Nothing.

Chapter 5

WITH ONE FOOT, Connie Latimer held open the door to the furnished Saratoga apartment, heaving herself and her groceries through. She was grateful that she had followed her intuition and chosen a place on the ground floor. She loved the old building - its history, its cozy corners, mullioned windows, and beautiful polished woodwork - but once again, the elevator appeared to be stuck somewhere between the second and third floors. She could hear Anton, the elevator operator, discussing it in excited terms with the other first floor tenant.

Connie put her bag on the cherry kitchen counter and glanced at her watch. In fifteen minutes, she would go to pick up Egan, and then they were off for supper out and an evening at the ballet.

She smiled to herself. Egan was enthralled with the dance class she had started four days ago and would love seeing the New York City Ballet at the Saratoga Performing Arts Center this evening. Lawn tickets were easy to come by, but for this, Egan's first experience, Connie had splurged on indoor seating in the fourteenth row. Egan would love it.

When she had visited Saratoga the winter before, it had seemed like a sleepy little upstate town. She'd come for a teachers' conference in February and there wasn't much going on. But the signs for the track and the arts center had intrigued her, and the brochures she'd picked up casually mentioned the rich and famous who clearly thought Saratoga worth their time.

So, why not a vacation there?

She wasn't disappointed. The place was busy and congested, exciting, stimulating. She'd been astounded at the throngs packing the summer sidewalks and the prices she'd needed to pay for in-season tickets. Even the apartment itself had been pricey.

But the SPAC performance should be thrilling, and Connie couldn't wait to see Egan's excited eyes at curtain time.

She began removing groceries from the bag and squelched the irritation rising in her. Aaron should be here going to SPAC with them.

Not for the first time, she wondered if the ultimatum she had given him was a little drastic for the situation. But, damn it, she was sick of it. He thought nothing of packing up and leaving them whenever a good writing offer came along, sometimes with no notice at all, and often, she was sure, unnecessarily. She couldn't even count the number of times she had been left holding his theater or concert ticket and had been forced to invite some friend or other to take his place, or cancel the baby-sitter and give the tickets away altogether. She was sick of calling friends to change dinner plans made months in advance, sick of dealing with plumbers and repairmen by herself, and sick of going to Egan's school functions alone, like some sad, single mom. And mostly she was sick of fighting with Aaron about it.

And now, to try to cancel the summer plans they had made months ago. Well, he could cancel. She had every intention of enjoying herself without him.

When she had married him, she hadn't seen this selfish streak. Well, that wasn't entirely true. She had seen it and loved him so much that she'd ignored it. She was paying for it now. Her anger was as much at herself as at him.

And the invitation to the lake for the summer had been the last straw. He knew she detested wilderness vacations, and he had gone right ahead and arranged a photo essay that would take him away from her and Egan, away from Saratoga, and into the woods. For half the summer.

Well, she had topped him on that one. "Go ahead to the woods, Aaron," she had said, her eyes burning. "Go muck around up at the lake, and have a great time. In fact, Aaron, stay two months. You might as well, because Egan and I are going to Saratoga for July and August."

He had been shocked, of course. It never occurred to Aaron Latimer that his wife might follow through with some plans of her own. Well, he could live with it and see how it felt to be abandoned at a moment's notice. She and Egan would go to plays and concerts, the ballet, museums, and the races when the season started. Saratoga was rich in history and culture, and if Aaron wanted to miss it all to wear rubber boots and buffalo plaid shirts and go glopping through the muddy forest, well, that was fine with her.

She had made herself agitated again. She breathed in deeply and looked around her new quarters. Beautiful polished cherry furnishings, tasteful taupe carpeting, original artwork on the walls. She had chosen well. Saratoga was a lovely town, and this was a fabulous old building, near the shopping areas and restaurants, a few minutes' drive to the track and Arts Center. She would enjoy introducing Egan to the wonderful cultural things she enjoyed, and she would make some inquiries soon about a girl who might be trusted to come in and sit for Egan so she could occasionally enjoy those pursuits alone or in the company of other adults, if she should meet up with any friends. She looked forward to doing exactly what she wanted to do.

She kicked at the creamy ecru ottoman in her rented living room. "Damn you, Aaron," she said. It had been five days and she missed him. It was always like this when he left to do a photo shoot, and being in one of the most exciting cities in the state didn't help. She might as well be at their house in Syracuse, mowing the lawn and weeding the garden. No place seemed right without Aaron.

She had refused to give in on the phone question. She admitted to herself that her stubbornness was childish, but she would not spend her days waiting for his calls. She kept her cell firmly off. She was most vulnerable when she heard his voice, and in the evenings, when she listened to his endless seductive messages, she had to force herself not to call back. She was relieved that he was okay, but she knew he would hear the loneliness in her voice and use it to convince her to scrap her silly summer plans. Before long she'd be packing her bags and whistling a happy tune while she loaded herself and Egan into the car and set her GPS for Spruce Lake.

It couldn't be that way. He was neglecting them more and more, and she wanted him to see how it felt. He could be the one to give in this time.

He was a proud man and a forceful one, and it wasn't easy to take a stand against him like this. He had been upset at her decision, but she had held firm. She fully expected to enjoy her summer and let him know in September whether or not she intended to return to him. He would just have to get used to the idea.

Whether or not? Connie grimaced. She knew there were no

two ways about it. Whatever he was and whatever he had done to hurt her feelings, she was still in love with Aaron.

Connie glanced suddenly at the clock, grabbed up her purse, and checked her hair in the mirror near the door. She would be just in time to get Egan, bring her home, get her ready for the ballet, and leave again.

She forced a smile as she let herself out of the apartment and locked the door behind her. If it killed her, she would have a wonderful evening.

Chapter 6

IT BECAME HIS MIDNIGHT HABIT to drift near the abandoned camp, hoping to see the girl again. He was never disappointed.

Who could she be and how did she manage to vanish each night while he observed her from his silent canoe? Her crying bothered him; there was something familiar in the sadness, and he shook himself, refusing to accept that buried part of him that crept, now and then, to the surface.

Again he examined the shoreline by day, even pulling his boat onto the beach and climbing out, peering under the watery ferns and straggling bushes, searching for a footprint, a sign of her humanity, evidence of her late night walks. There was no depression in the sand, no broken stalk or withered leaf or trampled blade of grass where she had left a trace of herself behind.

It didn't make sense.

Frustrated, he returned to his own shore and spent the afternoon brooding over his silent typewriter, willing occasional stubborn words onto paper and cursing the blank sheet staring back at him.

Another midnight, and Aaron canoed to the east shore again, determined to get closer to the girl who wandered the abandoned beach, her lantern held high. It was becoming difficult to work; he was, he admitted to himself, more than a little distracted by the mystery of the girl at the Dunn camp.

A pair of loons shrieked to each other, their doomed, repeated cry echoing in the stillness, then dying away. His paddle dipped silently; stars pricked the sky overhead.

He reached the state-owned parcel, where the trees drooped low over the water, leaves touching the surface here and there in quiet rings. He moved his boat forward as far as he dared, within feet of the Dunn property, then felt around for a suitable tree limb, fastened his rope, and tested it. It would hold. He would sit here waiting in the dark until she appeared. It was an eerie feeling; he knew without question that she would come.

He felt sleep crouch upon him and forced himself to hold his head up. Slowly his eyes closed; he was half aware that he was drifting lazily under the night trees, the bow of his canoe bumping gently against the exposed roots and rocks embedded in the dirt along the shore.

A weak cry jolted him suddenly, the throaty sound of a young girl in sad distress. His eyes flew open; the darkness confused him momentarily, and then he forced himself to sit stock still.

There on the beach, the girl in the light-colored gown walked away from him in the soft glow of her lantern. His breath caught in his throat at the sight of her long hair waving down her back. He had once known a girl with hair like that, a girl in his high school class whose memory seared him with guilt when he allowed her to creep into his thoughts. He closed his mind to the memory and concentrated on the girl before him.

Her steps were sure and light, but slow, going away from him down the beach. He watched her retreat, reached up to untie his rope, dipped his paddle into the water, and silently moved his boat forward, gliding into a rocky V on the waterfront. He was squarely in front of the abandoned camp now and smelled traces of a sour dead animal odor. With his left hand, he searched the ground for support and scraped his knuckle on a rock. He grasped the rock, held himself steady, and threw the rope with his other hand to twine it around a tree trunk fallen over into the water. He reached beneath the rough trunk and grabbed the rope. Cold water soaked through his flannel shirt, and he shivered as he wrapped the rope securely. His canoe anchored, he could now watch her, unobserved, hidden in the dark shadows.

At the end of the beach, she turned and began the walk back, her crying shallow, weak, and pitiful. She held the lantern aloft and as her eyes gazed at the channel past him, she stepped into the frigid water. It swirled her dress around her ankles, and Aaron lifted his hand automatically, then quickly stifled that same impulse to protect and rescue her from herself. The abrupt, swift movement of his hand caught her attention and she started suddenly, then stared directly at him and took a step toward him onto the beach.

She is looking at me, he said silently, I know she is looking at me.

Her face was golden in the flickering lantern light. Her eyes were pained, her cheeks tear-streaked. She looked very young. Aaron guessed her to be in her late teens. Her full lips and wide set eyes complemented the gold of her complexion, and her dress was frilled around the neckline and wrists with some kind of lace. The fabric clung around her damp calves and stuck to her bare, wet feet. Wet pine needles and bits of sand and dirt clung to the skin of her ankle and to the hem of her gown.

He was afraid to move, to breathe, for fear she would disappear. Could he be imagining this? The wind suddenly lifted her damp gown and puffed the hem out around her ankles, then let it fall limply again. Her big, sorrowful eyes continued to stare into his.

Without meaning to, he moved. Sitting in one position for so long, his leg had cramped. The knee he had hurt in the woods days before suddenly spasmed, hitting against the gunwale of the canoe. He let out a small gasp of pain.

She heard. Her eyes widened in fear; she turned gracefully and, with one swift movement, ran lightly into the trees and onto the overgrown lawn. He reached out, too late, and saw her briefly on the broken steps leading into the abandoned camp. The lantern flame vanished, and so did she, and Aaron realized with certainty that the girl would not return this night.

The air suddenly felt chilly, his arm clammy and cold in the soaked shirtsleeve. He slapped at a mosquito and plunged his arm underwater again to release his canoe rope from the fallen log. Then, in utter darkness, shivering, he stroked toward home, glancing all the time over his shoulder, sure there would be no change behind him, but afraid to take his eyes away all the same.

Chapter 7

HE HAD BEEN AT SPRUCE LAKE for a full week. He had chopped wood until the sweat ran from him in greasy rivers, positioning logs on the old stump on the side lawn, thwacking them in half with an ancient ax, then stacking the cut wood alongside the woodshed. He sat now, cooling in the shade while he contemplated the best way to build some kind of an outdoor shower.

A pump was in place, and cold lake water gushed freely into his kitchen and bathroom sinks. The kitchen had been remodeled in the thirties and again in the seventies, but the half bathroom was an afterthought, fitted out with cast-off porcelain fixtures. It worked, but barely. And there was no shower.

He knew there were a few lengths of PVC piping stored in the woodshed, maybe left over from the plumbing installed years before. If he could tap into the existing plumbing, add a faucet and some valves, he figured he could fix something up right outside the kitchen wall. He wouldn't bother with privacy walls or curtains; if any squirrels wanted to get an eyeful, that was okay with him. He wondered if the lake store might sell any of the parts he needed. He was running low on supplies anyway and made a mental note to search out plumbing items when he went for groceries.

It was a five mile walk to the lake store, and even with the packbasket it should be an easy hike. His sore knee felt better, and Aaron looked forward to the outing.

Wednesday dawned nice and sunny with a hint of a breeze. He took stock of his food and other essentials and made a quick list, which he tucked into his back jeans pocket. He hoisted the empty pack onto his back and set off, smiling to himself. Yes, he was a twenty-first century Noah John Rondeau all right; his step was buoyant.

Spruce Lake was the first of a series of lakes which made up the Colson Chain of Lakes. By channel, it connected to Sentry Pond, a small body of water with a few residences along its north and west shores. To reach the store, Aaron would simply head south on the Spruce Lake Road that passed in front of his camp, then veer west. He would follow similar roads that wove in and out of the shorelines of Sentry Pond, Little Trout Lake, and Eastern Bog. The scenery was pretty; summer cottages and colorful boats lined up along the banks, while trees of dusky green, lime, and violet-blue colored the mountains beyond.

Cars trundled past him, a few slow-moving souls giving him friendly waves as he walked along, and he paused briefly at Little Trout Lake to watch summer residents flash by on water skis. Aaron breathed the good air deeply, satisfied and contented, and resumed walking, taking in the rustic scenery.

An irregularly-shaped island in the main waterway of Eastern Bog was guarded on one side by jutting rocks and circled now by a contingent of mallards dibbling in the cool water. Aaron looked forward to making a trip to the bog later to photograph wild cranberry and milkweed, feeling optimistic that he might find both there. In fact, he had decided to gather some of the edible plants he intended to write about and see if he couldn't concoct a whole meal for himself using only the plants native to this area. He knew he could make a salad out of trillium and cook the greens of the touch-me-not; he had tried them before. Pine needle tea would be new to him, though. He wondered how it would taste.

He readjusted his empty packbasket, surprised that it felt hot and uncomfortable. He estimated he had walked close to five miles; the store wouldn't be far.

Of course he could have driven, but he was determined to try living the primitive lifestyle he had proclaimed in the first few paragraphs of his article. It invigorated him and put him in the right frame of mind for his work here.

Aaron's step slowed as his thoughts took a new turn. The work, in fact, was getting to be a problem. He had managed to spend a few sunny afternoons hiking through the woods behind the camp and had taken some nice photographs that he believed would work well in the project, but the real writing seemed to be coming slower and slower. It was his concern about Connie and Egan. And the strange ghost girl across the lake. Not that he believed Connie would really leave him, nor that the girl he had seen was really a ghost.

He jutted his chin purposefully. It was ridiculous to spend such a fine morning worrying about things that would resolve themselves. Connie would come to her senses; of that he was sure. And the girl across the lake, well, if there were ghosts at Spruce Lake, then it was news to him. There must be some other way to make sense of her. But what other explanation was there? Aaron wondered how he might find out.

He passed the big, two story boat storage building and trudged up the wide wooden steps of the camp store porch, depositing his woven ashwood pack on the oiled floor. Perhaps the cool weather was lifting and he would be treated to some warm, summery days after all. He certainly felt warm now. He removed his flannel shirt and tossed it into the empty pack. The tee shirt he wore felt sticky with sweat.

He and Chris had made many trips here as children, waiting in the car while his mother picked up milk or vegetables or a box of matches, accompanying her inside occasionally for an ice cream sandwich or a candy bar. The place hadn't changed much.

The building was sided with irregular slabs of dark wood, and a green-painted railing enclosed the big porch that overlooked the road. Bundles of daily papers and bushel baskets of fresh produce lined the railing. A concrete path led down one side of the lawn to the docks and gas pumps at the water's edge.

A few rafts, canoes, and small rowboats hung suspended from the porch roof by pulleys; from each hung a yellowed price tag. Oars and paddles were displayed in a worn, locked case.

Just beyond the store Aaron could see the twisting, rocky inlet to Big Trout Lake, buoys marking the most perilous areas for boats. Summer camps and some winterized cottages dotted the shorelines, and the sounds of lawnmowers and motor boats buzzed the morning air.

The light breeze had cooled him some. Lifting the pack, Aaron entered the store and wandered through the cramped aisles, choosing food and supplies and picking up a couple of small notebooks for research. He was pleased to find a meager selection of plumbing items and selected the things he hoped would work for his shower. Behind the counter, the rosy woman at the cash register smiled her thanks to another customer and beamed at Aaron as he deposited his purchases on the linoleum countertop. Near a display of touristy balsam pillows and cedar boxes stamped *Big Trout Lake, NY*, one local resident sat at a lunch counter eating a pastrami sandwich dripping with mustard.

"Staying at Big Trout, are you?" the storekeeper asked as she rang up Aaron's items.

"No, Spruce Lake," he answered. "I'm Aaron Latimer, George Latimer's son. The big yellow camp on the west shore."

"Oh, sure," she said, recognizing the name. "Beautiful spot. I read one of your articles, I think." She peered over at the gray-haired customer sitting at the counter. "Remember that article, Foster? In *Nature Digest*, wasn't it?"

"Oh, the one on animal tracks," Aaron said.

The pastrami sandwich was laid to rest on the plate before the elderly man, and he turned a slow head toward Aaron and nodded. "Yes, nice pictures," he said. "Very interesting article."

"Thanks," Aaron said. As always, it pleased him that someone had seen his work, recognized his name.

The storekeeper offered her pudgy hand and shook his. "Cathleen Parnell," she said. "Did you boat over?"

"No, I walked it today. Maybe the boat next time." He was arranging things in the packbasket, trying to position a loaf of bread without damaging it, using his shirt to cushion items. He counted out money to pay for his purchases. "The Dunn camp over there on Spruce Lake?" he said. "How long has it been abandoned?"

Cathleen Parnell thought a moment. "Quite a few years," she said at last. "I wasn't here at the time, but there was some kind of tragedy, a daughter who drowned."

Prickles came up on Aaron's bare arms. "I thought I remembered something like that," he said.

"Is that right, Foster?" Cathleen Parnell asked the man at the counter. "Wasn't it a daughter? Or a niece?"

The older man wiped his mouth on his sleeve and nodded. "Daughter," he said. His canvas jacket was too warm for the weather and showed signs of many years of comfortable wear.

"A pretty girl, I think," said Cathleen Parnell. "There used to be a picture of hers hanging in the store." She glanced around. "I guess somebody took it down after a while."

"A picture?" Aaron asked. "You mean a photo of her?"

"No, I mean a picture she made. A painting of a lake scene. It was very pretty; I don't know who has it now."

"Oh, she was an artist then."

Cathleen Parnell shrugged. "I don't know about that, but I

31

did see the one painting. It was nice. Small." She indicated its size with her hands. "Any signs of life around that camp?"

Aaron stifled an involuntary shiver. "No, it's caving in, in fact. Kind of a sad old place." He hoisted his packbasket onto his back and started out the door, calling back a thanks to the storekeeper. The pack was heavy now and cut into his shoulders. He removed it awkwardly and adjusted the canvas straps, then resettled it more comfortably. He would have to fashion some pads to cushion the straps.

His walk was slower now with the full pack, and the hot sun felt merciless on his head and arms. It wouldn't be a bad paddle, he thought, through Spruce Lake and Sentry Pond, then along the shores of Little Trout and Eastern Bog. If he picked the right day, he guessed he could probably do the whole trip, both ways, in less than three or four hours, depending on the wind. He would choose a sunny, blue sky day and buy lunch at the store, make an outing of it.

Yes, next time, the canoe would make more sense.

Chapter 8

BACK AT CAMP, he stashed his purchases in the kitchen, made himself a sandwich, and sat down near the telephone to make a perfunctory call to Connie. He wasn't surprised that she didn't answer. He had been here over a week with no word from her. Well, she had told him pretty clearly that this summer would be on her terms. It was annoying, though. How was he supposed to know that she and Egan were okay? He left a brief message, adding it to the other messages he had left. It was getting kind of ridiculous, and he was beginning to feel a little foolish. Maybe this would be his last call.

He took his sandwich out to the porch and ate with his feet propped up on the long railing, gazing at the Dunn camp across the way. A girl who had drowned. It wasn't possible . . . .

In the brilliant sunshine of afternoon, the idea of a ghost seemed preposterous, and he scoffed at himself as he recalled his own tension, the chill that sometimes came over him when he thought of the girl on the Dunn beach. The camp looked so innocuous from here, a small brown cabin like so many others that circled these Adirondack lakes. But at this cabin there was a flickering lantern light, there was a strange young woman who cried each night with tightly closed eyes, who appeared and disappeared without warning. There was desolation in the air, and a colder feeling when he approached that shore.

Aaron sat up straighter in the rocking chair and planted his feet firmly on the porch floor. These thoughts would not get the article written, and he was way behind schedule already. While there was still enough light, he would get some pictures. He deposited his lunch dishes into the kitchen sink, hung his camera strap around his neck, slung his tripod over his shoulder, and hiked into the woods behind the camp.

He came to a stand of bracken that caught his interest and

screwed the tripod into the camera, then kicked a few sticks aside so the tripod stood steady. The shadows were minimal, and he liked the way the afternoon sunlight danced on the bracken ferns.

Peering through the telephoto lens, he could tell he would need more light, so he adjusted for a slower shutter speed. Would the shot be crisp enough? He wanted the oblong, leathery-looking leaflets to jump from the page.

A slight breeze whispered among the tree branches and he waited it out patiently, watching the ferns sway idly. Any little movement would ruin the shot, making it blurry or fuzzy. When the breeze died away, he peered through the viewfinder, pleased at the image. He squeezed the remote trigger, ensuring a clean, still photograph.

As the minutes wore on, the light changed almost imperceptibly. Again, he tested through the viewfinder, concentrated on the dappled shadows, the smooth, rigid stalks supporting their blunt-tipped leaflets. Another breeze, a waiting, a second shot, and then a third.

After he had taken eight or nine pictures, he was satisfied and stepped aside, but another thought had occurred to him. The tender young shoots would be great to cook for his special dinner. With milkweed, trillium, and pine needle tea, the addition of bracken shoots would help him create a feast for a king.

He knew bracken fern had been known to cause illness, that it was carcinogenic, but so were grilled steaks, and he'd never turned them down. Cooking the fiddleheads would destroy the carcinogens, he knew, so he could easily avoid any lightheadedness, fever or nausea. Anyway, he would only be eating a few.

Aaron grimaced a little, not convinced he wanted to eat even that many, but he admitted that preparing the natural meal would give him an opportunity to write a light description of his culinary attempts, something that would lend color and a touch of humor to his suffering article.

He poked among the ferns and found plenty of young, pale green fiddleheads newly risen from the earth. At eight inches tall, they would be tender and eminently edible cooked as a vegetable. He snapped the stalk at the base of each shoot, set the stalks aside, and gazed again at the hardy full-grown bracken.

Again he readjusted his shutter speed, played the familiar

waiting game with the breeze and sunlight, and took half a dozen more photographs.

He had taken a whole roll of film and felt pleased with his work. He removed the camera from the tripod, folded in the legs, scooped up his tender bracken shoots, and headed back to camp. It had been a productive afternoon.

The camp kitchen was bathed in shadowy light as he stowed his equipment on the corner of the counter and carefully piled the shoots on the table for later.

When the telephone rang, he rushed to the living room, grabbed up the receiver, and was relieved to hear Connie's voice. "How are things going, Aaron? How is the article coming?"

"It's all right. It's about time you called. I miss you guys. I wish you and Egan would come up here." Her answer didn't surprise him. They had been over it before and she hadn't changed her mind. She had planned on summering in Saratoga; she intended to do so; she needed time to think; she was serious that some changes were in order.

"Did you get my messages?"

"I did, Aaron, but I told you not to expect me to call right away. If it's an emergency, say so."

"It's not unless you count how much I miss you."

"Oh, Aaron, I miss you, too. I don't even know if this is the right thing to do. I just feel as if I have to."

"Con, I'm going home one day next week to do some developing. Maybe Wednesday. Do you want to meet me? We could spend some time together at home, maybe get a sitter for Egan and go out for lunch."

There was a hesitation before she answered. "I don't think so. Will you have much free time, do you think? Won't you probably spend the whole day in the darkroom?"

He would, most likely, but obviously he would take some time for her. "I want to see you, Connie."

He could sense her backing away. "No, I don't want Egan to miss her classes."

"I'll come to Saratoga then. You name the day and place; I'll meet you."

The silence lengthened while she considered.

"Connie, this is very bad for my ego," he said, trying to make light of it.

"I'm sorry, Aaron," she said finally. "I can't. I'm afraid you'll try to talk me into leaving here . . . ."

"I wouldn't do that," he said. But they both knew he would.

"No," she said more firmly. "Please don't insist."

"What about Egan?" he said. "Can't I even see my daughter?"

He heard the breath that Connie exhaled slowly and knew she was trying to stay patient. "You've been away from her before; you'll both survive this time, too."

"Fine, have it your way," he muttered. "Saratoga must be tons of fun."

She ignored him. "Do you want to talk to Egan?"

He did, of course. She put Egan on and the little girl spoke shyly to her father. She was taking some kind of enrichment classes this summer. It was like Connie to manage to enroll her even though she wasn't a resident of Saratoga. Yes, Egan said, she liked the classes, they were in horseback riding and dancing. She went every morning at nine o'clock.

"We went to the ballet," she said. "I liked it, Dad."

"I'm sure you did, sweetie. Did you get lots of pointers for yourself? I bet you've been practicing all over the place since then, haven't you?"

Egan giggled. "Yep." Then, "Daddy, how come you're staying at a lake and we're having our vacation without you?" Her small, familiar voice touched him and he struggled for an answer.

"It's just for a few weeks, honey," he said.

"But, Daddy, I miss you. I want you to go places with us."

"I miss you, too." It wasn't the first time he'd been separated from his family; Egan ought to be used to it by now. A pang caught him by surprise and he squelched the little gnawing guilt that leapt within him. "I have to work, honey. We'll all be together soon, you know that."

He talked with Connie about it. She sent Egan into another room to play and spoke to him candidly.

"She can tell it's different," Connie said. "I don't know; kids are very perceptive, Aaron. She senses this time is different."

"Only because you've given me this ultimatum."

"And I mean it." Her voice was brittle. "We're not going to come running up there just because it's where you feel like being." She sighed, exasperated. "Don't make me get into it all again."

"But I love you, Connie. I don't see why you want to make it so complicated."

"Oh, no. Don't you dare twist this around so that it's my fault."

"It's not your fault, Connie. But I couldn't pass up this assignment; it's a good one. I thought you'd understand that." He wondered if his misery showed in his voice. "We'll do it whatever way you want."

She was silent, listening.

"As soon as this article is finished-"

She interrupted him, impatient. "You never change," she said. "I've heard that how many times before? And after this article there'll be one in Connecticut in September, and then one in Ontario after that. And you'll be gone again. You're away from us more than you're with us. It isn't fair to Egan or me. It isn't fair to any of us, Aaron."

"I know. I miss you. If it bothers you that much, I'll stop doing the articles. I'll work in a library or something or get a job in a photography shop." He wondered if those options sounded as pitiful to her as they did to him. "It can be different."

"You can show me that in September, if that's what we decide."

Her words were so cold. He clenched the old-fashioned black telephone receiver more firmly and was surprised when he heard the gentle snuffling on her end. She was crying. "Connie, for God's sake," he let out a breath. "Bring Egan up here. It's beautiful here. She would love it."

"She has classes." She sniffled.

"Skip the stupid classes. I'll teach her things here. We'll go canoeing and have picnics. We can hike." He knew even as he said the words that he was pushing his wife further away. Canoeing and hiking were the last things she wanted. She had told him clearly that wilderness adventures were not for her. She wanted hot showers, modern appliances, level sidewalks under her feet. He had known that when he married her. It had certainly been no secret.

"No, Aaron. I have to go."

"Wait a minute. You won't come here, and you won't let me come there. That's not fair." He sounded like a little kid on the ballfield whining about the rules of the game. He knew it, but he couldn't seem to keep the complaining tone out of his voice.

"It's fair, Aaron," she said.

"Don't hang up, Connie."

"I have to go."

"You don't have to go. Wait."

"No, I do, really. I'll call you later. Take care. I love you,

Aaron." Her voice was quiet, wistful. The line went dead. He stood staring at the telephone, then replaced the receiver.

He wandered around the room, picking up trinkets and putting them down again. His gaze fell on the shelf of athletic trophies above the bookcase. All of them were his; he could make out his name stamped onto the brass nameplates, and he knew anyway. His father was very proud of those trophies, proud of Aaron, and Connie had been impressed, too, the first time he had brought her here.

Her attitude lately wasn't really fair. She had known his job when they'd married, known his strengths, his weaknesses. She'd vowed to take him for better or for worse.

Aaron pulled out a chair and sat down unhappily at his writing table. He glanced down at the last words he had written and thought briefly, then began pecking out words on the old typewriter.

The milky juice of the milkweed stem is bitter, he typed. *Its mildly toxic characteristic* . . . . He managed to write half a page before he sat back and reread what he had written. Dry. Dry and dull and nothing he or anyone would pay a magazine's cover price to read. He pulled the sheet from the typewriter and crumpled it to the floor.

He started again, and managed a lighter tone, even injecting some humor into the paragraphs. That was better. He was okay now. Soon he was engrossed, writing quickly, his mind shooting ahead while his fingers flew over the typewriter keys. His agitation from Connie's call began to abate. The sick feeling of dread that had tried to sneak up on him while he listened to his wife dissipated easily. Things were fine between them. She just needed a little time to figure that out.

Chapter 9

HE HAD SPENT TWO HOURS crawling around under the camp, gluing, fitting, adjusting, and attaching, and had ended up with a makeshift shower that did exactly what it was supposed to do. He'd stripped off his dirty clothes eagerly, stood under the faucet, and turned the valve.

Icy water shot out in a solid stream, and Aaron yelped at the shocking cold. Well, his showers would certainly be quick. He soaped himself, gave his hair a haphazard washing, and rinsed off, his teeth chattering.

Now, dressed again, and feeling clean for the first time in nearly two weeks, he made himself a bowl of cereal and sprawled on a porch rocker, eating lazily. He was surprised by the sound of a vehicle approaching and then annoyed when he recognized the driver of the gleaming red sports car pulling in next to his dark blue SUV. Peering over the railing, he watched with distaste as his brother emerged and gave him a slight wave of the hand. Chris went around to the back, opened the trunk, and pulled out a soft canvas bag and a pile of books. His tweed sport coat looked incongruous in the dirt parking area, and his khaki pants were wrinkled from the drive. Chris was slighter than Aaron, a small, compact man with darker hair and smaller features. Thin-rimmed glasses sat timidly on the bridge of his nose. Aaron forced himself not to grimace.

Veronica stepped out of the passenger side and held the seat forward for two children who scrambled out testily, fighting over the plastic toy from a Happy Meal.

Aaron groaned.

"Hi, Aaron!" Veronica called. He gave his sister-in-law a reluctant wave.

Chris and Veronica trudged up the winding path carrying the parcels, the children arguing hotly behind them. Veronica stepped gingerly around wet leaves and sticks, navigating exposed tree roots and the old railroad ties that twisted up the bank and helped level the steps. Her sandals were becoming muddy around the edges. With one hand, she clutched her wraparound skirt closed as the breeze kept catching it and flying the panels around.

"How did you know I was up here?" Aaron asked his brother.

Chris laughed. His gaze slid from Aaron's face and landed on the sturdy beam behind him. His eyes behind the glasses looked round and slightly jagged on the edges, like carelessly cooked pancakes. "We didn't know," he said. "Honestly, I haven't been up in probably three years, and I picked today. Have you been coming up all summer? Or are you staying here? Where's Connie?"

"She had to take Egan to Saratoga. She's in some enrichment classes there." It felt good to twist it in a little. He was proud that his Egan had tested as a gifted student, whereas Chris's two were lucky if they made it to average.

Chris looked around appreciatively. "Same old place. You took down a couple of trees."

"Small ones. They were starting to block the view."

"Do you have any coffee, Aaron?" Veronica asked with a smile. "I've been dying for a cup, but Chris was in too much of a hurry to stop."

"We did stop," Chris corrected her. "You decided to want it after we stopped."

"I'll make some." Aaron went inside the camp, letting out a full breath. At least they didn't have suitcases. He could be thankful for that. Veronica followed him into the kitchen. "Did the kids bring their suits?" he asked her. "Swimming's great in the morning." Not that he would know these days. It had been years since he'd swum in Spruce Lake. He hadn't done much swimming at all in maybe fifteen years; somehow it had lost its appeal.

He fished coffee and a filter out of a cupboard, filled the coffee carafe with water, measured, poured, and turned the machine on. The coffee began to bubble and drip. Veronica chased down her sons to encourage them to take a nice morning swim.

Aaron leaned against the counter briefly, enjoying being alone. It didn't last. The older of Chris's sons came into the kitchen, letting the screen door bang shut behind him. "Uncle

Aaron, where should I change into my suit?"

Aaron pointed to the staircase beyond. "Any room you want except the last one." The boy bounded off and up, and Aaron could hear him up there, opening and closing doors.

When the coffee finished, he went to the screen door and looked out. Chris was sitting in a rocker, his loafered feet propped up on the porch railing, telling Veronica about some hassle he had encountered at work. Veronica sat next to him rocking away, listening intently to every word he was saying.

"Well," she said now, righteously, "if he's going to be disrespectful of you that way, I might just have to speak to Uncle Robert myself."

"Don't do that," Chris entreated her. "I'll handle it."

"Well, it bothers me that some . . . hired help-"

"I said I'll take care of it, Veronica. Just let me."

It was typical of Chris that he had floated into a job as accountant for his wife's uncle. The hardware store they ran was small, and Chris had ended up living in a compact ranch house just two blocks away from it, a boring shoebox of a building that Veronica had chosen. Chris had dropped out of college after some fruitless switching of majors, and good old Uncle Robert had certainly been happy to find a spot for him at Bob's Hardware, oblivious to, or maybe aware of the fact that his niece's husband was basically wasting his talents.

Aaron felt irritation prickle him as he thought of Chris's easy, unthinking acceptance of everything in his life. A stupid wife, boring kids, a job with no chance of promotion or recognition. Chris did the bookkeeping, kept the payroll, and worked out the taxes of Bob's Hardware in the nothing town of Forked Flats, and, on the rare social family occasions he shared with Aaron, acted perfectly content with his miserable choices.

He should have made something of himself, Aaron thought for perhaps the fiftieth time in his life. He would have been a perfect MBA candidate but hadn't even bothered to finish his Bachelors degree.

Aaron pushed open the screened kitchen door slightly. He could see his cereal bowl sitting on the railing before Chris and Veronica, his breakfast getting soggy and warm. "Coffee's ready," he said shortly. He'd be damned if he was going to serve them.

He sat at his oak table and occupied himself pouring over guide books, making penciled notations and trying to look busy. "What are you doing?" asked his second nephew. He could never

41

keep their names straight, Rory and Jeff or maybe Jeff and Rory.

"I'm doing research for an article I'm writing."

"You mean for a magazine?"

"M'hmm."

"I wrote an article for my class newspaper." The child looked at him, waiting, and Aaron was forced to look interested. "It was on page four. I thought that was pretty good."

Aaron nodded and returned to his work. The boy wandered away.

"Good coffee, Aaron." It was Veronica standing at his elbow, reading over his shoulder. "Thanks for making it."

"You're welcome."

She put a hand over her mouth to cover a smile. "Oops. Sorry. I shouldn't be disturbing you while you're working." He noticed that her hair was redder and bushier than the last time he had seen her.

"It's all right. I really do have to get this done, though." Why were they here? It was all he could do to be superficially polite.

"I love this place," Veronica was saying. "I always wish Chris would bring us up here for a week or two in the summer. He gets off the week of the fourth and can take an extra week whenever he wants to." She meandered from wall to wall, examining the family photographs, the taxidermied birds and fish. "He never wants to, though. He won't even stay tonight. We got reservations in Speculator instead." She looked over the rows of old pottery bowls in a sideboard and glanced up at the line of trophies above the books. Reaching up, she tilted the first one toward her and read the nameplate silently.

It wasn't Chris's, if that's what she was hoping. Aaron could have told her that no honors or prizes had gone to Chris Latimer in school. Chris couldn't be bothered to achieve.

Veronica came back to Aaron's desk again. "That's kind of silly, isn't it? Spending money on two rooms when we could have stayed here?"

"He must prefer it," Aaron said. Thank God.

"He brought some books up," Veronica said. "That's why we stopped. There's an old album. Somehow we had it at home, but he said it belongs here. He remembered it from when you were kids. Pictures of some of the old relatives. There's some of you guys in there, too."

"Sounds interesting. I'll have to look at it later."

"Veronica?" That was Chris, hollering from the porch,

wondering where his wife was with the coffee.

"I'll be right there, you old bear," she said playfully and wandered off to the kitchen.

Aaron rested one elbow on the table top and placed his chin in his hand. The mantel clock said ten fifteen. He wondered how long they would stay.

Chapter 10

THEY STAYED FOUR HOURS, long enough to make lunch out of most of his supplies and irritate the hell out of him with their questions and comments.

Chris had urged Aaron to the dock after lunch to talk and catch up on family news. Reluctantly, Aaron went. They must be planning to leave soon; maybe Aaron could hasten that if he could keep Chris from going back to the camp. He could see Veronica and the children up the bank, taking their damp swim things off the clothesline and stuffing them into plastic bags for their drive to Speculator.

Chris was digging into a bag of potato chips he had taken from his car. His sons had made short work of the whole chips, but there were salty crumbs in the bag's bottom, which Chris was magnetizing to one damp finger and licking off. Aaron remembered that Chris had always liked the little, salty crumbs the best. So typical of his brother to choose the crummy little broken bits.

"I was surprised to see your car in the parking area when I drove in," Chris said.

"Not as surprised as I was to see you get out of that sports car," Aaron said.

"It's a beauty, isn't it?" Chris laughed, peering into the bag. "I had my eye on that car for a while, and then I got another raise at work, so Veronica said to go ahead and get it. It's not very practical, but I enjoy driving it around."

"I didn't mean the car, Chris. I meant that you're here."

Chris exhaled loudly. "The camp is half mine, Aaron. They signed it over to both of us." He crumpled the empty bag and tossed it on the bank, away from the water, then tipped back in the webbed folding chair he sat in. The toes of his leather loafers bent and unbent as he balanced himself. "You may live closer, but I have every right to be here."

"No one said you didn't."

Chris sighed and allowed a long pause before he said, "The Dunn camp looks deserted over there. Is there anybody around?"

Aaron lied smoothly to his brother. "No, no one's been there in years."

"Sad place. Remember when the girl was found?"

"No," Aaron said shortly. He refused to discuss the strange occurrences at the Dunn camp with his brother.

Chris looked at the dock below his feet and at the strange, dappled shadows in the water below the wooden slats. "I remember we found snakes under there."

"I remember," Aaron said shortly.

A silence hung long between them. Then Chris took a sudden breath and said, "There's no point in trying with you. You've been rude since we stepped out of the car, Aaron. You obviously wish we hadn't come."

Aaron didn't bother to answer.

"I'd like to ask that you at least be polite to Veronica."

"I'm always polite to Veronica. Kindness to our loved ones is a family trait."

The metal tubes of Chris's chair banged down on the wooden dock. "Damn it, Aaron, why can't you put the past behind us? Everyone else has." He softened his tone and peered into Aaron's face. The look was almost timid. Like a shy schoolgirl, Aaron thought with contempt. "Look, you're my only brother," Chris said. "I would like to have a friendly relationship with you, but you make it very hard. Do you want to talk about this animosity you feel for me?"

Aaron leaned back in his chair and stretched his arms over his head. "No, not really, Chris," he drawled. "I think the time for talking is long past."

"It's never too late to purge yourself of hateful feelings."

"How ironic to hear that coming from you."

Chris stood up in agitation. "When I saw your SUV here, I thought, good, maybe an opportunity for Aaron and me to talk together like adults, set aside some of the differences between us, but you can't, can you?"

"No, I can't," Aaron said honestly. They had skated close to the topic over the years, invariably introduced by Chris in his fainthearted way, but Aaron had always cut the conversations short. Today was no different.

Chris grabbed up the empty potato chip bag, stalked up the bank to his shiny new car, and threw the bag in. His family met him there, and Veronica noisily ushered the boys inside. "Thanks for lunch, Aaron!" she called cheerily.

Aaron waved vaguely, then turned his back, settled into his lawnchair, and gazed across the lake. He heard the car start up and roar down the road and stomped out the little flare of guilt that bubbled up.

Yes, Chris was his brother, but there was nothing else that could ever draw them together.

Chapter 11

AARON WAS CONVINCED that the girl had seen him at least twice now as he hid in his canoe in the murky waters near her cottage. Both times she had peered at and through him and then darted away, her lantern extinguished in a snap of black night. He'd stared, too, trying to determine if she were real. It was too incredible to believe that the Dunn girl's ghost was haunting the shores of Spruce Lake.

He didn't even believe in ghosts. And when he saw her, he was not consumed with fear or dread. No, this ghost, if she was one, evoked pity in him and an overwhelming curiosity. Night after night, it was not until after she vanished that he felt suddenly surrounded by the rotting smells and crushed evidence of a long gone humanity. He would shiver inside his clothes and look to the inky sky for an explanation that never came.

Maybe today he could get some answers.

The weather was perfect for a rigorous outing, and he decided to paddle to the lake store. As he centered an empty cardboard carton for supplies between the gunwales of the boat, he breathed in the good mountain air. The pewter morning sky was already turning to a bright robin's egg blue, and the water lapped softly against the sides of the boat as he dipped the paddle in, moving swiftly with the current.

It took only minutes to paddle the length of Spruce Lake. Sentry Pond, although larger, was a calm, easy paddle, too. It pleased him to travel along with dragonflies and a pair of wood ducks, and when he reached Little Trout Lake, Aaron pulled his camera from its drybag, loaded it with film, and began shooting the water lapping against the boat, the mountains looming up green and blue on every side of him. He felt small and awed floating in his little boat. He breathed the clear air into his lungs, allowing himself, finally, to think.

He didn't want to lose Connie. He admitted he had neglected their marriage, but he had never been unfaithful, had never given her the slightest cause for worry. It was just the traveling. He needed to for work, he kept telling her, but even as he said it, he knew he could easily have turned down some of those assignments. Aaron Latimer was a name that some people knew, and, he admitted proudly to himself, he had reached a point where he could pick and choose.

No, he hadn't really had to go running off to Colorado last fall or to Boston this spring, or to any of the other places in between that had beckoned to him and to which he had raced, excited at the idea of new sights and sounds. If he were honest with himself, he knew that he had chosen to take those trips. He found the lure of change appealing.

In the early days of their marriage, he had assumed she would travel with him, would put him ahead of all other interests and be with him, by his side, his helpmate, lover, and confidante.

He had expected too much.

She had enjoyed the students in her math classes and refused to take her few personal days to travel with him just because he decided it was time. And her summers, before Egan, had been filled with conferences, workshops, and planning meetings. She had no intention of giving those up. So she stayed behind, planning lessons, writing curriculum, and amusing herself. He wasn't even sure how.

That had worked for a while.

But with the birth of Egan and the responsibility of both work and child, Connie had reverted to a very old-fashioned standard. She couldn't imagine leaving her daughter with someone else and had solved the problem by taking a leave of absence, stretching it to the maximum and eventually resigning altogether. Connie had never regretted her decision and loved being a full-time mother.

He approved and had hoped they'd both travel with him. Although she tried, Connie soon discovered that moving a baby from place to place, three weeks here, four days there, was exhausting and counter-productive. So he traveled alone, leaving her with a baby, then a toddler, and now a six year old who obviously couldn't just sign out of school for days or weeks at a time. And Connie refused to leave her.

Again, he approved. Connie was doing everything right, and he felt chastised and even a little ashamed that it had come to this. If Connie was right, then he was obviously wrong.

He would change, he told himself. He would make it clear that Aaron Latimer was no longer available for photo opportunities or research that took him far from home. He knew it was the right decision, yet he couldn't bury a spasm of irritation. What right did she have to dictate how and where he could work? Every right, he told himself. She was his wife, the mother of his child.

A sudden roar shocked Aaron out of his thoughts. He dropped his paddle and had to fish it out of the water. Deep in thought, he had approached a bend in the channel and startled a ruffed grouse that flew not two feet before his face. He exclaimed and leaned back, rocking the boat violently, then twisted his body to see the bird land on the opposite shore. Three more grouse followed, excited wings flapping, a huge noise whirring overhead. By the time he grabbed his camera, he was too late, and the boat was rocking crazily. He settled back on the caned seat again, caught in a breath, and wished Connie had been here to see that. But Connie, he knew, wouldn't have cared to see it.

Were they really the ideal couple some people thought them? Maybe they weren't compatible at all. Had they married too soon? Tension bit through him at the thought of going through life without her. No, their marriage was right. They just needed to make some compromises.

Chapter 12

THAT CONNIE HAD AGREED to marry Aaron in the first place was one of the truly humbling facts of his life.

It was only six months after he had met her, and they'd chosen a breezy, cold Saturday morning in March to fly a kite on a hill outside the city because he had insisted. She had never flown a kite before and believed she hadn't missed out on much, but he had been amazed that she'd never felt the tug of the string in her hand or experienced the surge of power as the kite billowed and danced among the air currents. At his urging, they bought a kite, and he instructed her in the ordinances of kite flying, the kitemaster's gospel according to Aaron Latimer.

She had, of course, ignored his careful directions and had run with the kite wildly, laughing and joking all the while, watching it rise rapidly and soar crazily off balance. It had been only a matter of minutes before the kite string was entangled in a low tree branch, the colorful kite drooping alongside the trunk.

And instead of feeling shamefaced or contrite, Connie had laughed and admitted that he was right, it was fun.

He set to work trying to untangle the string, bending his head into the mess of twine, picking at it with his ungloved fingers. "It would still be in the air if you had listened," he said.

"Oh, well," she said. She stood near him, wrapped in a shearling jacket, watching him concentrate on plucking at the threads. The air was brisk, and the sun was pale and lemony above them, and he was surprised when she placed her mittened hands on either side of his face and lifted it to hers. She kissed him softly with her cool lips, and the lingering quality of the kiss surprised and pleased him; she was affectionate, of course, but not effusively demonstrative.

"You know what, Aaron?" she said, her face still close to his, her breath slightly frosty. "I love you."

He caught his breath and tried to drop the string, still tangled about his fingers. It wouldn't slip off, and he grabbed at it and pulled clumsily with one hand while he held her close with his other arm. She giggled and tried to squirm away.

"No, stay," he said. The kite string finally loosened and he shrugged it from his hand. It hung vertically down the tree trunk, moving slightly as the wind touched it. He enclosed her in his arms and kissed her. "Say that again."

"That I love you?" she said smiling. "Sure. I love you, Aaron. I do."

She had never said it to him before, although he had been foolishly proclaiming his own love for going on two months. He couldn't stop smiling as he held her on the sunny field, covering her face with kisses, the early spring ground hard under their feet.

They had done the best they could disentangling the battered kite and its string from the tree, and they carried it back to her apartment, stowing it, huge and ungainly, in her pantry, then set about making scrambled eggs and toast for lunch.

He set silverware, glasses, and napkins on the kitchen table, then sat watching her whisking eggs and reaching into the freezer for a loaf of wheat bread. He admired her long, slim legs in jeans, her salmon colored sweater, the flat shoes she wore. She took plates from the cupboard and looked over the selections in her wine rack, chose a bottle of chardonnay, uncorked it, and poured it into two glasses. She held one out to him with a smile and he took it.

As many women did, she wore the top two buttons of her sweater unbuttoned. It was not a particularly risqué adornment, but for some reason, today, since she had told him she loved him, it was driving him crazy. Every time she turned to look at him, he would find himself staring at her shapely neck and throat, and his own throat would dry up, making conversation practically impossible. Other women might wear clothes that were conspicuously tight or short, cut seductively low or outrageously high, but Connie needed only to leave her top two buttons undone and he was sent into a fit of passion that would have surprised her if she'd known.

Connie sipped from her glass and caught his eye, then peeked down at her modest sweater, as if maybe she had left something undone down there. "What are you thinking about?" she asked him. She sounded slightly suspicious, but also a little amused.

"Sex."

She turned back to the scrambled eggs, turned the burner off, reached for a wooden spoon, and began serving the eggs onto two plates. "Oh, really."

"M'hmm."

"I see."

The toast was up and she placed it on the plates and carried them to the table. She laughed and kissed the top of his head as she put his plate before him. "Eat up, tiger," she said. She sat down opposite him.

Those top two buttons continued to tantalize him, and he couldn't keep his eyes off her neck, her arms, the swell of her breasts enclosed in the salmon-colored sweater.

"That was fun, Aaron," she said. "It's too bad the kite died. We could get another one, I suppose."

"Yeah, in a few years maybe. I usually only fly a kite about once every ten years." He took a bite of scrambled eggs and discovered he was ravenously hungry. The wine tasted good, and she had placed honey, butter, and peanut butter on the table for the toast. He always ate his with jelly, but he tried it with peanut butter and discovered a new favorite food. He leaned back and looked at her.

"Connie? I'm still thinking about it." He surprised even himself with the blunt admission. He was never this forward with women, had cultivated a studied aloofness that kept him a good, safe distance. So why was he willing to throw it all aside for modest, schoolmarmish Connie Beckett?

She gave a nervous little laugh and stood up from the table, came to him and kissed him. He put his arms around her waist and nuzzled his head into her sweater. She disengaged herself and removed their plates from the table, carrying them to the sink.

"Then you'd better stop thinking," she said lightly, then gave him a frank look. "I guess I better be up front about this, Aaron. There won't be any sex. It's a decision I made a long time ago."

He licked his lips, wondering if it was the wine or the conversation that was making his throat so dry. He removed the butter from the table and put it in the refrigerator. Then he looked at her squarely. "Do you mean ever? For life?"

She laughed again, greatly amused. "I hope not." She looked at him and took his hands in both of hers. "I'm waiting, Aaron. I intend to be married first. It's not a completely novel idea, even these days."

He had had no idea, had assumed their chasteness was his own doing, and discovered that he was impressed by her fortitude even as regret nipped at him.

"That's probably disappointing to you," she went on, and when she glanced up at him, her eyes were large and serious. "I assume you were thinking about it with me in mind."

"You know I was. You said you love me."

Her tone became more serious and she looked away. "I do love you, and that is a fact. I've never loved anyone else so much, but this is important to me." She gave a tiny shrug and pursed her lips, meeting his gaze.

He nodded wordlessly.

She brought his hands to her lips and kissed them briefly, then let go. He caught her hands up again, feeling humbled, and tried to squelch the less than pure images of Connie that were popping into his mind, the less than pure memories of his one and only, sadly concluded sexually-motivated venture.

"Connie," he said, still holding her hands, looking away from those two pearly buttons that tantalized chastely. "There's something about me that you don't know."

She looked at him in surprise and smiled mildly. "I'm sure there are lots of things I don't know."

"This you should hear, though." And for some reason, he found himself plunging headlong into a story out of his past that made him ashamed whenever he thought of it. He was testing her, he supposed. She had said she loved him, but if she knew this - and still stuck with him - well, it would certainly be a fine test.

"In high school, I had a girlfriend, Katrina. She . . . there was a day when she . . ." He discovered it was nearly impossible to go on.

"Aaron, whatever it is, it probably doesn't matter," Connie said. "The past is the past." Her voice was low. He could tell she was not at all anxious to hear Aaron Latimer's true confessions, and he wondered if he was crazy to tell her.

He lunged ahead. "She was pretty sure she was pregnant at one point," he rushed on. "We'd only been together once, and when she told me, I basically refused to be responsible."

Connie was quiet, watching him, ingesting it.

"I insinuated that maybe it was someone else's baby. That it might have been just about anybody's. I knew better, but I talked myself into thinking it might be."

"Oh," she said. She had quietly disengaged her hands from his. "What happened to the baby?"

"There was no baby. I just gave her a couple weeks of terror and let her go through it alone. She hated me after that, which I deserved, of course."

"I guess so," Connie said.

"I was scared. But I hurt her, badly. I shouldn't have done that. But, anyway, I just wanted to tell you because that was actually the only time. I wanted you to know."

"Why?" she asked. "Why did you want me to know that? Lots of people have sex all the time, with everybody, like there's no tomorrow." And then, "Were you serious about her?"

"Well, as much as you are in high school, I guess. I mean, we were just kids, but the way I ran and left her alone. It was my responsibility. It makes me sick to remember it."

But he did remember it. Katrina grasping his arm under the trees near the school athletic field and whispering her terrifying secret, scared to death. "What am I going to tell my father?" she said. Her words were sniffly and low. He wondered how long she had been crying to herself.

He had felt deep fear stiffen him, and tried to brush it off. "Oh, I doubt it's even true," he started. "We only-"

"You doubt it?" Katrina had nearly shrieked, then lowered her voice; she didn't want to draw the attention of others circling around the football field or standing in little groups, their classmates sitting not twenty yards away, cheering and sipping cocoa in the stands. "How can you doubt it?"

"There was only that one time," he said. And only that because he had talked her into it.

"What should we do?" she asked him quietly. Her hand still grasped his arm, afraid to let go.

"I don't know," he said irritably. "What makes you so sure? What makes you think it's mine anyway?"

Her arm dropped and she stared at him, aghast. "I never did that with anybody else. You know that."

A sudden loophole burst upon him, and he followed it ruthlessly. "How do I know? Your reputation-"

The slap hit him hard and stung viciously, and he raised a hand to his cheek as he watched Katrina stalk away. A couple of kids on the bleachers turned to look. Aaron walked stiffly off the school grounds and didn't stop until he was home in his own room.

Well, Katrina Jeffers *had* had a reputation when he'd met her. He had found out later that it was undeserved. He was captivated by her sweetness, loved her smile and her pretty, long wavy hair. He had genuinely cared for her. Her innocence when the two of them had somehow ended up with their hands inside each other's clothes in her house one summer night had matched his own. The sight of her, half dressed and as unsure as he was, had given him a sense of bravado, and it hadn't taken much to talk her into it.

"Please, Katrina, please, you know I love you."

She had given in, trembling and awkward, as he was. Later, shaking with fear, they had both promised that it would never happen again until they were married. They had meant it, too.

The great irony, of course, was that there was no baby, never had been, just a false alarm, and when she sought him out a week later to tell him, privately this time, he had been incredibly relieved.

"Thank God," he had said to her, and smiled a little, putting his arms around her.

Her eyes were ice. She shook him off and stepped away, and hurled one word at him before she stalked out of his life for good. "Bastard!"

Chapter 13

CONNIE'S EYES were downcast as she listened, and Aaron worried that his direct honesty might have been a big mistake after all. It had seemed, for some reason, necessary to share his most shameful secret with her; now he wasn't sure that had been wise.

"Why are you telling me this, Aaron?" she said finally.

"I don't know," he said truthfully. "But I want you to know I'm not that person anymore. I would act differently now. I regret what I did back then."

"Sleeping with her? Or abandoning her?"

"Both. She was the only one, ever. I never put myself or any girl in that position again." Because he had too much self-control for that and had learned his lesson well. A baby? Children? Abortion? Adoption? The thought of any of them was enough to reign him in. He'd heard too many smirking stories about foolproof methods that had turned into someone's bouncing bundle of joy.

"What if it happened now?" Connie asked him. "What if you made love to some girl and she ended up pregnant? What would you do?" She sounded curious more than anything.

"It would never happen now," he answered positively. "I wouldn't let it. I mean, if it were you, well, I guess I'd marry you. Yes, of course I would. So there would never be an unwelcome baby."

"You sound very smug," she said quietly. "What if I didn't want to marry you? How can you be so sure you'll always be in such perfect control?"

Because he lived his life that way, he could have told her. Because it was the only safe way to be.

Connie was quiet the rest of that afternoon, and when he suggested dinner out and a movie after, she begged off, saying she was tired and really needed to get some things done. She kissed him chastely as he left her apartment.

He had blown it.

He called her the next day and the day after, halting, awkward conversations that left him moaning in fear that she was lost to him. On the third day, she agreed to let him come over and smiled demurely when she answered the door to a dwarfed Aaron hiding behind an armful of two dozen red roses.

"They're beautiful," she said. "Thank you." She placed them in water and positioned them on a table.

She had done it again, worn clothing that covered every inch of her and looked provocative as hell. This time it was a silky-looking scarf tied loosely at her throat, and, yes, the two unbuttoned shirt buttons that didn't expose a thing but made him burn with desire to know the mysteries that she kept so carefully concealed.

He decided he'd better get her to marry him soon.

It was the obvious next step since he couldn't sleep and couldn't eat, thinking maybe their relationship was destined to be strictly friendly and she might decide to wave good-bye at any moment, leaving him confused, depressed, and alone.

Broaching the subject was the hard part.

She had been sitting at her kitchen table looking through pictures on her laptop and invited him to sit near her and look, too. They were pictures of her trip to Scotland the previous year. He bent toward the screen, showing an interest.

"To you, they don't look like much," she said.

"Sure they do. Why do you say that?"

"Because you're Aaron Latimer."

He laughed, pleased at the compliment. "Well, that doesn't mean I can't appreciate good old-fashioned vacation pictures. They're good, Connie. They catalogue your whole trip. You look as if you're having a great time. Where are these ruins?"

"In Melrose. That's Melrose Abbey; it used to be the richest abbey in Scotland. We had soup near there. It was so good; I think we were all starving. I remember I almost left my camera behind." She clicked past a few photos. "Look, here's the River Tweed. That was taken in Melrose, too."

Aaron moved his chair closer to hers and gently turned her to face him. She stopped describing pictures and looked at him. He put one arm around her shoulders and kissed her. "Connie," he said. "I love you. I've never loved anyone else this way."

"I never have either, Aaron."

"When I told you about Katrina, I didn't mean to force you away from me. I just wanted you to know that I haven't been with a lot of women. I can't change the past. I'm sorry it bothers you so much."

"What bothers me isn't the fact of this girl, it's the way you treated her." Connie's guileless eyes stared straight into his, and he realized with a rush that he could never be as good as she was, could never measure up to the moral highroad she traveled.

"I was terrified. I was seventeen."

"How old was she? Didn't you suppose she was terrified, too?"

"I know she was, and I regret everything about that time. But, Connie, that was almost ten years ago. I would never do that now. I wouldn't abandon someone I cared about that way."

She was studying him closely, looking very serious. "No, I don't think you would."

"It sounds ridiculous to say it but I'm glad I told you, even if it changes things between us." He exhaled loudly and stood up, agitated. "I don't want any secrets between us, Connie. I need you and I'll always put you first. I want you to know everything about me, so you can make your decision with your eyes wide open."

"What decision?" she asked, confused.

"To marry me. I've never asked anyone before and I'm not very good at it, but I love you." Much to his own surprise, he was down on one knee, grasping her hands and begging her to be his wife. "Will you marry me? I promise to share everything I have with you. There won't be any other women, and I'll always love you. I need you, Connie. You make me happy."

Connie reached out a hand to his cheek, and he covered her hand with his own.

"Please," he said.

A flicker of a smile touched the corners of her mouth. "Yes," she said. The word was a tiny breath on the air. Then she paused, thinking. "There's one thing, though,"she said. "Do you want children, Aaron? Now that you're grown up? Because I do."

He gazed at her with wonder. Had she really said yes? He grinned broadly and scooped her up into a great bear hug. "Are you kidding? Dozens."

Connie laughed. "I'd like a short engagement, Aaron."

"Sure, that's fine!" He tried to reign in his enthusiasm. "I'm all for that."

"Good," Connie said, "because now that we know, I can't stop thinking about it either."

"It?"

"Sex, you goof."

Chapter 14

AS HIS CANOE neared the lake store, Aaron could see the three docks jutting into the water and smell oil mixed with gas. An older man sprawled in a deck chair conversing with a young guy sitting in a boat. The younger man held one firm hand to the horns of a cleat, keeping his boat steady before he left the dock. The oily residue floating on the water glittered phosphorescent purple, blue, and green in the sun.

Two or three other boats were pulled in, ropes coiled around moorings. Aaron paddled in easily, snugged his canoe to the dock, and stepped out of the boat. He greeted the old timer and headed up the path.

The man Foster was eating at the lunch counter again when Aaron entered the store. Cathleen Parnell beamed her welcome and made an official introduction. Foster Wolf nodded, and Aaron shook the gnarled hand he extended.

Aaron gathered up a few groceries and decided to look over the camp souvenirs. He bypassed the cedar incense burners and ceramic ducks and loons, but picked up one of the small heart-shaped cedar boxes. *Big Trout Lake, NY* was stamped on the lid. He piled it with his groceries, a gift for Egan.

Aaron took a stool at the counter and looked over the plastic-laminated menu, taking note of the changes in price; red marker raised a salami sandwich to four fifty and a cheeseburger to five forty-five. He ordered a bowl of vegetable soup, and Cathleen served him promptly. He caught sight of the heavy wheel of milky white cheese under glass. "Is that sharp cheddar?" he asked.

Cathleen grinned. "The sharpest." She cut him a generous wedge, placed it on oiled paper, weighed it, and left it unwrapped for him. Whatever he didn't eat for lunch, he could take home with him. She stepped behind the counter and rang up his purchases.

"So, you have the big place on Spruce," Foster recalled.

"Right. My father's family built it about a hundred years ago."

Foster nodded. "Prime piece of property you got. If you ever decide to sell it, be sure you check out the market value. Some of these places are starting to go for half a million. Without the land of yours, too. Probably built them for a few dollars, pulled the lumber from the woods, and drug all the fixtures up the banks by hand."

Aaron laughed. "There used to be a dump up behind our camp. My father would tell about reading the old Sears catalogues his uncles threw out."

"Surprised they didn't use the Sears in the outhouse," Foster mused. "Most folks did. All the camps had a dump, though. That was for the small stuff. Used to slide the burned out appliances out on the ice in the winter and when the thaw come, no more worries." He cackled happily at the thought of the Colson lakes, their bottoms littered with miscellaneous sinks and stoves, burned out refrigerators and ancient, worn out motors.

"Remember when we were talking last time about the Dunn girl?" Aaron asked Cathleen. "What more can you tell me about her?" Cathleen had brought out a cracked ceramic bowl filled with sesame rolls. Aaron took one, broke off a piece of cheese, buried it in the roll, and bit into it hungrily.

"You writing another article?" Cathleen asked.

"Not about that. I'm just curious."

"Foster could tell you more," she said. "You were probably staying here then, weren't you?" she asked the older man.

"Her name was Virginia," he said nodding. "I think they called her Ginny. It's been maybe ten, twelve years since she drowned. She disappeared from the camp one night and washed up on Big Trout a few days later. That's where my place is, and I was staying there at the time. Current must have caught her just right and drug her all the way down through the channels and into Big Trout Lake. A couple of fishermen found her there, tangled up in some weeds. Conjecture was it was a suicide."

"What did she look like?" Aaron asked. "Not the dead body," he added hurriedly. "I mean when she was alive." He wasn't even sure he wanted to know.

"Pretty girl, I think. Long hair, I remember, big eyes. All the Dunns were good looking." He turned to Cathleen Parnell.

"Weren't there other kids? Some brothers?"

She shrugged. "I have no idea. I just remember that picture that hung over there." She gestured to the wall above the cash register. "Virginia Dunn it was signed. What ever happened to it, Foster?"

He chuckled. "Well, that's no mystery. I took it home. No one around here wants it, do they? A picture made by a suicide?"

Cathleen looked at him, her hands on her hips. "Well, I guess not." She stared at Foster Wolf. "You just took it, Foster?"

"Problem with that?" He slurped the last of his chocolate milk and turned to face her.

Suddenly she laughed. "No, no problem."

"Is that because you knew her?" Aaron asked. "The reason you took the picture, I mean. To remember her by?"

"No, I liked the picture. It's a good view of the shore of Spruce Lake."

Aaron's thoughts were spinning wildly. The shore of Spruce Lake, and if she had painted it from her dock, as she probably had, it was a painting of his own land, maybe of his own camp. "I'd like to see that," he said. "Foster, would you let me have a look at it?"

Foster Wolf shrugged his canvas jacket sleeve up his wrist and peered down at his watch. "Sure, come right now, if you want. I'm over on Big Trout, Shore Road, fourth camp from the end. Called *The Wolf Den*. There's a sign on the boathouse."

Chapter 15

IT WAS AARON'S CAMP she had painted, his and Chris's. He held the watercolor with a trembling hand, admiring the pale hues that lent a shimmery quality to the paper. She had caught the mountain at dusk, the dock and rowboat, the yellow painted camp and shed, the ferns and wildflowers that clustered up and down the high, rocky bank. The mountain behind was in shades of green-gray, blue, and purple. Her name was in the lower right hand corner in a fine, small script: *Virginia Dunn.*

Foster motioned to the two overstuffed chairs flanking his gas heater. Aaron sat.

"How come you're interested in the Dunns?"

He wasn't sure how to answer, so he told a half truth. "The camp is abandoned, caving in. It's very sad, a shame to see the property going to waste like that."

"They never came back that I know of. After they found her, the family just packed up and left. People said she was kind of wild, had a reckless streak. An arty type. I imagine the gossip was too much for them. And looking out on the lake every day. They kept to themselves anyway, and with only two camps on the lake . . . ."

"My family hasn't used our camp much over the years, either. My brother sends his share of the taxes; we hire repairs when we need to."

"Sounds like another property going to waste," Foster declared.

Aaron shifted uncomfortably. "Well, my wife isn't the wilderness sort."

Foster nodded. "There was a rumor around that the girl, Virginia, wanted to get married and the family was against it. You know how people romanticize an unexpected death. Some were saying that she went out to elope that night and he never came, so she took her life."

Aaron swallowed. "Who was the boyfriend?"

And what was she looking for, lifting up on her toes, craning her neck toward the channel night after night, her lantern held high, tears coursing down her cheeks. Was there a fiancé coming for her that night? Did she go with him and something happened? Did he never come at all?

"Eddie Safford," Foster said. "He's a lawyer now down in Albany."

"Was he able to shed any light on her death? Did he see her that night?"

"No, he was home at his own camp over on Little Trout Lake. Oh, they don't have it anymore," Foster said as he saw Aaron's sudden movement. "You can forget canoeing over there if that's what you were thinking." Foster Wolf looked him over silently for a moment, then asked, "Don't you have a motorboat?" The question took Aaron by surprise. "Or a car?"

Aaron felt himself flushing, wondering how he appeared to this unpretentious man.

"No, no motor boat. I'm not here often enough to put one in. I do have a car, of course, but felt like a little exercise." He felt silly. It reminded him of his first conversation with Connie, when she had teased him about the woodsy shirt he'd worn for his book's jacket photo. Why was it that Foster Wolf could dress in a dirty, worn canvas jacket, but Aaron Latimer evoked ridicule just by canoeing to the store in an L.L. Bean flannel?

He busied himself examining Virginia Dunn's painting.

"Well, as far as Safford goes," Wolf was saying, "I suppose you could reach him in Albany, but that was a long time ago and he's got a family of his own now, I imagine. You doing some kind of a book?"

"No, no," Aaron assured him. "Just curious, looking out on the place every day." More than curious, Aaron admitted to himself, and wondered if he was losing his grip on reality. It was one thing to feel curious about a camp on the lake; it was another to start digging into old history that was none of his business. To investigate his own personal ghost.

He still held the little watercolor in his hands and looked down at it again. It was under glass, framed in rustic wood, little more than four slim slats tacked together. *Virginia Dunn*, scripted tightly in the corner, ensnared him.

"This is a great likeness of my camp," he said to Foster.

"Would you be willing to sell it?"

The older man looked at him in surprise, rose from his chair and came to stand behind Aaron, looking down at the painting. "Sell it? That wouldn't seem right, seeing how I stole it." He chuckled at his own bad behavior.

"I'd like it, though," Aaron said, "and I'm willing to pay you. How about twenty dollars?"

"Son, if you want that painting, go right ahead and take it. You don't need to pay me for it."

"Well, for the frame at least."

"You think that frame is worth twenty dollars?" Foster said in surprise. He peered at the makeshift frame more closely.

"Well," Aaron hesitated. The frame was worthless, of course, but he wasn't sure if the old man might have made it himself and considered it a work of art. Of greater concern was the possibility that Foster Wolf might ask for the picture back. Money would cement the deal. "Here, I'll give you twenty for it." Aaron fished through his wallet and came up with a twenty dollar bill. He set it down on a side table and anchored it with the corner of a book. He now owned the painting exclusively.

He was suddenly anxious to leave.

He could hardly control the excited beating of his heart and looked up to find Foster Wolf looking at him curiously. Was it obvious, he wondered, that it was the signature and artistry that had captivated him, rather than the subject of the picture? He realized he would have paid far more than twenty dollars for this little piece of paper painted by a girl long dead.

Hurriedly thanking Foster Wolf before the old man could change his mind, Aaron left the cabin and headed to the shore where his canoe was beached. He glanced at his watch and was surprised that the afternoon had slipped away. He wedged the little painting between a box of stone ground crackers and a container of oatmeal in the cardboard carton that held his groceries, checking to be sure it was firmly supported.

It took him two hours to paddle back to Spruce Lake, fighting the current and the wind, keeping an eye on the sun that was setting in the west much faster than he was moving toward home.

Chapter 16

IT WAS TWILIGHT when he arrived. He put away his purchases and flicked on the battery-operated radio in the kitchen, wondering if the reception here would be good. It wasn't. He turned the radio off.

The fiddleheads he had collected still sat on the kitchen table, and he boiled a few, just as an experiment, and ate them with his dinner. Not too bad, but he wouldn't want to make them a staple.

He watched the sky darken outside the kitchen windows and felt a happy stirring when the telephone rang and he heard Connie's familiar voice. He told her about his paddle to the store and mentioned that he'd met an older guy, Foster Wolf, and visited him at his camp on Big Trout for a while.

"That sounds nice," she said. "What did you buy at the store?"

He catalogued items for her; it was a lazy conversation, both of them avoiding the one subject that he desperately wanted settled, that Connie refused to talk about.

"What about milk and eggs?" she asked, "Things like that?"

"Well, I'll have to go back to get a few items. I couldn't get anything perishable and then canoe back in the heat. I'm using powdered creamer."

"Oh, Aaron." She laughed softly.

"I don't mind," he said. "I'd rather do it this way. Last week I hiked," he said righteously.

"It's a few miles, isn't it?"

"Yeah, about five, but I enjoyed the exercise."

"You couldn't have carried enough to last you long."

"Last time I drove back later to pick up milk and a few other things," he admitted. "I'll do the same this time."

He could hear the mirth in her voice. "Well, it's one thing to enjoy it, but when it's impractical-"

"It was good enough for people around here a hundred years ago. Why shouldn't it be good enough now?" He knew he sounded belligerent.

"Oh, Aaron," she laughed gently, "do you really think you're fooling the lake residents?"

He bristled. "What do you mean, fooling them?"

"With the packbasket and all. It's like you're creating some character who's bigger and better than life, drawing attention to yourself. Why didn't you just use the SUV? It's the twenty-first century, after all."

"Sure, and not all progress is good, Connie. I'm trying for authenticity here. It's all part of the article."

"Don't get your mucky-boots in a huff," Connie replied tartly, then laughed a bright, amused laugh.

Aaron felt indignant. "This will flavor my writing, Connie, just like the camera and the typewriter." He ran a hand across his face and took a breath. "Never mind. I don't expect you to understand."

"Oh, don't be like that," she said. "I'm sorry."

"I like carrying the supplies that way," Aaron insisted. "And I like using the canoe instead of the car. I like the exercise. It's better for the environment, too."

Connie chuckled softly.

"It's not a pretense," he said hotly. "I happen to think that sometimes the old ways made more sense."

"Okay," she said agreeably. "But powdered creamer in your coffee, yuck. I'm glad I'm not there."

"If you were here, you could drive to the store and get whatever you want."

Connie laughed a silvery laugh. "Or walk there with a basket on my head, wearing a nice big apron to fold my surplus supplies in."

She changed the subject. "We met the tenant across the hall," she said. "He has a cat, and Egan found it in the hallway. She was excited to have a pet so handy."

"Let me talk to her," Aaron said abruptly.

"All right," Connie said. "Hey, listen, I wasn't making fun of you, honey. I know you enjoy the wilderness things."

"It's okay. You've never minced words with me before, why start now?"

"Let me get Egan," she said.

Egan prattled on about Oboe the cat for five minutes before Aaron interrupted her to ask about the classes and the ballet, the museums they had visited, and the restaurants they had eaten in. "Sounds like Mommy's treating you pretty well," he said, trying to keep the miffed tone from his voice. What was wrong with him? Was he jealous that his wife and daughter could have fun without him? No, only that Connie had chosen to go ahead and enjoy a vacation on her own. The whole idea of being separated like this was stupid, and Connie was ridiculously stubborn for insisting they continue.

Well, fine. He would write his article, take some great pictures, enjoy the woods, and explore the lakes. If she wanted to act selfish and shallow, he would manage perfectly well without her.

By the time she came back on the line, he had decided to be magnanimous and forgive her for her obstinate lack of understanding. "Connie, I might as well go through the usual litany," he said. "Will you pack your things and join me here? I want Egan to see this place, and I want us to have a few weeks together before fall-"

"I know, when it starts to get busy again. School starting, you running off to Spain or Iceland, me keeping the home fires burning."

"It won't be like that."

"Aaron, I love you, but I don't want to talk about this right now. I need this time. I want to do the things that I want to do, with you or without you. Examining bear scat isn't on my list. If you want to be with us, give up the article and join us here."

"I could come for a couple days. What's the address?"

"Aaron, *no*."

He backed off. "All right, Connie. Call me tomorrow, would you?"

"I don't know if I can; we have a lot planned. I'll try."

He could sense her getting ready to hang up the phone and searched his mind for another topic to detain her. "Chris and Veronica were here," he said.

"Really?"

"He has a new sports car."

"Oh, nice for him. I haven't seen them in a long time. How did they happen to show up?"

"He wanted to return a photograph album or something. They stayed all day. They ate all my food."

"Poor Aaron."

He had never told her that he detested his brother, but she'd always known. He wondered how. She seemed to know everything about him, and that wasn't always a comforting thought.

Suddenly he felt very unsure of himself and more worried about his marriage than he had realized. "Connie," he said, "will you call me tomorrow?"

"I'll try, Aaron," she said.

He replaced the receiver on its cradle and stood staring at the phone, then at the clunky typewriter sitting on the old oak table. Maybe Connie had called it exactly right. He was doing everything the hard way and not impressing anyone. Foster Wolf had made the same point, subtly, when he wondered aloud why crazy Latimer didn't just travel the way everyone else did. Aaron grimaced, recognizing his posturing for what it was.

His glance took in the little watercolor hanging above his typewriter. He had cleaned the glass and the wooden frame, attached a new wire to the back, and positioned it above his writing table where he could see it easily. It was a good likeness of the camp, which sure appeared to be a pleasant place to bring your family. Why didn't Connie see it that way? Why was she so insistent on staying away from him for two whole months?

He looked over the selection of mildewed nineteen-forties novels crammed into a bookshelf and selected one. He settled into a lumpy, overstuffed chair and read three pages before he tossed the book across the room and sat staring out the window at nothing.

Chapter 17

THE TELEVISION WAS TUNED to the arts channel, and the hands of the tuxedoed pianist blurred as they manipulated the keys. Connie's eyes were fixed on the soprano trilling next to him, but her mind was racing.

She had been surprised to hear Aaron mention Chris's name. Connie had never pried into Aaron's past, had never insisted that he expose whatever wounds had been inflicted in his childhood years. That there were some she was sure; something caused him to need that quiet control over all situations, and she'd always suspected it had something to do with Chris.

She had asked about Chris once, only once, and Aaron's response had been curt. "Of course I like my brother. He's my brother."

"Well, you never want to talk about him; you never seem friendly on those rare occasions when-"

He had interrupted her, controlling his anger. "He's my brother, Connie." He had turned aside abruptly.

After that, she left it alone.

Whenever his parents brought up Chris's name, Aaron would become aggravated and move the conversation to safer ground. When they were forced to attend family events, she noticed that Aaron went out of his way to land in a different room from Chris, to sit at the opposite end of a table, to forego the activities Chris participated in and to participate in the ones Chris declined.

Aaron would tell her why if and when he wanted to, and she respected his privacy enough not to ask. Chris was a taboo subject.

She herself had met Aaron's brother and his family only a half dozen times in their nine years of marriage. Veronica seemed pleasant enough and the children typical of kids their ages. Chris, if anything, appeared timid around Aaron. Connie wondered- maybe it was that very timidity that Aaron had trouble accepting.

She knew very well that Aaron had not welcomed Chris's visit to Spruce Lake and was surprised he had mentioned it at all, then realized the obvious: Aaron had wanted to keep her talking, would bring up any topic, even one distasteful to himself, to keep her on the line long enough to sweet talk her into changing her mind about this Saratoga business.

Honestly, he was so transparent. She almost laughed.

Well, it hadn't worked.

The man who owned her heart and soul was finally trapped in a situation he couldn't control. Connie wondered why she didn't feel a greater sense of victory. When she had married him nine years before, could she have foreseen the unhappiness she was feeling today?

Their wedding had been the old-fashioned church variety, the two of them swearing lifelong devotion to one another and promising to accept children lovingly from God. Their darling Egan had been the result of that promise, and they had talked hopefully of more children, several more.

They'd had a gorgeous, brilliant June wedding day, and their outdoor reception in the park near her mother's home had been an event to remember. Flowers cascaded from every surface; cute, wholesome bridesmaids swished prettily in lace dresses; a group of Aaron's handsome college friends acted as groomsmen, ushers, and drivers. It had been a perfect start to what was supposed to be a perfect union.

Her own dress had been patterned after her grandmother's, with identical scalloped rows of tiny seed pearls and intricate flower appliqués covering the bodice and skirt. Aaron had looked so handsome, broad-shouldered and tall in his tux, and had whispered to her that there had never been a groom happier than he was at that moment. He had meant it; of that she was sure.

Do you, Aaron Richard Latimer, take Constance Mary Beckett, to be your lawfully wedded wife, to have and to hold . . . .

He did. And his eyes had shone with love when he said so.

So, what had gone wrong?

She flicked off the television in her Saratoga apartment, and the soprano disappeared into a silent black void. Connie hadn't heard a note of the aria, of any of the performance for the past half hour. She had been reminiscing about her beautiful, storybook wedding, her beloved, miraculous daughter who was playing quietly on the floor nearby, her husband who was, by choice, nearly a hundred miles away, closer actually than he often was during the course of any given year.

That's what had gone wrong.

She rose restlessly from the chair and paced to the kitchen, running her hand over the glowing cherry countertops. They were beautiful, but certainly no substitute for the man she wished she could touch right now.

No. She wouldn't allow herself to miss him. If he was her devoted husband, he should be acting like it.

And was he a worse husband than her father had been? A worse father than James Benjamin Beckett, who had unexpectedly left Connie and her brother and their mother one morning? He had simply disappeared that day. And shown up twelve years later as if he'd never been away.

Connie sank into one of the spindly chairs at her kitchen table and propped her weary head on her hand.

Her brother had been two and Connie six when James Beckett looked around their compact suburban ranch house, decided he'd had enough, went off to work whistling, and never came back until Connie had passed her eighteenth birthday. Egan was six now, she thought with a start. Maybe that fact had contributed to her decision to force Aaron's hand. Maybe it was her own panic that was begging Aaron to admit how important his presence was to their well-being as a family.

She didn't even remember the precise day her father had left. It never occurred to her that Daddy wouldn't be coming home for twelve years, and if she had questioned her mother about his absence at first, she had soon stopped asking.

Her little brother Stevie had been shuffled from daycare center to baby-sitter to nursery school, and it had fallen to Connie to pick him up and look after him when her own school day ended. She had cared for him in the summers, too.

Strangely, her mother never complained, at least not in front of Connie. Judy Beckett's most stinging criticism of her absent husband was that he was a very weak man, and when she said those words, her lip would curl and her eyelashes would flutter in disgust. Connie learned at six years old that weak men were the worst kind.

Judy Beckett spent her days at work, as a receptionist for a small Realty company, earning something close to minimum wage, but she enjoyed her job because it gave her a chance to dress up and meet the public. She had gone right ahead and moved up the corporate ladder to office manager, and then vice president of the company, and she had seemed happy enough.

She hadn't had any men friends, boyfriends, that Connie knew of, but had managed a cheerful facade, supported her children financially, and raised them very well, all things considered.

And she had taught Connie and Stevie, by her shining example, two principles that had stayed with Connie for the next twenty years: Respect yourself. And handle your responsibilities.

When James Beckett returned one fine day, his wife informed him that the family no longer needed him. It didn't matter to her that he now needed them. She politely closed the door in his face and sent him on his way.

Connie managed a Christmas card to her father each year, and had sent various snapshots of Egan over the years, but the ties were not close. She didn't despise her father, in fact pitied him if anything. He had met Aaron and Egan once or twice, had canceled several invitations to stay with the young, growing Latimer family, and had proven himself to be exactly what Judy Beckett called him: a weak, irresponsible man.

Connie had taken to heart her mother's rules for living and applied them to every decision she'd ever made: her choice of a career, her decision to leave that career, at least temporarily, when Egan was born, her choice of Aaron Latimer, a good man and a good provider, as her husband.

It galled her that Aaron seemed so lacking now in his sense of responsibility toward her and Egan. Clearly, he could have used a lesson or two from his mother-in-law. But, Connie mused resentfully, he was too busy putting his own needs first.

Exactly what James Beckett had done nearly thirty years before.

Was that the next step then? That Aaron would leave someday for a photo shoot and shoot himself clear out of her life? Had she, in fact, married someone just like her father?

If she were honest, Connie knew it would never come to that. Aaron loved her. But all those trips, so much unnecessary travel. So many nights when she had read herself to sleep - alone.

A vague, plaintive mewling interrupted her thoughts.

Egan had come into the kitchen and was tugging at Connie's sleeve, trying, with her child's small grasp, to force her mother up and out of the chair. "It's the kitty, mom," she said. "It's in the hall and I think it's feeling sad."

She let Egan pull her back to the living room.

The cat's meowing had grown louder - melancholy mews that barraged their door and intruded upon the quiet evening.

"Can't we check on him?" Egan asked.

"Honey, I'm sure he's fine. He has an owner. Let's let him take care of the cat."

"But what if he's not home?" Egan begged. "What if poor Oboe is hungry?"

"It's time for you to get to bed, Egan," Connie said. "I'm sure-"

"But he's meowing. Can't we check and make sure he's all right?"

Connie relented, opening their locked and barred front door and glancing down at the half-grown black and white kitten huddled there in the corridor, licking its own paws. Egan, fresh from her bath and soft and clean in her summer pajamas, began petting its velvety fur, coaxing it into their apartment.

"Honey, the cat belongs to Mr. Rime; you know that. I'm sure he knows it's out here. If you take it inside, he won't be able to find it and he'll worry."

Egan was torn. "But, mom . . . ." she began.

Connie was saved the trouble of arguing when the door across the hall opened and a young man appeared. Justin Rime smiled when he saw Egan intent on saving his cat.

"Oh, Oboe," he said, squatting down near Egan and cradling the kitten's head in his hands. "How did you get out here?" he crooned softly.

"Do you think he's hungry?" Egan asked.

"Could be. Want to come and help me feed him?" He smiled at Egan, then at Connie, inviting her, too. Connie followed cat, man, and girl into Justin Rime's apartment across the hall. His woodwork was polished, his carpet plush, his furniture and accessories more modern than those that had come with her furnished apartment. The room was tasteful, comfortable, and masculine, and it looked as if Justin Rime had set up housekeeping with an eye to staying for a while.

"How long have you lived here?" Connie asked him.

He thought briefly. "Two and a half years. You just moved in, right?" He peered at her with eyes that slanted down a little at the outside corners, giving him a soulful edge.

"Just temporarily," Connie said. "We're here for the summer to take in some culture."

"Well, you came to a good place for that. Have you been to SPAC yet?"

She nodded enthusiastically. "Just the other night for the ballet. It was wonderful. We have tickets for the orchestra, too."

They followed him to his kitchen, where he pulled the top off a can of cat food, emptied the fishy-smelling lump into a ceramic saucer, and placed it on the floor. Egan squatted down to watch Oboe eat, her little face almost even with the cat's as it lapped at the food.

Connie laughed. "Egan, you're about to climb into that bowl any minute. Back up a little and let Oboe eat, honey." She smiled at Justin and found him looking at her intently.

"I'm not in his way," Egan insisted.

Justin chuckled, turning to watch Egan and Oboe, then poured himself a cup of coffee from the pot still hot on its burner. "Would you like a cup?" he asked Connie. "It's decaf." His hand lingered on a second mug, ready to fetch and pour at her command.

"Okay."

"Connie, right?" he asked. She nodded. "And I've forgotten your daughter's name. I'm sorry."

"It's Egan. It's a family name from my husband's side."

"Is he . . . ." The question remained unfinished as he sipped from his cup and motioned her to a chair.

"Working," she said promptly. "He's a photo journalist. He's in the Adirondacks for a few weeks, researching and writing."

Justin Rime was very young, she decided, in his twenties, possibly thirty, certainly not older. His hair was dark and unkempt, his frame tall and slim, much slimmer than her broad-shouldered husband. He was serious-looking, not exactly handsome, but appealing, sensitive-looking. Yes, that was it. His eyes were large and deep and met hers over the coffee mug, frankly studying her face.

"Oboe has become a favorite at our place," she said, looking fondly at Egan, who now held the cat. Oboe relaxed in her lap, curled up and carefree, a fuzzy, black and white ball.

Justin chuckled. "Looks like he found a very comfortable spot, Egan." Egan grinned up at him, her soft child's hand gently stroking the kitten.

They traded trivialities while Connie finished her coffee, then she coaxed Egan up. The little girl reluctantly brushed Oboe gently from her lap and took Connie's hand. "Thank you for letting me visit Oboe," Egan said at the door.

"Thank *you*," Justin answered gallantly. "If Oboe ever gets loose again, I'll count on you to keep him safe for me." He smiled at Connie, said good night, and closed the door behind them.

"That was fun," Egan said as Connie tucked her into bed a few minutes later.

"Yes, it's nice that we have a good neighbor, isn't it?"

"I love Oboe," Egan said sincerely. "Can I get a kitten, Mommy?"

"Oh, I don't know," Connie said vaguely. "Yesterday you wanted a horse, Egan. Why don't you just enjoy Mr. Rime's kitten while we're here."

"He said I can call him Justin," Egan reminded her.

"Yes, you're right," she told her daughter, kissing her nose. "Go to sleep now." Justin *had* invited Egan to use his first name. A friendly gesture, she was sure, from a nice man who happened to be their closest neighbor. But, for some reason, that small familiarity made Connie slightly uncomfortable. She was glad to have a friend here, but a male friend?

"Good night, baby." She kissed Egan again, pulled the blankets up around her shoulders, turned out her light, and went into the living room to spend the rest of her evening alone, aching for Aaron, with the mindless noise of the television to keep her company.

Chapter 18

AARON'S STOMACH WAS CLENCHING; he was determined to make contact with the girl on the beach, to find out if they could communicate somehow. He was insane and willing to admit it.

Could she really be a ghost? The bits of the story he had learned from Foster Wolf were chilling; this had to be the same girl. He had looked so doggedly for signs of life over there, and there were none. She came and went on a breeze, turning the air cold around her, repeating the same motions as if she were caught in them, unable to change her destiny. He had heard her. And he had seen her. And, most alarming, yet exciting in some weird way, he was convinced that *she had seen him.*

At a quarter past midnight, the canoe glided across the lake as if on its own, and Aaron tied it, hiding it beneath the trees. This time, he climbed out of the boat and, without use of a flashlight, picked his way to the dilapidated outside steps leading up and into the Dunn camp. The rancid hint of some decomposing animal assaulted his nostrils, and within the bulging walls he could hear scurryings and scratchings. His stomach turned over as he sat on a step near the top. There was a moon, but he hid in shadows. Leaves rustled overhead, and he forced his eyes to take in the darkness, trying to make out shapes of things.

When the air turned cold suddenly, he strained his eyes, sure she was near. She was hazy for a second and then took shape, her pale gown clinging to her, her long hair in waves down her back, so like Katrina's had been. She walked slowly up the beach, then returned, holding her lantern aloft, stretching up on her toes, peering down the lake to the channel. She waded out into the water, and this time he didn't flinch, for he knew she would never go any farther. He watched her lower her lantern and start toward the rotten cottage steps. Her whimpering began, low and controlled. She stepped onto the first step.

Aaron could hardly breathe; her waist was at his eye level. She rose to the next step. He watched her gown swish around her hips and was sure he felt a flutter on the air. He had left plenty of room for her to pass, but wondered if she might float right through him. What would that feel like? Was he losing his mind?

When she stepped up onto the same creaky board he sat on, he reached out with his right hand and gently grasped her ankle.

Whatever he had expected, it was not the cold, marble smoothness that his hand now touched. The contact between his flesh and hers shocked him. There was no warmth and no life, but there was substance. The icy surface froze his hand, but burned, too, hot to the touch. She reacted to the contact with a very real gasp of terror, a low, hollow sound that echoed away on the mountainside. Her lantern swung precipitately, and she thrust it onto the step above, where it rocked crazily and finally righted itself, burning steadily.

He refused to let go; his fingers held her slim, cool ankle, slippery with lake water. She struggled against his hand, grasping her skirt and pulling away, trying to loosen herself, gasping pitifully.

"Virginia." He whispered her name, afraid to speak louder for fear of terrorizing her further. Her struggling stopped abruptly, then continued with even more fervor.

"Ginny, don't be frightened. I don't intend to hurt you." He gulped back a nervous laugh. How could he hurt her when the worst had already happened to her?

She struggled less.

"You've seen me, Ginny. You know who I am."

She stopped struggling, and briefly he wondered what she would do next. For some seconds she remained completely still. And then her skirt rustled and he felt shock rush through him as her icy fingers probed under his chin. He allowed her to lift his face, and she bent her own to peer into his eyes. He met her gaze, locking his eyes with hers. He stared at the strange shadows the lantern flame created on her face.

He still held her ankle, but he felt her body relax; her fighting had died away. "I know who you are, Ginny, and I don't think you meant to die. If you had meant to, I don't think you'd be here." He wasn't sure where that idea had come from, but it made sense to him, and when he saw the tears start in her eyes, he knew he must be right. "I'd like to be your friend, Ginny.

Would you let me?"

"Die?" she said. He felt himself breathing harder at the sound of her voice, cool and delicate, hollow, ancient, and musical. Her frozen fingers still touched lightly under his chin. Heat pulsed from her fingertips into his face, flushing his body. Tears dropped from her eyes onto his face below hers. He felt their cold, wet rivers trace over his skin and tasted salt as they flowed to his lips. He fought for composure, letting his left hand feel the damp, mossy step, his feet pressing solid earth, grappling to anchor his reeling senses. He forced familiar control and patted the empty step beside him. "Sit here, Ginny, will you, please? Will you sit beside me?"

Her head still bent, still looking deeply into his eyes, she sat, a small, weightless thing in the night.

He was afraid to let go, but holding her ankle was awkward now that they sat side by side. With his left hand, he searched out her hand, and finally grasped its cold, stony form. He intertwined her fingers in his, holding tightly, trying to ignore the icy burning that reached to the depths of each of his fingers and shot like daggers through all of him. Then he released her ankle and sat up straighter.

She sat stiffly beside him, her hand in his.

"Ginny? Virginia? Is that right?" he said.

She nodded yes, and his worst fears were realized. He was sitting in the damp, foul night, clenching a ghost by the hand, afraid to release her.

"They believe you killed yourself, Ginny," he told her. "But I don't believe that."

She didn't answer. For many moments, they sat, hands intertwined. He was afraid to let her go, sure she would evaporate into the air. He clutched her hand tightly.

A high-pitched trilling startled him. "A loon," he said. "There's a pair of them. I think they're nesting over in that marshy area on the state land." Raucous laughter nearly burst from him. Was he dreaming this?

"I've seen them," she said, "and heard them in the night."

Her matter-of-fact response sobered him. Stunned and mesmerized by the ethereal quality of her voice, like an echo, a lost soul, he gathered his wits and answered rationally, "Right. Me, too." He forced himself to breathe slowly, felt her nod almost imperceptibly beside him and wondered at the banality of their dialogue. The loon trilled again, haunting the still, black lake.

A little silence covered them. He felt her hand still in his, small and cold as ice.

"I've watched you every night for two weeks," he told her at last. "I'm sorry you're unhappy. Why do you walk down the beach and then look toward the channel to Sentry Pond? Do you walk into the water to get a better view?"

She twisted to stare into his eyes, then lifted the hem of her skirt a few inches. Its drenching water ran out in little rivulets. The lantern light specked glowing darts on her skin, showing him that her ankles were still damp. With her free hand, she took his right hand and gently placed it on her ankle again.

"No, no," he said gruffly, "I don't need to hold you that way. I was afraid you'd run off." She spread her cold hand over his warm, burning one and rubbed his hand up and down her ankle, then her shin. His hand burned and he could feel his breath coming in gasps. He pulled his hand away and turned to her. "No, Ginny, I don't want to touch you that way. I want to help you."

"How?" she asked. Her voice was a musical note, strumming far away. That she had a voice at all was a shock to him.

Obviously, he had no idea how to help her and realized he had said the words thoughtlessly. He was here merely to satisfy his own curiosity; he had no other goal. He rubbed his free hand across his eyes. "I don't know," he said honestly. "Maybe I can't."

"You could come tomorrow night," she said unexpectedly. "It's so hard to be alone each night."

"You haven't been alone," he said wryly. "For the past two weeks, I've been right here."

"Why have you?"

He wasn't sure. He shrugged. "Curiosity, I guess."

She smiled at him, and the lantern light behind and between them danced and glimmered in her eyes. "Will you come?"

Come again? To visit with a ghost in the deep, black night? He wondered why fear did not overpower him. "Yes, I'll bring you something," he said at last. "You aren't afraid of me, are you?"

"No, I'm not afraid."

The wonder was that he was not afraid of her. "My name is Aaron," he said. "I live right over there." He raised their intertwined hands and gestured across the lake. "Well, for a while anyway. I don't really live there, but I'll be here for a few weeks."

"I'm glad."

Her unexpected words touched him, and he smiled to himself. "I'm glad, too. I'll be here tomorrow."

"You're the man in the canoe."

"Yes, the one who hides under the falling branches and tries to be still and quiet so he doesn't disturb you."

She shook her head just slightly. "You're not still and you're not quiet, though."

He nodded. "I know."

Her light laugh startled him. "You thought about saving me once. When I went into the water."

"Yes, I didn't realize . . . . What's through the channel, Ginny? What are you waiting for?"

She didn't answer but raised his hand, and therefore her own, to her lips and nuzzled there for a moment. Her cold lips brushed his fingertips, sending hot pain through him. He looked down on her brown hair, her slender neck, and watched her place her cool cheek against his knuckles.

Uncomfortable, Aaron loosened his fingers, then let her hand go altogether.

The next second she was gone. The light went out immediately, and he turned quickly in both directions. Where was she? He felt for the lantern on the step above him, but his hand felt nothing but springy moss and damp, rotted wood. The lantern, too, had vanished.

He moved stiffly on the dank step. He was very cold suddenly. How long had he been here? And had he really been deep in conversation with the ghost of Virginia Dunn?

He stretched his fingers. He had felt the hot, frigid smoothness of her skin; he was sure of that. He raised his hand to his nose and cheeks. Right there, her tears had coursed over his skin; he had tasted their saltiness. Hadn't he? He turned around and peered into the darkness. Behind him, the camp was black. The carrion smell overpowered him suddenly, and his stomach lurched. Squealings from inside the building jarred his nerves and made his skin prickle.

He must be crazy. What was he doing here, sitting cramped and alone in the foul night air on the steps of a bleak, abandoned camp.

He shivered as he shoved off in his canoe and pulled his flannel shirt tighter around him.

Chapter 19

THERE WAS NO WAY he could relax with every nerve in his body taut; he felt like a spring about to snap. It was one o'clock in the morning, but forget sleep. The best he could do was to curl up on a porch rocker wrapped in one of the old family quilts and stare into the blackness across the lake. Was she real? A ghost? Some kind of figment his crazy imagination had concocted? Two o'clock passed. Three o'clock. Four.

Her skin burned him. But how could that be when she was so cold, so very cold?

The sun began to rise at five o'clock. From the porch, he watched, his eyes bleary, as its slanting rays bathed the mountainside in amber and green light. He saw the glints on the water, the millions of tiny diamond specks that pricked the surface.

He could feel the agony of the sleepless night in his muscles, but the shower he had rigged up behind the camp sounded cold and uncomfortable, and even though the lake looked inviting, something within him balked at the idea of diving in. He had loved swimming here as a child, but found the idea distasteful now.

Finally, he went inside and changed his clothes. For today, clean clothes, a damp hairbrush, lots of toothpaste, and a cup of strong black coffee would have to do.

When the telephone rang it startled him, and he stared at it. Another jarring ring and hesitantly he picked up the receiver.

"Aaron, it's no good."

A relieved breath escaped him. What had he thought, that the ghost of Virginia Dunn was calling?

"Connie, how are you? How's Egan?"

"Oh, we're fine, Aaron, but this is just not right. I miss you so much, honey. I hate it when we're apart." She laughed self-deprecatingly. "And that's exactly the problem we're trying to fix."

He sat down and allowed the relief to come over him. She missed him. The experiment wasn't working. "Are you coming here?" he asked hopefully.

"I don't know . . . . Maybe. Give me three reasons why I should." It was an old way between them and he laughed appreciatively.

"You only need one, Con. I'm here."

"Yes, conceited old you."

"Well, why wouldn't I be? I look at my wife and figure I must be so damned important to have won you." This was good, the old conversations, the same old banter between them. "Connie, do you think I'm pretentious?" he asked.

"Yes," she said. "You know I do. I told you that the week I met you. Why are you worrying about it now?"

"I just want to be sure your feelings for me haven't changed."

He heard her light laughter on the other end and leaned back in his chair. Exhaustion overcame him, and he allowed loose relaxation to warm his body as he listened to his wife's familiar, loving voice over the phone line. Then, not thinking, he made a mistake that would change everything. The way they were talking, confiding in each other right now, the easy way they had with each other, the course of their summer and their lives would be radically tested by the words he said next.

"Connie," he said, "the weirdest thing happened last night."

"What was it?"

"I . . . . You're never going to believe this. There's a ghost here . . . ."

There was a pause while Connie considered. "A ghost?"

"I met a ghost last night," he said. "I'm not kidding. I talked to a ghost."

"Really, Aaron?" The fun was gone from her voice, and she sounded reserved, as if she had taken a firm step back.

The good feeling inside him fizzled and disappeared. What had he thought, that she would take it at face value? She didn't even like the idea of spiders and squirrels, and he was expecting her to accept the idea of a ghost? He didn't answer her, couldn't speak. He had no idea what to say.

"Aaron? What are you talking about, a ghost?" He heard her skepticism, her worry, and, yes, the tiny flicker of annoyance that she couldn't quite hide.

"Yeah, a ghost," he said uncertainly. Please believe me, he begged her silently. He wanted desperately to have her know. How could he bear this burden alone?

"Tell me about it," she said more calmly. "Is this a joke or something? Did you see something?"

"It's true, Con. I saw a light across the lake," he said, "at a camp where a girl drowned ten or fifteen years ago."

"Well, people were there, then-" Connie started.

"No, no. That wasn't it. There's no one there except-"

There was dead silence on the line. His stomach began to ache. "It's the writing," he finally said. "I'm really tired and you know my imagination."

But Connie had grasped onto another idea, one even more frightening than squirrels or spiders, and certainly more threatening than ghosts. "Did you say a girl drowned in that lake?"

"It was years ago," he said.

"Oh, Aaron, I can't bring Egan there. She can't swim. I'd be worried every minute."

He flung himself on the chance to change the subject, to discuss something sane and normal. "She'd be able to, Connie, if you'd let her go to the Y for lessons."

"She's too young for that. We've talked about it before. You know how I feel."

"She's not too young, Con. They have a preschool program. If you had taken her, she'd be able to swim now, and you'd be able to trust her around the water."

"Right." Connie made no effort to hide her exasperation. "If *I* had taken her."

He realized his mistake, and, unsure how to repair the error, he said nothing.

"And you know that for those beginning classes, they expect a parent to get into the pool," Connie said.

"I know, I know." She was reminding him of his own shortcomings, and of another thing - her own terror of the water. Egan had not yet learned to swim because Connie had never learned. And Aaron, of course, had made himself far too busy to commit himself for the weekly sessions.

"But, Connie," he said gently, trying to deflect her attention back to safer ground, "this girl who drowned. It was different. They were special circumstances. She was trying to elope, they say, and it may even have been a suicide. I'm not sure how it happened but I-" He caught himself before the dangerous words tumbled from his mouth.

But I'm planning to ask her, he had almost said. I'm just going to put the question to Virginia Dunn herself.

Connie would come to Spruce Lake, then, oh, yes, and drag him off to be committed to an asylum. He almost laughed. This was something he could never expect Connie to understand. "Are you still there?" he asked, and he knew immediately that Connie had caught the change in his tone, the insane mirth ready to explode into laughter.

"What's going on, Aaron?" she asked soberly. "This isn't funny if it's some kind of joke." She was distant now and sounded irritated and suspicious. "Aaron?"

"No, of course it isn't."

"You said you talked to a ghost. What does that mean?"

"It doesn't mean anything. Forget I said it. Is Egan up yet? Can I talk to her?"

Connie sighed unhappily and put their daughter on. Aaron was preoccupied and exhausted and said all the wrong things to her. Egan, impatient with the distance between them and annoyed at his distraction, became whiny and demanding. It required Connie retrieving her cell phone to smooth things over. She didn't ask again about the ghost at Spruce Lake, and he didn't offer an explanation. Why not, he thought ruefully. Why not one more complication springing up between us? Neither did she renew the topic of coming to Spruce Lake. She would not be bringing Egan along to cavort through the forest with Aaron and recreate their happy little family.

He suggested it vaguely, but already knew her answer.

When he finally hung up, he felt worse than he had in days. Connie had been so close to seeing things his way, to giving in and joining him here, and he had destroyed it. Big time. Ground it down and stomped on it, crushing into pulp all the good feelings between them, as only Aaron Latimer knew how to do.

He sat at the typewriter and stared at a sheet of paper with three typed lines on it. He waited for words to appear, for some kind of inspiration to strike. Nothing happened.

He needed sleep. He needed Connie and Egan. He needed to get this article finished so he could leave this place and concentrate on his family and win them back. He did not need, had never needed, a slight, young female ghost with hair like Katrina Jeffers'. A ghost in a long, flowing gown who nuzzled her lips against his hand and searched deep into his soul with her big, teary eyes. A ghost with liquid silver in her touch.

He gave in to his tiredness and went upstairs to the bedroom he had staked out for his summer-long solitude. Fully clothed, he lay down and fell into a troubled sleep.

Chapter 20

CONNIE YANKED EGAN'S HAIR as she brushed the tangles out. It was seven in the evening; Egan was clean and scrubbed and smelled of soap in her blue bunny pajamas, but even her sweet, freshly-bathed scent did nothing to soothe her mother.

"Ouch," Egan cried. "That hurt, Mommy."

"I'm sorry, sweetie."

"Let me do it," Egan said.

"No, no," Connie reassured her. "I promise I'll be gentle." She pulled the brush carefully through Egan's hair and gave her daughter a quick hug. "You can play with your puzzles for a few minutes before bed if you want to." Egan ran from the living room. In moments, she had dozens of wooden puzzle pieces scattered about the kitchen floor and was happily sliding various horse shapes into corresponding cut-outs.

Connie stood in the living room fuming and then flung herself into one of the matching blue velvet chairs flanking her fireplace. What on earth was going on with Aaron? What did he mean, he had seen a ghost? Didn't it just figure that Aaron would discover a ghost at Spruce Lake?

But did he really believe he'd seen one? What on earth was happening to him?

She squelched the flicker of worry beginning to build inside her and gave in to annoyance instead.

Was this some new trick to get her to change her mind? If so, she didn't see how. She didn't believe in ghosts, and neither, she'd thought, did her intelligent, sensible husband. So why did his voice shake when he brought it up? Why had he sounded so strange? And had he been quietly laughing at her? What was wrong with him?

The Latimer camp rose in her mind's eye. It was a pretty place and worth a small fortune, too, with its unspoiled waterfront and intense privacy. Most people would have jumped at the chance to spend the summer there, spotting loons and herons and even bald eagles, breathing the mountain air, enjoying the clean, clear water, and taking in the beautiful views.

But Connie wasn't most people and had no intention of 'vacationing' at Spruce Lake, and if she had called Aaron in a moment of weakness, it had certainly passed now.

The place gave her the creeps, and it had nothing to do with ghosts.

If Aaron had asked her to drop everything and accompany him to Boston or Newport, would she have gone? Was it really Aaron she refused to see or was it his family camp?

It was both, she admitted. Yes, she was upset with Aaron and the selfish freedom that took him away from her so frequently, but there was more to it than that. To give up Saratoga for Spruce Lake, well, she couldn't. She couldn't possibly.

The wilderness, she admitted to herself, scared her.

Her mother had taken them camping once when Stevie was four and she was eight. It had seemed pleasant enough with the quiet breeze dancing among the high, leafy treetops and the blue sparkling water inviting them in to swim. Their tent site was right on the lake shore, the woods behind and across the road, and when Stevie had wheedled long and hard enough, Judy Beckett had finally given in and settled in to watch and applaud him as he splashed in the water.

But Connie had always shied away from the water, too afraid to try, and she had no intention of trying it at the scary, unknown campsite lake, with its black, faraway bottom that she couldn't see. So she had asked her mother if she could play in the woods instead, right across the road from their campsite. She would be fine there, and she would be careful. Her mother could almost, not quite, but almost see her from her lounge chair on the waterfront, and after all, Stevie was smaller, so she needed to keep a better eye on him.

"Don't play in the road," her mother had cautioned her, an unnecessary warning. Connie knew enough not to play in the road; hadn't she been Stevie's caregiver for two years now? And traffic here was practically non-existent anyway.

So she had played by the side of the road, gathering stones that pleased her with their gold-flecked surfaces and smooth shapes. She strolled into the dappled woods, drawn by a shock of green. Just beyond some big rocks she stopped to examine what might have been animal tracks. They led her down a slight dip to a cluster of tall trees that provided a pretty, canopied shelter.

There had been mushrooms there, and she'd gasped in delight at the fairy rings they made, growing in tight circles. She knew enough not to eat them or to touch her hands to her face if she fingered them. She was a cautious child, and even touching them seemed dangerous beyond her imaginings. So she simply looked, admiring their crisp, fluted gills and smooth, brown caps and pretending they might be homes to elves or a family of forest sprites.

She walked farther into the woods, lured by another clearing where a few wild daisies grew. These she could pick, and she did, plucking out the petals one by one to see if *he*, whoever he was, loved her even now, years before she knew his name or face.

When Connie realized she was lost in the woods, a stillness overcame her. She knew she could find her way out if she simply thought. She peered overhead and around her, tried to notice markings on trees and rocks, and wandered a little this way, then that. It was moments before sheer terror overwhelmed her. She hadn't meant to wander so far from the road's gravel edge, but now when she looked around, all the trees looked the same, horribly familiar, yet not.

Ahead was a clearing, and sure that it must be the road again or maybe the grassy area of the campsite pavilion, she had run to it. But no, it was just a little forest clearing with more trees, more rocks, more dead leaves underfoot. There were no daisies here, but then she had plucked them all, so this might be the same clearing. But it might not.

She had tried to circle back again and thought a certain rock looked familiar. But once she got to it, she wasn't sure after all. She ventured beyond the rock and found herself at the top of a dense hillside, thick with brush and leaves, where blown down trees created a prickly web.

This was not familiar at all.

She cried and screamed for help, but no sound answered her. She could hear the whisper of leaves in the trees, and sometimes a roar that made her think there might be a waterfall nearby. She searched for it, but didn't find it, so decided that it must have been the wind. She screamed again and shouted until her throat hurt.

She had finally made herself so lost, hoarse, and afraid that she had stopped under a giant tree, curled up on muddy pine needles against a cold, damp rock, and cried herself to sleep.

When she awoke, it was evening. She could tell because the light had changed. She shrieked for her mother and Stevie, waiting for someone to hear her and come to find her. There was no sound except the wind through the trees.

Had they missed her? Was anyone looking for her?

As the sun burned red behind the thick growth of trees and underbrush, Connie watched it sink beyond the forest, and then, as her heart pounded in terror, darkness shrouded her.

She had forced her eyes to stay open long past the time when she might usually have slept. Every noise scared her; every rustling in the underbrush caused cold panic to prick up on her chilly, exposed limbs. Mosquitoes buzzed around her ears and nipped tiny, stinging bites on her arms and legs.

Her sleep, when it finally came, was fitful, and dressed in just her cotton tee shirt and shorts, she shivered throughout the night. With every snuffling noise, her eyes blinked open and she cried anew. She was sure she heard some heavy animal lumbering through the woods, and she tried to curl up smaller, to stay quieter, letting her tears come as her terror mounted. She felt strange featherings on her arms. Insects? An animal's hot breath? There was a metallic taste in her mouth, and she was so afraid to move from her dark, damp spot that she wet her pants, then cried in shame and horror.

It wasn't until morning that she fell into a real sleep.

Large, rough hands had awakened her gently. A camper, culled from his tent along with dozens of others, had stumbled upon her as they formed a search grid. He'd picked her up, and his shout of excitement had terrified her at first until other searchers joined the camper, who carried her, trembling, back the two and a half miles she had traveled.

She was dirty, scared, and relieved. Her pink shorts were ripped and ragged and smelled damply of urine and earth; her hair was tangled and bristling with pine needles, dead leaves, and dirt. Bug bites, raised and red, swelled and itched on her bare skin.

Her mother had cried and hugged her, both their noses running, and had thanked the searchers a multitude of times, assuring Connie that they would never go camping again.

And they hadn't. Just the thought of being in the woods terrified her, and if she hadn't exactly told Aaron the whole story, she had certainly dropped enough hints about her aversion to the wilderness. It was selfish of him to keep insisting.

What kind of parents would they be if they dragged Egan off to the Adirondack forest, putting her in possible danger from who knew what wild animal or other terror? Bears, foxes, coyotes. Tempting her near the water's edge, putting her in the way of mosquitoes and snakes. Connie shuddered.

Aaron had no idea what he was asking.

Chapter 21

VIRGINIA DUNN, once she had acknowledged Aaron, ensnared him.

When he tried to talk himself out of re-visiting his ghost, he was surprised how painful such an idea was. How could their one brief conversation have enslaved him so completely? When he recollected sitting alone on her cottage step, smelling the decay and hearing the mice gnawing away at the interior, the memory horrified him. When he recalled her face with its delicate features and her voice, so hollow and forlorn, like a haunting melody, he felt his insides turn weak. He ignored his heart, telling him not to go, and his mind, which should be plotting ways to win back Connie, and his soul, which didn't believe in ghosts anyway, and he followed the weakest part of his nature into his canoe and paddled swiftly to the opposite shore of the lake. He simply wanted to see her again. He arrived at twelve fifteen.

It was cold on the dark beach, and she was there, but she interrupted her own routine this time. She walked up the beach and back and then turned to smile at him, holding her lantern before her face. Her mouth looked full and soft, and her eyes were bright. She came to him and set her lantern down, then took his hands in her frigid, unyielding ones. He stood there gazing into her eyes, wondering how on earth she had bewitched him.

He felt as if he'd known her for centuries.

She led him to the camp steps, holding his hand. He made a feeble attempt to steal his hand back, but she held it firmly.

He gave up easily and allowed her to caress his fingers. "I tried to tell someone about you," he said at last.

"And?" That reedy quality, the echo of an ancient time.

"It's hard to explain you," he faltered.

"Virginia Dunn," she said solemnly, "age twenty. Never

married."

"Why, Ginny? Why never married? What happened?"

She shrugged, deflecting his question. "You told me you had something for me. What is it?"

"I'll show you. Come with me." Exaggerated shadows interrupted the lamplight which lit their way to his canoe. He lifted a plastic bag from under the seat and removed her painting, dropping the bag back inside the boat. He wondered if she would remember it, if she would even be able to make it out in the darkness.

She held it near the lantern and gazed at it, recognizing the picture at once and dancing with it delightedly on the shore. He watched her, absurdly happy that he had pleased her.

"Then it is your work? I thought it must be."

"Yes, it's mine. I sat on the dock for days," she said. "And every time the light changed, I grew frustrated all over again and had to add a new color to the mountains." She peered at the picture as the black night sifted around them. "It came out well, though, don't you think?"

"Yes, I like it," he said.

"I like it, too." She laughed sweetly. "Thank you for bringing it. It used to hang in the lake store. How did you get it?"

"I bought it. I'd like to have it back, Ginny." He hoped she hadn't misunderstood. He didn't intend to give her the picture.

Her soft brown eyes looked up into his, and he felt his heart stop. "Why do you want it?"

"Because . . ." he said, then realized he didn't know how to finish. "Just because."

She handed it to him. He rewrapped it in plastic and placed it carefully in the bottom of the boat, then leaned back against one of the trees along the shore, watching her. Lantern light played on her features, exaggerating them, mesmerizing him.

"I would have learned what to do about that - the changing colors - if I had kept on with school," she said. "I only had one year. It wasn't enough."

"Did you quit school, or . . . ."

Her head was cocked to one side, thoughtful. "I don't remember. Why would I quit school? I was studying art. I wanted to be an artist."

He smiled at her. "I heard that you had a wild streak, Ginny. Is that true?"

"A wild streak?" She considered briefly, then giggled. "No. I

93

pretty much do what I want, though." She peered up at Aaron. "Like asking guys out. Like convincing my teachers to let me do projects on subjects that no one else thinks of." She tilted her head slightly and smiled at Aaron, then began a seductive dance down the beach, shimmying, shaking the skirt of her long gown. He watched her, fascinated. She came dancing back to him, and he caught her arm to stop her.

Ginny looked at him in great innocence. "I talked one of our teachers into letting us draw from nude models."

"Ah, you're a true artist."

She shrugged. "Sure. I knew it was a good idea. The teacher was a prude, but it wasn't fair of him to force his own inhibitions on us."

Aaron laughed. "So you did have a reckless streak."

"Well, I'd hardly call it that," Ginny said. Her eyes turned thoughtful. "Come here, Aaron." She held her arms up, waltz style. "Dance with me on the beach."

"No, I'm no dancer." He also felt about sixty years older than Ginny. He shook his head as she began to dance alone, moving to a rhythm only she could hear.

"I know you're not," she said, swooping by him. "You always thought you should learn, but you never got around to it. You just didn't have time."

He stared at her. "How do you know that?"

She stopped dancing and cocked her head sideways. Her eyebrows knitted together. "I don't know, but it's true." Her face cleared and she smiled at him, moving off, her arms lifted to some dashing, imaginary partner. "Isn't it?" She looked back at him coyly.

He nodded and watched her as she danced off down the beach into the dark, then returned to him. She laughed, swaying before him, breathless and radiant, her eyes closed as she listened to the music in her head.

"Were you engaged to Eddie Safford in college?" he asked.

Ginny stopped moving and looked at him suddenly. "How do you know about Eddie?"

"Someone told me. He was your boyfriend, wasn't he? Your fiancé?"

"I don't think we were engaged yet," she said vaguely.

"Why did you go out that night?" he asked. "Did you meet him?"

He instantly regretted asking. She stared at Aaron, and he

could see damp tears begin to form on her eyelashes. "Ginny, I'm sorry," he said.

Tears began to flow from her eyes; she wiped them away with one hand and approached him. "Hold me," she said quietly. "Please." Awkwardly, he put his arms around her, feeling the polished skin beneath her gown. Her back was smooth and cool, and he felt the length of her body pressing close to his. His hands crept up her back to her neck, getting tangled in her long hair, Katrina's hair. He held her head in a caress and tipped her face up as she looked deeply into his eyes, crying softly.

"Why did you run away last night?" he asked. "Don't you trust me?"

"Should I?"

"Of course you should. Why would I hurt you?"

"You will, though," she said quietly. A large breath escaped her. She loosened herself from his hold and wiped at her eyes with her hand. She walked back to the cottage and he followed, catching her hand in his, sitting next to her on the steps. His fingers gently massaged hers. The feel of her cool flesh soothed him; the burning pierced him. She is real, he told himself. I am here, and so is she. This is real.

He pushed aside any other thoughts, burying them.

"Tell me who you are, Aaron."

"You know." He searched for something to tell her and added, "I'm a writer and photographer."

"Oh, Aaron," she breathed excitedly, "are you really a photographer?" Her tears were gone as quickly as they had come. The impetuous, carefree Ginny was back. "Can you take my picture?"

He was taken aback. Could he? He had seen photographs that claimed to be of ghosts. He wondered. "Well, of course," he said. "Yes, let's try it. I'll bring my camera sometime."

She snuggled in next to him, forcing his arm around her slim shoulders. Her other hand played with his fingers. "Your arm is very warm," she told him. "It's nice. Tell me more."

"I'm not sure what you want to know."

"All about you, your family. I have two brothers, Royce and Timmy. I haven't seen them lately. Do you have brothers?"

He felt a clenching inside and forced himself to answer casually, "Just one brother, Chris."

She leaned away from him a little, her eyes searching his face. "You don't like him much."

"That's not true," he answered quickly. "He's my brother. I love him, of course."

"Yes?" She peered into his eyes. "It's a strange kind of love, though."

Strange wasn't the word for it, Aaron thought. In his mind he saw Chris averting his eyes, fleeing from Aaron, both of them pursued by never-ending waves of fear and guilt and regret. He clenched her hand harder. "God, Ginny," he said, "I . . . ."

"Yes?" She was peering at him, waiting for him to finish.

"I hate him, I guess," he mumbled. He was startled at his own words. Why had he told her that? He had never told anyone that, not even Connie. The admission left a dreadful taste in his mouth. "I didn't mean that," he said.

"No," she said, and her words carried the wisdom of the ages. "You love him, Aaron."

He could feel his breath coming hard. He had never breathed a word against his brother to anyone, but inside . . . . "And I have two parents, just like everybody," he said, desperate to escape his mixed-up thoughts of Chris.

"You like them pretty well, don't you?"

"Of course I do."

"And?"

"That's all, I guess." Why wasn't he telling her about Connie and Egan, the two most important people in his life?

Because he was sitting here at midnight with his arms around an appealing young girl, that was why. Because she was melting into him and reading his mind, and any minute he was probably going to kiss her if he wasn't careful.

Abruptly he pulled away from her and stood up. She sat up swiftly, surprised and hurt. "You're so beautiful, Ginny," he said, his breath coming fast. "I don't know what happened to you, but I'm sorry it did. I don't understand you. And I sure don't understand myself lately. I can't stay here now; I have to leave."

"I loved *my* brothers," she said simply. "They were littler than me, and I just keep remembering how they cried and cried."

He stalked toward the canoe and stepped into it solidly, then felt the crunch beneath his foot. He had cracked the glass covering her painting inside its plastic bag.

He pushed off with the paddle, his eyes all the time on Ginny Dunn standing on the weedy lawn before her camp, a circle of moonlight shrouding her. Her white gown billowed around her feet in the slight breeze; a bewildered sadness shadowed her face.

Hurriedly, he paddled out to deeper water, and then headed across the lake.

He didn't look back.

Chapter 22

THE NOVEL Connie had been trying to read seemed flat and uninteresting, and her thoughts kept wandering. When she heard a hesitant knock at the door, she put the book aside willingly and opened the corridor door. Justin Rime stood there, looking very young and a little sheepish. His hands were thrust into his pants' pockets, and he gave her a lopsided smile. "I'm looking for Oboe," he said. "He keeps getting away from me."

Connie looked vaguely around the living room, knowing full well the cat wasn't there. Then she smiled at Justin. "We haven't seen him," she said, "but come in if you like."

He entered easily and stood beside her as she closed the door. Egan came out to see who had knocked, wound herself around Connie's legs, and grinned up at their neighbor.

"Have a seat." Connie gestured to a chair. "I'll put some coffee on."

"No coffee for me, thanks," he said. "I'm on my way out in about ten minutes. Remember the friend I told you about? Cabbie Moracca, the pianist?"

She nodded. Justin had told her about him several nights before, when they had bumped into each other in the hallway. An old friend of Justin's, Cabbie was traveling from city to city, entertaining, hoping to make his big break or at least keep body and soul together by playing his music.

"He's playing this week at a coffee house. It's not much of a place, but I promised to go and lend support." He gazed at her face and said thoughtfully, "Would you like to go?" Then he spotted Egan's damp hair and pajamas and laughed. "No, guess not."

"Please, sit down if you like," Connie said. "Let me just take Egan in to bed. She's had a busy day and ought to get to sleep. Egan, go pick up your toys and I'll tuck you in."

Obediently, Egan ran to the kitchen and returned with a box of puzzle pieces. The cover was askew, the wooden pieces protruding at angles. "Be right back," Connie said to Justin.

"Is Justin looking for Oboe?" Egan asked as she climbed into her bed and slipped under the covers.

"Yes, his kitty seems to have escaped again. Don't worry; I'm sure he'll find him."

Egan covered her smiling mouth with her hand, just as a soft mewling sound escaped from under the bed. Connie's eyes went round as she stared at her daughter. She bent and pulled a cut cereal carton from under the bed. Egan had lined it with a pillow case, and Oboe stretched luxuriously, his front paws hanging over one edge of the box, his tail over the other. "Egan! Did you bring the cat in here?"

"Not really," Egan said innocently. "He followed me in."

"You used scissors to cut this?"

Egan nodded guiltily. The scissors in the kitchen drawer were sharp. Using them without permission was strictly forbidden.

"That was wrong, Egan," Connie said. "I'm disappointed. Do I have to keep the scissors out of your reach?"

"No," Egan muttered.

"I need to trust you, Egan." Connie paused. "And what will Justin think of you taking his cat?"

"I didn't hurt him," Egan said. "Besides, he said I should take care of Oboe whenever I find him. Remember, Mom?" Her eyes began to tear up.

"I know, honey, but he was worried. Think of how you would feel if it were your cat and someone just took it." Egan pressed her lips together and ran a little hand down Oboe's soft fur.

"Get out of bed," Connie told her.

"What are you going to do?" Egan asked. She disentangled herself from the bedclothes and stood before her mother. Her little face looked worried.

"I'm not going to do anything. You are. You have to tell Justin you're sorry. Come on."

Connie picked up the flimsy cereal carton with Oboe purring inside and followed her daughter to the living room. Egan stood silently before Justin, tears hanging on her eyelashes. Justin suppressed a smile as he looked from Egan to Connie to Oboe, who stretched and meowed, his tail swinging over the side of the cereal box.

"I'm sorry I took Oboe," Egan whispered. She wheeled around and fled back to her bedroom.

"Justin," Connie said helplessly, "I'm so sorry. She loves your cat, but there was no excuse." She handed him the box.

He was grinning. "Hello, Oboe," he sang. He looked into Connie's eyes and gestured toward Egan's open bedroom door. "Oh, it's nothing. Will you let her come back out for minute ?"

"Sure." Connie called to her daughter. Justin placed the carton on the floor and sat next to Egan on the couch, regaling her with his own tales of boyhood mischief. Egan laughed and eventually scampered back to bed.

"I hope you won't be too hard on her," Justin said. "I doubt she'll grow up to be a thief."

Connie laughed. "Well, thank you for being understanding. Are you sure you won't have some coffee? Oh, wait, you have to go watch your friend." Why was she feeling so flustered? It was very embarrassing to have him standing here smiling at her when Egan had plotted the theft of his kitten and brought it off so well.

"I have to get going," he said, wandering toward the door, balancing his cat in its box. "Would you come tomorrow?" he said suddenly. "Both of you. I'd like you to hear Cabbie play. It would be more fun for me if you both came, and he would appreciate the audience."

Connie shook her head. "No, I don't think so. Egan has to get up for classes every morning-"

"Egan would enjoy it," he said. "So would you, I think. Cabbie's an outstanding musician. We can go early, at six, and then have supper someplace, and she'll be back by nine-thirty, I promise." He grinned at her. "Say yes, Connie."

It was hard not to. He was persuasive and seemed so pleased at the idea that they would go with him to hear Cabbie Moracca play. Egan had stolen his cat, after all, and that made it very hard to disappoint him. And his friend needed an audience. Besides, didn't she want Egan to have as many cultural experiences as she could fit into one short summer?

"All right," she said hesitantly. It wasn't a date, after all. It would be silly to refuse because of Aaron, sitting up there at the camp, chatting with ghosts. "Yes," she said again more firmly, "sure we'll come. We'd enjoy it."

Justin grinned. "Excellent. Six o'clock then." He opened her door to leave. "Oh," he said, noticing the pillow case under and over Oboe. The kitten's head was shrouded in the pale blue cloth. Justin laughed and peered around the covering. "Are you in there, Oboe?" he asked. He pulled the kitten's tiny face from under the pillow case, tightened the cloth around its head like a turban, and grinned at Connie. "My own Cat in the Hat," he said. He lifted the pillow case and shook it out. A number of black and white hairs clung to it. "I think this is yours." He handed it to Connie, smiling. She took it and closed the door after him.

By the time she had undressed and slid between the cool, clean sheets, Connie had stopped feeling so sure of herself. What would Aaron think of her taking Egan and going off with some man to a coffee house? It was a perfectly innocent outing, but it sounded all wrong. She would cancel. She would go across the hall and tap at Justin's door first thing in the morning and explain that she just couldn't go.

By one o'clock in the morning, Connie was convinced she would not be sleeping this night. Justin's innocent, delighted face when she had accepted his invitation contrasted in her mind with Aaron's hurt, annoyed one when she had announced her plans for the summer. Why was she comparing them? One was some guy who lived across the hall. The other was her husband, for God's sake. Egan's father. Egan's *absent* father. Connie punched the pillow and tried again to get comfortable. She couldn't.

She reached for her cell phone and cradled it in her hand, making a sudden decision. This nonsense with Aaron was about to end, right now, ghost or no ghost. She would call and tell him they would leave in the morning. How could they solve their problems if they stayed miles apart all summer? She was his wife and belonged by his side. She was acting ridiculous, clinging to her own foolish, selfish plans when she could have accompanied Aaron on his assignment and been a help to him . . . . Besides, she was worried. Something was strange in his voice lately. And was it possible he was even hallucinating?

She glanced at the vintage Seth Thomas clock on the mantel in her bedroom. Five after one. Well, she would wake him. She smiled to herself. This was a call Aaron wouldn't mind being awakened for.

She punched in the number for the Spruce Lake camp and let it ring four, five, seven, nine times. Frowning, she pressed the disconnect button.

She ignored the faster beating of her heart and told her hands to stop shaking; she had pressed a wrong number somehow. Concentrating, she tried again and listened to the phone ring eight, ten, fifteen, sixteen times. She punched the disconnect button, turned off her phone, and flung it aside. It drifted down in among the coverings on her bed.

She looked again at the clock across the room. It was five minutes after one in the morning. Where was Aaron?

Chapter 23

GINNY'S FACE LINGERED in Aaron's mind as he approached his own dark cabin on the west shore of Spruce Lake. He would stop going over there; it was a complication he didn't need in an already complicated summer.

As he beached the canoe and picked his way up the steps in the dark, he heard the ringing of the rotary phone through the camp's open windows and all thoughts of Ginny were banished. It was one o'clock in the morning. Why would Connie call now? Something must be wrong.

The ringing had stopped by the time he reached the camp.

In great agitation, he dialed Connie's cell. Her familiar voice invited him to leave a message.

"I'm here, Connie," he said. "It's about one o'clock. Call me back."

Sleep was a joke. He rehung Ginny's painting, running his finger gently down the crack he had placed there, a long, clean break going from top to bottom, dividing the glass roughly in half.

The break in the glass bothered him, a crack in the façade. It gave the pictured camp a distorted, broken quality. Like my mind, Aaron thought. Like the rift between Connie and me, like the stupid, crazy feelings I can't seem to control.

He kept expecting any minute to hear the telephone shrill again. Why would Connie call him in the middle of the night unless something had happened? To her? To Egan? His heart spasmed. And there was no way he could reach them except to leave a pitiful message on her phone.

At Connie's foolhardy insistence, he could not reach them.

Forcing a calm he did not feel, he pulled his chair up to the typewriter. The same three lines had been staring him down for days. The reference guides were still open to the same illustrated pages. He thrust the books aside roughly and sat staring at the wall ahead of him, at the little watercolor of his wilderness retreat, painted by a hand that was long dead, a hand he had held and caressed this very night while his wife, far away in Saratoga, called and let the telephone ring and ring and ring- and received no answer.

Chapter 24

WHAT A FOOL SHE WAS. She had even considered canceling her harmless plans with Justin because Aaron might not approve. She had been oh, so ready to give in and go running to Spruce Lake. She was disgusted at her own lack of fortitude.

It was two in the morning now, and Connie had been pacing and fretting for fifty-five minutes. She had hoped, yes *hoped* that Aaron would try to call her back and had turned her phone off for that very reason. It would serve him right to get her voicemail. Where had he been at five after one in the morning?

Oh, of course, she had nearly forgotten that Aaron Latimer did precisely what he wanted to do whenever he wanted to do it. And what exactly was that in the middle of the night when his wife was approximately one hundred miles away? She glanced at the clock. She should let him suffer a bit longer.

Abruptly, Connie pulled her cell phone to her, clicked it on and called the cabin again. She dismissed the possibility that Aaron was sick or hurt or that some calamity had befallen him. This was, she was sure, just more of the same - thoughtless, selfish Aaron Latimer doing whatever he felt like doing.

Aaron picked up on the first ring. She didn't speak for a moment. "Is that you, Connie?" he said. "Is everything all right?"

She found her voice. "Yes, great," she said shortly. "Except that I called you an hour ago and was surprised to find you'd gone out." She sounded shrewish, and she knew it. God, how she hated women who nagged their husbands. She had tried so hard not to be one of those, and now she had succumbed. She made a gallant effort to speak in a calmer voice. "Where were you?"

"I was outside," he said. "I heard the phone but I couldn't get to it in time. I called you right back. Didn't you hear my message?"

"You were outside?"

"I was, um . . . ." There was a pause while Connie waited. She was sure Aaron was trying to decide what to say. "What if I told you I saw the ghost again?" he asked.

"I'd say you should come up with something better," she snapped. Then, "What's wrong with you, Aaron? Did you eat something weird that you got in the woods? Are you getting enough sleep?"

She could almost see him licking his lower lip, a gesture she had come to know well. Usually, that telltale sign of nervousness would appear when he had to discipline Egan or explain to an editor that he had changed his approach on an assignment. His voice would stay firm, and he would always come out on top, but there was that tiny gesture, his tongue massaging his lower lip for just those few seconds before he spit out the modified plans that would change the entire layout of the article or announced to Egan that she would not be having dessert that night.

She had seen it countless times - when he demanded a refund in a store, when he talked on the phone to the newspaper carrier or garage mechanic who did not quite measure up to Aaron's expectations.

She couldn't recall when he had been nervous talking to her, but she sensed it now.

"I was out of the camp for a while, Connie," he said. "That's all."

"Out where?" she repeated, hating the tone of her voice.

"I was in the canoe, Connie."

"At this time of night. Aaron? Doing what? Looking at the stars? Or what?"

"Yes, I was. Since there aren't many lights up here, the stars look brighter and bigger."

Well, it made a grudging kind of sense. Aaron was the type of man who would decide to canoe at night, just because he could. She had always admired his strong will and independent spirit, so why become upset about it now? It was one of the things she loved about him, wasn't it?

Connie let out a held breath. "Oh, well, I felt bad when I couldn't reach you."

"I'm sorry."

Wasn't he going to ask why she had called? Had they grown so distant that he didn't even care? She swallowed her hurt and concern. "Well, how's the photo essay coming? Are you getting a lot of good shots?"

She was surprised that his pause was long and thoughtful. "Not that great, really," he said. "As well as can be expected, I guess. It would go a lot better if you were here."

"I'd be in your way."

He was silent. For a few moments, so was she.

"Did I wake you, Aaron?"

"No, no. I was trying to write, then I went out to the porch, just looking at the stars."

The stars again. How much stargazing did one man need to do in a night? "Well, okay," she said.

"Why did you call so late, Connie? It couldn't have been too serious or you would have said so by now."

She heard the patience in his tone and hesitated before she answered him. She had changed her mind about joining him. Should she tell him about her plans with Justin? Aaron sounded so far away somehow, and a part of her was sure it was a ruse designed to make her worry.

She would wait and tell him later. "No reason," she said. "I just felt like hearing your voice, I guess. I'll call in a few days."

"Connie?"

"What?"

"Before you hang up, I love you."

She felt a spatter of relief. "I know that, Aaron. I love you, too. Maybe this separation wasn't a good idea, I don't know. But we'll straighten it all out."

"I hope we do," he said.

"But we'll wait 'til daylight," Connie said. She tried for a lighter note. "Decent people should be sleeping right now." She waited, wanting to hear Aaron's reassuring voice once more. He had just said he loved her. Well, she knew that, of course. But something was gnawing at the edges of his words. And he hadn't even asked after Egan. What on earth was going on at Spruce Lake? Irritation crept upon her again. Yes, she was sure of it; he *wanted* her to worry so she would change her mind. Well, it wasn't going to work.

"Good night, Connie," he said.

"We'll talk later, Aaron," she said stiffly and clicked off her cell phone. She went to bed, but her thoughts collided throughout that sleepless night and all through the next day.

As she drove Egan to her classes in the morning, she thought about her husband and her daughter, the life she had planned, the people she had chosen because she loved them. With all her heart, she loved them. She was sure that Aaron could use time away from her, too, so he could gain some perspective, see what was happening to their marriage. She hoped he would recognize how it felt to be the one left, that he might actually miss her. He said he did, but he'd sounded so strange. If he thought he was seeing ghosts, maybe he needed serious help. But what could *she* do? Well, for starters, she shouldn't have a fit just because he didn't answer the phone one night.

When she picked Egan up later, she had convinced herself that Aaron was fine, that he was playing on her emotions, and that her upcoming evening with Justin Rime wouldn't hurt anything. He was a family friend, a nice guy, a neighbor; he worked very respectably in a used book store in Saratoga, and he wanted to show her a first class pianist and amuse Egan with an evening's entertainment. What was so bad about that? He certainly hadn't made any improper comments or passes at her.

She needed to lighten up.

As she brushed out Egan's hair and arranged it with two small butterfly clips, she chastised herself. Would she be turning mental somersaults if this were old Mr. Crafton, who lived next door in Syracuse? Of course not. If Frank Crafton had invited her and Egan to see a musician, she would have gone without a second thought. So what difference was there, just because Justin was young, sensitive, a good-looking bookseller who wanted their company for an evening.

Connie swept aside her reluctance. She loved her husband, and they all knew that - Aaron, Justin, herself. It wasn't a date; it was an outing with a friend.

At five forty-five, exhaustion had caught up with her, and she admitted to herself that she felt tired and shaky. She dressed hurriedly, fixed her hair, and debated about perfume. How ridiculous. If she were going out with any of her women friends at home, she would wear it. She spritzed some on.

When she opened the door to Justin, he stood there, carefully combed and eager. "Ready?" he said. He looked down at Egan, putting his hand on top of her head. "You're going to love this," he said to the little girl. His eyes brushed Connie; he smiled in appreciation and said to her, "You look great, and you smell good. For dinner, I know a place right in town where the service is fast, and we can get really great pasta. Is that okay? Would Egan like that?"

Connie nodded in agreement and found Egan's hand, which

she clasped firmly in her own. She couldn't help wondering why she suddenly saw that sweet little hand as a life support, why she clung to Egan as a drowning victim might cling to a passing board, why her six year old child looked to her, for all the world, like a very inadequate chaperone.

Chapter 25

SLEEP HAD BECOME A LUXURY in which Aaron rarely indulged. If, as Connie had said, decent people slept at night, then perhaps he wasn't such a decent guy anymore.

He hadn't actually lied to her. He *had* been in the canoe, and it was true that the stars were brighter here at the lake. His was a sin of omission.

He had noticed that when he was with Ginny, it was hard to think clearly about Connie. He tried to picture his wife, walking along city streets beside him, the sun glinting off her hair, the day they had moved into their house in Syracuse, a house they had chosen together because she loved the neighborhood and because it had the perfect darkroom for him. He could see her in the back yard with Egan years ago, tucking her newborn into her screened crib, Connie taking their baby out and jouncing her on her knee; the many days he had arrived home just as she was turning up the driveway with Egan tucked securely into her stroller, or Egan toddling beside Connie, clutching her hand. Himself, arriving home after a three or four day absence; Connie, busy in the garden, leaving her flowers to come and kiss him hello, letting him know how much he was missed. Or later, Egan running down the driveway as he drove up, clutching a school drawing, so excited to see him that she could hardly wait until he stopped the car. Connie watching from the porch, smiling, looking beautiful.

He loved those images, and here on his own side of the lake it was easy to recall them. It occurred to him that his best remembrances of Connie were drenched in sunshine. If there had been dark, rainy days in their nine years of marriage, he didn't recall them.

He shuddered, realizing that he had never seen Ginny except in the blackest night.

When he visited Ginny, she sucked his entire concentration, and thoughts of his life and his family seemed hazy at best. He would sit with Ginny or stand near her on the dark beach, and the sunny images of Connie and Egan would retreat like part of a distant, already completed past, something he had loved, but that wasn't necessary or important anymore. Even when he was determined to tell Ginny about his vast love for his wife and daughter, something made the words stick in his throat.

It would make things so much easier if he could talk to Connie. Maybe she could help him understand this spell Ginny had cast over him.

What a ludicrous idea.

He abhorred himself for going to the cottage across the lake, dreaded the setting sun when he knew he would stand gazing over the water, waiting for night to fall so he could slip across the cool depths to Ginny.

Each night he made his way to her camp, and hesitantly, when she asked, he told her bits about himself. He was always surprised at the feel of her body beneath the gown as she leaned into him or as he held her at arm's length to keep her at a distance. She should be figmentary, a vapor. He should be able to walk right through her, see through her. But he couldn't. She was maddeningly solid.

Ginny had begun sharing as much as she could remember of her childhood and her last days. He encouraged her, but recognized that to press would be to wound her. Slowly she had learned to trust him, and now she relied on him completely. He found this responsibility terrifying.

Would he hurt her as he had hurt Katrina Jeffers? As he was, even now, driving a wedge between himself and Connie? Well, it wasn't the same thing at all, of course. Connie was a living, breathing woman, pulsing with life, and with claims on him. Katrina had been the same. Ginny was different, a firm body disguising a shimmering vapor, an elusive cloud. How could he hurt her? She was already dead, after all.

Finally, he came to accept the fact that he would not keep away, so he found an excuse that helped him justify his longings. He was becoming convinced, or had convinced himself, that Virginia Dunn needed him to make her terrible existence a little more palatable. He told himself it was for Ginny's sake that he paddled across the lake at night, that it was impossible that she could have any hold over him in the long run.

Chapter 26

THEY WERE IN HIS CANOE, and he had just pushed off from shore to take her for a midnight ride. He sat in the stern, steering, and Ginny perched in the bow. He didn't expect her to paddle, and she didn't offer. She sat erect, like an old-fashioned ship's figurehead, leading him under the black sky. The moon's reflected light made a golden haze around her head. Otherwise she was as black as shadow.

She turned her head slightly to speak to him. "Should I wear a life jacket, Aaron?" she asked sweetly.

He was taken aback. "Why would you?"

"I never learned to swim," she admitted. "It seems funny, all these years at camp, but I was always too afraid." She leaned down and felt for the life vest in the bottom of the boat. "Do you want me to put it on?"

"I don't think you need it, Ginny." He clenched his hands into fists to stop the trembling there and steered the boat to the western shore.

"Can you swim, Aaron?" she asked. Her voice was a hush in the stillness.

He nodded, then realized she couldn't see him in the dark. "Yes."

"Oh, I never see you swimming."

"No, I haven't gone in years." They glided peacefully along his waterfront. "Look up there, Ginny," he said quietly. He had left lamps burning to light his way back, and they could make out the lines of his camp, high and imposing under the silver-black trees. "That's where I live, at least for right now."

"But you haven't been there all this time," she said. "You wish you could love it, don't you?"

"I don't know what I wish," he said weakly. "I guess I appreciate it."

"Do you?" she asked.

"Don't I?" he repeated. He let them drift slowly past the property, now and then dipping his paddle into the inky water. "I don't know what I think anymore," he said finally.

"I painted it because I thought it was beautiful," she said. "You see that, too."

"I guess I do. Anyway, your painting is beautiful, Ginny," he said. "You're very talented."

"I have other pictures." She turned to him suddenly. He heard the enticing, girlish quality in her voice. "Would you like to see them?"

"Sure I would," he answered quickly, without thinking. Then it occurred to him. "Where are they?"

"In the cottage," she said. "I'll take you in and show you when we get back."

His mouth tasted coppery; he was pretty sure he didn't want to go inside Virginia Dunn's lakeside cottage. "I won't be able to see them, Ginny," he said. "It will be too dark in there. Even with a flashlight or lantern, I think it would be too hard."

"Oh." It was a disappointed sound, a hush in the night.

A sudden thought gripped him. "Unless you would take me there in daylight." An opportunity to see her in sunshine? It might be worth it. "Could we do that?"

Her posture was suddenly rigid. Aaron could feel the decided shift in the boat and waited for her response; she remained silent.

"Wouldn't you like that, Ginny? To see the sun for a change? Maybe to see what I really look like?" He could sense her terror. "Why does that frighten you?"

"I don't know, but it does."

"Is it possible for me to see you during the day?"

"It's possible," she said grudgingly.

"Then let me come tomorrow," he pleaded. "Just this one time."

"Aaron, I'm afraid."

"Please, Ginny."

Finally, she agreed. "But in the woods, please, in the shade, not in the sun."

"That's fine. At noon?"

She was silent briefly, then giggled softly. "Aaron, I won't know when noon is. Just come when you want to. I'll know you're there."

113

Chapter 27

AARON WAITED on the state-owned land on a smooth, level spot created by an outcropping of rocks. He was there at eleven-thirty and was ashamed at the boyish fervor he felt. Like a first date. He buried the thought of Connie that popped into his mind, along with the intention he had once had of bringing Egan here to watch for deer. He knew that once Ginny appeared, those thoughts would dissipate.

He stood on the rocky ledge and leaned against an oak tree, waiting for her and wondering if her fear had caused her to change her mind. Or maybe ghosts couldn't just appear whenever they felt like appearing. She had said she'd know when, but daylight was foreign to her. Maybe there were certain rules, certain natural principles . . . .

And then he saw her, a shimmering image that took his breath away. She came slowly through the woods, tripping lightly over roots and leaves, looking around her in wonder and surprise at the dappled leaves and hushed summer colors. "It's so beautiful," she said when she reached him. "This must be where the deer feed. Sometimes I see them coming toward my camp from this direction." She reached up shyly and handed him two wild daisies she had picked.

He found it impossible to answer. She wore the same gown as always, and in daylight he was astonished to see that it wasn't white at all, but pale blue. It was a nightgown, in fact, a girl's cotton nightgown with lace at the neck and wrists. Her hair, which he had thought was brown, was more blonde, a shining cascade down her back, and her face, which had looked seductive by lantern light, was the pretty, innocent face of a shy, young girl. She had said she was twenty. She looked fifteen.

By contrast, he was sure he looked every one of his thirty-six years, and even though the clothes were clean, they were camp clothes, his usual tee shirt, jeans, and plaid flannel shirt. That was pretty much all he'd brought to Spruce Lake. Suddenly he felt badly dressed. He wondered if she saw him that way.

"You came," he said finally. "I was afraid you wouldn't."

"But you wanted me to," she said, as if that explained everything. "And I want to show you my pictures."

"You brought flowers." He said. He held them to her face and she wrinkled her nose at their wild, sour scent, then smiled at him. He handed them back to her. "I should have been the one to bring flowers." It made her laugh, and he felt his heart expand.

"Here," he said. "Sit here, Ginny." He swept off a place on the flat rock with his hand, and demurely, she sat down, holding the daisies. Her feet were bare and he resisted the urge to touch her ankle to see if it was still cold, still made of firm granite. "Can we talk a while before we go back to your cottage?"

She settled back comfortably, leaning into the shadows made by the rocks behind her. "Last time, I was telling you about my brother Royce," she said. "He was six when I saw him last."

"And he was the hot-headed rebel," Aaron filled in.

"Yes, I wonder whether he still is." She sat thoughtfully for a moment, the sun burnishing her hair, her sleeves pushed up in the midday heat. Her arms were pale and creamy in the afternoon light. Suddenly she looked at Aaron and a sly smile played on her mouth. "You promised you would talk about Chris," she said. "It's time."

He bowed his head and tried to think how to begin. "Well," he started, "first of all, I'm still trying to decide if I hate my brother. I'm positive that I don't love him."

"Really?" She sounded surprised.

"Why do you assume I do? I never gave you any reason to think that."

She looked genuinely surprised. "I don't know why. I just know it."

"Well, you're wrong, even though we were very close when we were little."

She smiled engagingly. "Tell me the things you did together. About the hobby horses and bikes."

He darted a look at her. He had never mentioned either pastime. Well, they were common enough; most kids had a hobby horse and virtually everyone had owned a bike.

He began to tell her. He and Chris had galloped around the living room of their house in Buffalo with hobby horse heads attached to sticks. On summer days they rested their horses under the privet hedges and stretched lazily beside them, watching clouds or observing ants. They'd owned matching red bikes and had raced them up and down their quiet street, living on their bikes, feeling the power of the machinery they controlled. The family occasionally came to Spruce Lake, and they'd always stay for a few days; the drive was too long not to. They used to ask to bring the bikes but their father was adamant. "With a whole lake to play in?" he would scoff. "A whole mountain?"

"We used to play in the woods, of course," Aaron said.

"We did that, too."

"Up behind the camp, we'd wander around back in there. We built a teepee once. We gathered up all the dead limbs we could find and leaned them all against a sturdy trunk, circle style. We had friends who'd come up with us." Chris had friends. After a while Chris had always invited along another playmate. Aaron's rough and tumble diversions didn't interest him much. They were two very different brothers with different personalities and interests, but that hadn't mattered when they were little.

"You were so happy then," she said.

"Yes, I was."

"But later . . . ."

He hesitated. "What about later?" Later, when Chris had refused to look him straight in the eyes, when a nervous, averted glance had been Chris's usual expression whenever the brothers met.

"Well, something happened, right?"

He glanced over at her slight shape. She was leaning back against the rock, fingering the daisies, keeping herself in shade, while he sprawled out next to her in the sun. "I never said something happened."

"What was it?"

He pulled a stalk of timothy from the ground and switched it in her face. She giggled and reached up to flick it out of her way, grabbing his hand.

"You are a witch, Virginia Dunn," he said playfully. "Can you read minds?"

"No!" She sounded astonished. Then she thought for a minute. "I don't think I can."

"He was jealous of me," Aaron said suddenly, and found himself surprised that he had spoken aloud. He explained. "I was

116

a year younger, but I was bigger. I always beat him at sports. He was no athlete, but it came naturally to me."

"You're very strong," she said agreeably.

"And I was faster and . . . well, just better at everything physical. So, we used to rough-house the way brothers do. He could never beat me at any game or sport, and it must have really bothered him because one day, one day . . . ."

She was staring at him, and she raised her hand to his face. "Shh. It isn't necessary to tell me that part," she said. Her cold fingers stroked his cheek, sending hot liquid through him.

The words dried up in him and he clasped her hand suddenly and kissed her fingers. Her full lips parted; her other hand crept around his neck. He let out a sudden breath, felt a tightening in his chest. "Ginny," he said, "you're like a marble statue." His voice was raspy, coming from somewhere deep in his throat. "It's as if you're caught in time."

She sat up quickly and so did he, but he leaned over her and into her. His arms went around her protectively, possessively, and he could hear her ragged breathing as she struggled for control. "You're so cold," he breathed. "Cold like a rare stone polished by water." His hand circled the back of her neck, and he tilted her head up. His mouth was inches from her face.

"Not inside," she said. "Inside I'm warm and real. Inside I ache sometimes."

"When I touch you, I freeze and burn, Ginny. I don't understand it, but I can't stay away."

"Then . . . ."

He tightened his hold on her and brought his lips down on hers roughly. She struggled for a moment, then gave in to his kiss, flinging her arms around his neck and exploding with passion as he swept her up into his arms. He could feel her searing into him. Each place he touched felt icy, then flaming. He lay her gently down on the cool rocks beneath them and knelt beside her, feeling her tremble, seeing her eyes wide with trepidation. He caressed her cheek with his hand, feeling its ice burn him, and bent to take another kiss.

The sudden intrusive screech of a flicker brought him abruptly to his senses. His head shot up as the bird's raucous, repetitive ki-ki-ki assaulted him. He saw its speckled breast as it darted off, wheeling into the blue sky. A sweep of wind parted the trees above unexpectedly, slashing an opening that suddenly filled the little clearing with hot sunshine.

Ginny gasped and threw her arm over her face, scrambled to her feet and backed away from him, out of the sun, into the cool shade. Her daisies lay on the rock, discarded, wilting.

"Ginny, please," he started.

She flitted into the woods and away, leaving him frustrated, horrified and ashamed at what he had almost done. Rasping for breath, he plummeted down the wooded bank, startling a grazing deer that leaped aside as he passed. He slid and fell until he reached his canoe, scraped it badly on rocks trying to untie it too fast, and paddled wildly away from the waterfront. He rushed across the lake, his canoe an arrow headed for the western shore.

By the time he reached his own camp, he had calmed somewhat. Never again would he go there. He had been saved this time, but what of the next time, and the time after that? He wandered aimlessly around inside his camp, lit a fire in the fireplace to shake off the chill in his heart and soul, sat at his work table staring blindly at pictures of creeping snowberry - useless, bewildering full color plates in the guide books he had brought along.

He needed Connie, but Connie apparently had stopped needing him. He hadn't heard a word since their last call three days before. He admitted that their last conversation had left him quiet and drained, wondering if there was any hope at all for them. What must she have thought, calling in the middle of the night and finding no one home.

Aaron shivered before his blazing fire, hugging his arms tighter across his chest, clutching his upper arms with his hands. And the one thing he wanted, no, needed to explain to her, the reality of Virginia Dunn's ghost, was just one more subject Connie would not tolerate.

Damn her! A phone that she actually answered would have helped him countless times. He'd have called her daily, hourly, instead of leaving a series of progressively shorter messages that she ignored. He'd have begged her to come to him, would have driven to Saratoga and forced her to leave her anonymous apartment, wherever it was, and brought her here. Which was exactly what she didn't want him to do. Time apart to think and consider. Well, it served her right that he had found himself bewitched by . . . .

Reeling, Aaron stumbled to a chair and sat down heavily, holding his head in his hands. A ghost, bewitched by a ghost. And allowing it to happen, inviting it, making every effort to see her and touch her and hold her. He was trapped, and it terrified him.

How could he have let this happen?

And what on earth was he going to do now?

Chapter 28

ARE YOU STILL SEEING GHOSTS, AARON?" Connie's sarcastic words crackled over the telephone line. She sounded on edge, and he wondered how angry she was. God knew she had every right to be.

"How's Egan?" he asked. He had realized too late last time that he hadn't even asked about her.

"Fine. How's the ghost?" Drilling, insistent.

He gave what he hoped was a reassuring laugh. It came out a little burst of panic. "There was a light at the abandoned camp across the lake," he said. "There must have been kids over there. I'm sure it was nothing." It chilled him that the lies slid off his tongue so easily. He didn't recall ever lying to Connie before. "Do you believe in ghosts, Connie?"

"I don't know." He sensed that she was creeping her way carefully. "I've never seen one, but that doesn't mean they don't exist." A nice, safe non-answer.

Well, at least she was open to the possibility. He'd get her up here, take her across the lake at midnight, they'd knock on the rotten door of the Dunn camp, and Ginny would answer, ghostly and vague in her summer nightgown, while forest animals scrabbled on the couches and chairs behind her and crept slyly into rotting holes in the walls. If that didn't set Connie screaming and shrieking back to civilization in a hurry, he didn't know what would.

He decided to change the subject. "Where's Egan? Is she up?"

"She's asleep."

"How is she?"

"She's fine, Aaron. She's happy."

A prick of jealousy stung him and he chastised himself. Why was he jealous that his own daughter was happy? Was he that far gone? "Well, that's good," he said.

"Yes, she's having fun. We do a lot of interesting things, and this place I found for us is perfect. It's a beautiful, historic building, and luckily we're on the first floor." He sensed she was chatting in this friendly way to keep peace between them. If they discussed her building they could avoid all the topics that seemed too fragile to touch.

"The elevator always seems to be stuck between floors," she went on. "It saves Anton a lot of work, though. Most people just resign themselves to using the stairs."

He would play along. One thing he knew was that he didn't want to fight with her. "Anton? Sounds like a hairdresser."

"The elevator operator. He's an older guy. He and his wife live upstairs. I hear him in the hall venting to Justin a lot."

"Who's Justin?"

Her pause was just long enough to make him wonder. "The guy who lives across the hall. The one with the cat. I know I mentioned him."

"Yeah, I remember the cat. Egan liked it." Connie laughed, a sound Aaron hadn't heard lately. What was so funny about the guy across the hall with the cat? And why was he feeling so suspicious? Because he had kissed the ghost of Ginny Dunn, that's why. Guilt breeds mistrust. He forced his next line. "Does he let her play with the cat?" he asked.

"It's in her room with her right now, in fact, having a sleepover. Egan actually stole the cat a few nights ago."

"Stole it?"

"Well, he came to ask if we'd seen it, and Egan had hidden it under her bed, cut a box down for it and everything. He was very understanding about it."

Aaron felt a knot tightening in his stomach. New people, a cat, a beautiful new apartment. And Connie was chattering on as if she were enjoying her new life without a thought for him. It hurt.

"Well, who is this guy Justin?" he asked. He tried to keep his tone casual. "What does he do? How old is he?" A decrepit, aging grandfatherly-type, he hoped, a nice older gentleman who was looking after Connie.

"He's our neighbor," Connie said guardedly. "He's young, maybe thirty, probably younger. He works in a shop that sells used books."

He hated himself, but he asked anyway. "Do you see much of

him?"

"Yes," Connie said. "Yes, we see a lot of him. He lives right across the hall. He's a very nice guy, Aaron; we've become friends. Egan likes him, too." She paused. "But not as much as she likes Oboe."

"Well, I don't like him," he muttered petulantly.

"You don't even know him," Connie said quietly.

"Connie, are you and Egan ready to come up here and join me yet?" He tried to make it flippant; it came out desperate.

"I think about it, Aaron," she said seriously.

"I'm glad you do. Are you coming then? I really need you, Connie."

"Have you considered coming here?" she asked. "Those were our original plans, after all."

"Give me your address."

"Oh, no. Not without a firm commitment. Date and time of arrival, and exactly how long you plan to stay."

"I have an article to write, Connie, and research that has to be done here." He fought off the guilt creeping up his throat. Article? Ha! He rarely bothered with it lately. "It would make more sense for you to join me," he said. It might give him the steady influence he needed to get back to work. And it would keep him safe from the enchanting arms of Virginia Dunn. "Will you?"

She sounded defeated. "I don't know. I have bad feelings about coming there, about the lake itself, separate from the thing between you and me."

"I know you hate coming to camp," he said. "You always have. It's the rustic nature of the place, right? Why else would you . . . ." He stopped himself from rambling on and asked her bluntly, "Why don't you like it here?"

"The wilderness spooks me, Aaron, the animals and things that I don't understand. Flying squirrels, insects, moths, mice. I feel like things are watching me sleep, crawling over my clothes."

"The building's pretty sound. We don't get that much inside here-" he began.

"I'm just not used to it. I'm a city girl; you've always known that. And I love modern conveniences, of course. I know I sound shallow, but I really like my washing machine and dishwasher."

"I have a microwave oven here."

She laughed appreciatively. "Well, that's good for a start, but I can't take a shower in it."

"I rigged up a shower outside, Connie. It's not bad."

"I bet it isn't heated."

"No, but it's invigorating."

She laughed. "Oh, yes, I'm sure." Her voice became serious again. "But there's more, Aaron. I've been thinking since we talked last week, and trying to figure out why I'm so reluctant to stay at Spruce Lake with you. And I realized it's not the lake or the camp as much as it's you."

His heart plummeted to his belly, and he caught at a sudden gasp of air. He was choking, drowning. "What?" he said so quietly he wasn't even sure he'd really said it. He dreaded the words he suspected were coming.

"Every time we've gone there together," Connie said, "you act different. It agitates *you* for some reason, and that makes me uncomfortable."

He'd been sure she would say she didn't want to see him, but this was different. He felt mild relief. Connie had sensed his aversion to the lake as Ginny had.

He thought for a moment. "I guess that's true."

"Then you're aware of it, too," she said gently.

His voice was husky with emotion. "I suppose so."

"Well, why, Aaron?" She was solicitous, anxious to share it with him.

He felt grateful, delivered by some miracle from a fate he could only imagine.

"Did something happen there?" she asked. "What is it about that place that makes you so tense?"

"I wish I knew. If I knew, I could fix it maybe." Another lie. Why couldn't he tell her? Maybe he should fasten a piece of chalk to a string and make a slash on the wall by the telephone each time he fabricated another whopper to poor, gullible Connie Latimer, the unsuspecting absent wife who was far too good for him.

He knew why Spruce Lake distressed him, of course. He knew that his organized mind had locked it away and latched it tightly, shutting it up inside layers of other memories, like the nesting Chinese boxes on the bedroom dresser upstairs. His past was behind him, safely buried.

But the Chinese boxes, once you began to open them, would give up their mysteries easily and lie spread over the dresser top, all their secrets revealed. Right now, the boxes were closed up tight, but Ginny was prying and Connie was prying. And when he

123

started to open up, what would happen?

He needed to be very, very careful.

"Things from the past can alter us," Connie mused, as if she could see his thoughts. "Sometimes we don't even realize it. Do you remember me telling you I got lost in the woods when I was eight? It was near one of the campsites at Piseco. Well, it was a lot more frightening than I ever told you. It was terrifying."

"Sure I remember. You were lost all night, weren't you?"

"Yes, but it wasn't a case of rubbing two sticks together and finding moss on the right side of a tree. I was scared to death. I expected to die in those woods. The sounds and the darkness." She stopped, thoughtful. "And being alone, that was the worst part. Feeling as if I might be by myself forever, even if I could somehow stay alive. In fact, I began to think I'd rather die than try to survive all alone."

"Connie, honey." He wanted to reach out and hold her.

"I really miss you when you're away from me, Aaron. I don't think you realize what it's like for me. When you travel for your work, I'm not myself until you get home again."

Why hadn't he seen that? Had his strong, independent wife covered up so well? Or was he simply not paying enough attention? "I'm so sorry, Con," he said. "I'm going to try to make things different."

"I want to believe you Aaron, but you've said that before. I'm afraid it might be different for a while, and then . . . ." He could hear her sniffling on the other end, then crying softly, and he berated himself for whatever part of this was his fault. He had always believed he didn't deserve her, and he didn't feel any differently now.

"Don't cry, Connie. I love you, you know."

"And I love you," she said, "but I'm more confused than ever."

"It's the end of July, Connie," he said. "It's been a month, that's long enough. Bring Egan up here. If your goal was to make me miserable, you succeeded. Let's get back on track."

"Of course that wasn't my goal," she said unhappily.

He was pleading now. He wanted his wife with him and was getting sick of having to beg for her company. "If you come here, we can talk and maybe straighten some of this out. For God's sake, Connie, I can't sleep. I can't even write the stupid article. The writing would sure go a lot better if you were here."

Sudden silence from her surprised him.

"Connie?"

"Is that why you need me?"

"No, that's not what I meant."

"I don't think I'll be coming, Aaron." She was distant now. What kind of monster was he that he'd sent her so very far away.

"Connie?"

"Write your article, Aaron. We can talk more another time. I have to go," she said.

"Well, call me at least, will you?" he said, resigned. "Can you call every day so I can hear your voice at least?"

"I don't know. Maybe."

"Better yet, come," he said. "I want to be with you." If he had lied to Connie earlier, he knew he was telling the truth now. "I need you."

Chapter 29

AARON CONCENTRATED on writing for three days and accomplished little except the knowledge that he was focused, doing what he was supposed to do. He wrote mechanically, then read it over, ripped it up, and hurled the torn sheets into the blazing fire.

The lack of sleep was catching up with him, and his mind was a whirling dervish. He had kissed Virginia Dunn; he had lied to Connie. In his thirty-six years he had never felt so weak or alone, so completely at the mercy of something outside himself. His head throbbed painfully, and a sense of exhausted stupidity overtook him, dragging along with him from bedroom to writing table to kitchen.

His food supply had run down, and he satisfied the need to keep food in his system by cranking open a can of ravioli or baked beans when he thought of it. It didn't occur to him to wash the can opener or rinse and bag the greasy empty cans. They piled up on the kitchen table. The food tasted bad to him, and he left most of it sitting on the plates.

He would find himself staring at a mug of drinking water in his hand and then remember to place it in the microwave and set the control for two minutes. He used the same teabag two, three, even four times; to replenish the supply meant a trip to the lake store, and he didn't trust himself to go there; he dreaded questions about the Dunn camp and couldn't be sure he wouldn't give himself away by bringing up her name too many times. Ginny. Ginny.

He could survive without going to the store anyway, and getting there sounded like a long and arduous journey, a great effort for very little gain. He hardly recognized himself as the proud nonconformist who had easily hiked the trip with his authentic ashwood basket a few weeks before.

A run-down feeling became his constant companion, and he found himself wavering between chills and a feverish sweat. He couldn't get warm, even though the thermometer on the porch showed temperatures in the seventies. To offset the chill, he wore two shirts and extra socks and drank tea when he thought of it.

And then he would break into a sweat, mopping at his face as he sat gazing dully at the silent typewriter keyboard. He would peel off the flannel shirts and warm jacket, and, sweating profusely in jeans and a tee shirt, stare blankly at the clean white sheets of typing paper. And the chills would start again, and he would wrap himself up once more.

Now and then, he roused himself to make another cup of tea or to throw another log on the fire.

By day he thought of Connie, willing her to call him, to come to the lake, to rescue him, to save their marriage. At night he tried to sleep, and when he did, he dreamed fitfully of Ginny.

The next time Connie called he would insist, he would demand that she answer her cell phone. It was ridiculous that he couldn't reach her in an emergency. A spasm of guilt leapt up and he stifled it quickly, but not before it took hold of him. In his trips from home, his three week excursions, his four day forays, how careful had he been to always leave her his current hotel phone number? Not very. And had he left his cell phone on so Connie could reach him? Rarely.

There were many changes that needed to be made, and, Aaron was discovering, they all needed to come from him. He had won and married the woman he loved and then set about destroying the very thing he cared most about.

Now he wondered why. He was 'decent,' or had always thought he was; he truly loved Connie and Egan and wanted to be with them. So, why? He knew the answer lurked somewhere inside him, but he did not possess the strength or brains or courage or whatever it was that would help him pull it out.

He wandered out to the camp porch and peered up at the sun setting over Spruce Mountain. He shivered with fever, pulling his jacket tighter, and gazed at the camp across the way. He had no idea if Virginia Dunn still kept her late night vigil on the beach before her horrific ruined cottage. These days, at the midnight hour, he found himself inside with windows closed and doors securely bolted, staring at crisp, clean sheets of paper. He could not write, but at least he was safe. No flickering lantern light, no eerie, whimpering young girl's cry could reach him inside his own four walls. He was determined not to give in to her bewitching spells again.

Back inside, he examined Ginny's painting on the rough wooden wall above his writing table. It was a pleasant ornament for his camp, and that was all. He told himself that it meant nothing to him, but caught himself stealing glances at it as words for the article continued to elude him. The long, sharp crack down the center of the glass was a good reminder: whatever he was feeling for Virginia Dunn might seem magical right now, but was bound to shatter and break him in the end. He only needed to keep telling himself that.

Stay away, and all would be well. All would be well.

Chapter 30

THE DUNN COTTAGE was prettier than he'd imagined, with fresh flowered wallpaper on the kitchen walls and attractive, comfortable furnishings. He sat at the polished kitchen table and watched Ginny fuss with plates and silverware as she brought lunch to the table. Her eyes were bright and her smile lingering.

Aaron glanced down at the covered platter before him and laughed. It was like an old movie, the shiny silver cover with its bright handle that he must lift to view the wonderful meal beneath. He received a happy nod from Ginny. Her eyes were sparkling with love. He lifted the cover.

Bile rose in him as he jumped up. His chair clattered over. Aaron stared at the steaming pile of squirming maggots worming in and out of the decomposing meat. He looked up and stared at Ginny.

Her face drooped and began to drip like melting tallow. She swiped at her eyes and blobs of her skin came away in her hands. Those hands! They were skeletal now. Why hadn't he seen that before?

"Doesn't it look delicious?" she asked in her hollow voice. Her grin showed hideous yellowed teeth, and her smile pulled her skin back taut, until it cracked and broke, the pieces raining down in small chunks onto the tabletop. She was a picture of death, a ghoul in a lacy nightgown.

"Aaron?" The rasp of her voice jarred him awake.

Aaron sat up quickly. He was in his own bed at camp, trembling and hot. The bedclothes were tangled and damp; his skin felt slick with sweat. He glanced around the familiar room, saw his boots by the door, yesterday's clothes hanging from pegs in the wall. Moonlight bathed everything in a soft, luminous glow.

The dread began to subside, but the images lingered. Ginny

in his nightmare was a ghoul, her beautiful face decayed by death. But it was only a dream, he assured himself. He knew how Ginny really looked. He knew that she was . . . .

Aaron rubbed a hand over his face and tried to breathe more evenly, forcing himself to put the nightmare behind him. From his upstairs window, he could barely see across the lake, could hardly make out the line of trees ridging the mountain. Her cabin was not visible at all.

But was that a light? He stared across. He had forced himself to avoid Ginny, but now he watched from behind the brittle safety of window glass. The light moved down the shore to the left, rising, returning, disappearing. And did he hear something, or was it just the wind in the old rafters? No, he heard a wail begin, a hollow crying, muffled and doomed.

It died away in the night.

Aaron twisted to see his bedside clock and made out the numbers by hazy moonlight.

It was quarter past midnight.

Chills shook him. Aaron grabbed the bed covers and pulled them up. He burrowed in, and fell into a torturous sleep.

Chapter 31

AARON SAT at his kitchen table wrapped in a quilt, sipping weak tea, and wondered if he'd picked up a flu or virus at the lake store. Maybe Foster or Cathleen had given him some kind of bug; he hadn't been in much contact with anyone else. Or could it have been the fiddlehead ferns that affected him like this? He knew raw fiddleheads could cause fever, lightheadedness, even hallucinations, and the mature bracken was even worse. But he'd taken only the tenderest shoots. Hadn't he cooked them enough? He was sure he had, and he'd only ingested a few.

He glanced at the brittle, drying pile of young shoots on the table. So much for his authentic Adirondack meal. He turned away in disgust.

He had spent the last three days struggling to write and fighting to banish the pictures of Ginny that crept into his mind. When, finally, the nurturing sleep that had eluded him for days tackled him, he could barely drag himself up the stairs and fall into bed. He fell asleep immediately and slept for fourteen hours.

It was Connie's face that awoke him, a floating vision of her that ducked and smiled coyly, just out of his reach. He sat up startled, fully awake, and realized it was late morning. The chills had left him and the fever had finally broken. He made his way downstairs cautiously, feeling like a recovering invalid.

The camp was a mess. The fire had died out, and crumpled papers with burned edges poked up out of the ash. A few unintelligible sheets of typing were stacked carelessly by the typewriter. Aaron skimmed them and grimaced. Worthless. His three days of illness had not produced genius; that was apparent.

He made a half-hearted effort to pick up the clothes and blankets scattered around the floor and wiped off his kitchen table with a dirty, damp cloth. He stared at the smelly cans, the crusty plates and forks, the mugs with their ringed tea stains. He exhaled an exhausted breath. He would take care of it later.

His glance fell on the stack of books Chris had brought, and he fingered them thoughtfully. He picked up the photo album, opened the screen door to the porch, and sat down in his favorite rocker. Pictures of his father's uncles sitting on this porch, pictures of his father as a child holding a boat he had made. Aaron turned the pages listlessly and paused when he came to a photograph of himself and Chris, six or seven years old, their arms around each other's necks, best friends grinning for the camera. He turned the page.

His breath stopped. Virginia Dunn smiled up at him, a little out of focus, her long hair lifted by wind. She held tightly to the hand of a little boy, and both of them sat on a dock, dangling their legs over the edge, with the Dunn camp a shapeless blur in the background.

He peered at Ginny's likeness and then at the boy. This had to be one of her brothers. Aaron peeled the picture from the page and read the back. *Dunn kids,* no date, no further explanation. He recognized the writing. His mother had labeled this picture, probably with as much information as she knew, and he assumed his father had taken it from the boat on a trek around the lake. He had seen the two sitting on their dock, had probably waved and smiled, and had snapped the shot as he motored by.

There were others in the album - one of his father and some neighbors at the boat launch on Big Trout, some kind of a picnic at a camp he didn't recognize, his parents and a few other people on the porch of the camp store.

There were no others of Ginny.

He replaced Ginny's picture in the album and brought it to the living room, where he stuffed it into the bottom shelf of an overfull bookcase. He looked around again at the disorder in the camp but felt too tired to do anything about it. He returned to the porch and collapsed into a rocker. Whatever flu had gripped him, though, seemed to be gone; maybe now he could finally think.

Chapter 32

HE WOULD GO TO GINNY.

He was shocked at his intention to see her once more. It was not what he wanted to do, but his resolution was weak against the iron claw that gripped his will, twisting it so that seeing Ginny was the only goal he knew.

He chided himself. No, that was not the way to get out of this mess. He must never go there again.

But considering it sent a shivering thrill up his spine.

He stopped the motion of the porch rocking chair suddenly as his justification began to bloom, a slick, black bud, enticing and frightful.

Ginny might be able to help him, a sly, eager part of his mind suggested. She had that weird knack of almost reading his mind. She was a listener, could draw him out. Hadn't she made him face his angry relationship with his only brother? And he knew now that something deep inside him had made him run from his perfect marriage, run to Maine, to Calgary, anywhere to escape his loving family. He had never mentioned his marriage to Ginny, but he was convinced that it was because of her that he could now see himself as he was, a very flawed man.

But why *this* flaw, he wondered. What possessed him? He needed to look deeper. Ginny could help him.

No, Ginny could not help him; that was insane.

Aaron resumed rocking. He wiped his brow on his shirt sleeve. Was it the heat of the evening sun or a remnant of the previous days' illness that made him feel so weak and warm? Or was it his crazy thoughts?

It was Ginny's fault that his soul was tortured. Connie had been ready to give in and come to the lake but had pulled away when he had stupidly mentioned Ginny's ghost.

Well, then, Ginny owed it to him to bring Connie back. He

could give Ginny the opportunity to help him. She had to help him.

Would he have the courage to see her again? The ability to leave once he got there? He wasn't sure, but he hoped.

Ginny would show him why he was bent on destroying himself. He would go to her.

More likely she would manage to destroy him altogether. He would not go.

He sat on the porch watching the dusk settle. Pink and violet light hazed over the top of Spruce Mountain; the evergreens beneath glowed green and blue and gold like Christmas trees lit by flaming candles. He observed the light dappling the water, turning it a deep midnight blue at this evening hour. The trees ringing the edge of the lake cast wavery reflections on the water, some glowing green and lush, others bent by harsh winters and old winds, their dead branches sweeping the lake's surface. He heard the water lapping against the shore and saw his scraped canoe lying dormant where he had beached it hastily, days before, on his last frantic race across Spruce Lake.

He forced himself to think logically. It wasn't necessary to remember Ginny's wide, almond-shaped eyes or recall her smooth, translucent skin. What he needed was to remember the one thing she had that might be useful to him now – her peculiar intuition, a gift brought by death. He could use her, trick her into helping him. The thought left a sour taste in his mouth.

Instead, he would tell her honestly that he needed her help, that his motivations were pure. He would beg for her guidance. And he wouldn't touch her. Touching her would be deadly.

The sun was setting lower now. He took stock of all the reasons not to visit Ginny tonight, and there were many. Then he considered the one and only reason for going. For the sake of his marriage and his sanity, he would go. He was convinced she could help him if she chose to.

His decision made, Aaron clenched his hands into fists and summoned strength. He would go tonight. He told himself it would be his last visit, but he shuddered weakly. He had become such a liar lately.

Chapter 33

I CAME AT NIGHT because I didn't want to scare you, Ginny.

Aaron had thought, not said the words, as he stood several feet away from her in the dark, afraid to move any closer. She stood on the rocks along the shoreline, facing him. The moonlight above created a soft halo around her head. Her lantern sat on the top step of the cottage steps, casting weird shadows around them. Her eyes were flames.

"I liked the day," she said simply, as if answering his unspoken words. "I liked the flowers, and I liked the way you looked in the sun."

"But night is better for us," he said, aloud this time. "Surely you can see that. You're very beautiful, and I was taken by that. I frightened you, and I'm sorry."

She met his eyes frankly. "I was only afraid because it was new to me." He saw her turn aside and wondered if her face might have tinged suddenly with a faint blush. "Eddie wanted me to, but we never did. Something happened. . . . I don't know . . . ." Her large, innocent eyes sought his.

"I had no right to touch you. I don't blame you for running away," he said.

"But I've changed my mind." She took a step toward him.

"So have I, Ginny." The words tumbled from him. "I've changed mine. You know that kiss between us never should have happened."

"You liked that kiss," she said.

He admitted it. "Of course I did, but that doesn't make it all right."

"I never had sex," she said to him frankly. "I want to see what it's like."

"Well, we can't, Ginny," he said with an effort. "I'm married, and I love my wife."

135

"I don't mind," she said hollowly. He was suddenly recalled to the first time he had heard her speak, the ancient, reedy quality of her voice, his shock at the timelessness of it, his awareness that he was listening to a ghost.

He decided not to pursue the meaning of her ambiguous words.

He peered into her face, shimmering and beautiful in the darkness. "I'm married," he repeated loudly to convince them both. He forced Connie's face before him and selected a memory, Connie opening the door of her apartment to him when he had first known her, when the mystery of her had been as magnetizing as Ginny was now. "And anyway . . . ." He raked a hand through his hair and exhaled, turning from Ginny and sitting on a rock near the cabin. "I can't believe we're having this conversation, Ginny. You're a . . . You're . . . ."

She looked at him expectantly, clueless and unaware. "I'm what? Not pretty enough? Not old enough?"

Aaron grimaced. This was nuts. He was explaining to a ghost why it would be difficult to seduce her in the usual way. But it sure had seemed plausible several days before. She might remind him with her cold, marble skin how impossible such thoughts were, but he couldn't deny the heat that pulsed beneath that cool surface.

"You're pretty enough," he said. "But you're very young. And I'm married, that's the most important reason."

"But, Aaron," she said plaintively, "I love you." She sounded like a spoiled child trying to get her way, and, for a second, he caught a glimpse of the living, breathing Virginia Dunn - pretty, impetuous, a little headstrong, artistic, affectionate, and maybe slightly spoiled. And drowned before all of her childish and grown up qualities fused together to create the magnificent mature woman she might have become.

Sadly, he turned away from her.

"Aaron?" Her voice was tentative. "Don't you love me, too? You can stay with me, you know."

He started and jerked back to face her.

"You could," she insisted.

And he would see things as she saw them, a distorted, hazy view of reality. To spend eternity here with her, and never act among the living again. What did she mean? How could that happen? He would have to . . . .

Aaron shook himself, shocked at the path his thoughts were

following.

"Ginny, can we just be together here as friends and talk?"

"Wouldn't you like to stay with me, Aaron?"

His horrified face gave her his answer.

She walked toward him, past him, walked up the steps and sat down near the top, where the rotting door of the camp listed on its hinges. She rested her head in her cupped hand and watched him through the dark veil of night. The lantern burned behind her, outlining her in a foggy shroud.

They sat quietly for several moments, she on the step, he on a rock a good, safe distance away. She sat hunched, bent over, her thoughts a burden. Suddenly she surprised him. "Listen," she said. A tiny melody trilled from her lips, sounding like morning birdsong, a cheery tune. "That's a song I used to sing. It's pretty, don't you think so?"

He smiled at her. "Yes, you have a pretty voice. You have lots of talents. It's not really singing, though."

"But it's music, Aaron. I made it up. I sang it when I was happy. I used to sing it to Royce and Timmy when I took care of them when they were little. They're a lot younger than me. I haven't sung it in a while."

"No."

Suddenly she smiled at him and sent a trilling cadence out into the night. The notes skipped out over the water, running up and down an octave, then stopped. "I feel happy when you're here, Aaron," she told him. "When you kissed me, I felt very happy about that." She turned away again, gazing toward the channel.

"Ginny, please," he said. "I have a wife and daughter, and I love them."

"The way I love Eddie."

"Yes." He swallowed the insane jealous lump that formed suddenly in his throat. "Exactly like that."

"I miss Eddie," she said sadly. She rose, came to him, and stood over him. She brought his hand to her lips, and he felt a tear drop there. She needed protection and sympathy; he longed to hold her in his arms and whisper to her that he would make everything right for her.

It would be a lie and a cruelty. He concealed the impulse and sat perfectly still, squeezing his eyes shut, then opening them, in control.

"What did you mean that they said I killed myself?" She

formed the words slowly, as if trying to determine each one's exact significance. Her lips still grazed his fingers.

"That's what people think happened to you."

She shrugged, an impatient gesture. "I don't understand that at all. It wasn't like that."

"I believe you. I don't think you wanted . . . whatever happened that night."

When she spoke her voice was so low he could hardly hear it. The words sounded wrenched from her. "I wanted Eddie, and they didn't want me to have him."

"Your parents?"

She nodded sadly. "So I told them if they made me go back to school I would kill myself." She looked down at him suddenly, surprised. "I had forgotten that! No wonder they think that!"

"Did you mean it?"

She dismissed that idea and laughed. "Of course not. I was being dramatic. I told them I was going to elope, too. I never would have. Eddie wanted to be engaged, and they thought we were too young."

"Why did you leave the house that night?"

"Oh, Aaron," she said suddenly, "I'm so tired. Don't make me talk about this." She pulled him to his feet and leaned into him; he stiffened. "Please, Aaron," she said, "don't do that. Please just let me rest right here. Be soft to me like you were before."

"Ginny . . . ."

She tilted her head back and laughed; he could see amusement deep in her eyes. "You might as well kiss me, Aaron," she said. "I know you want to."

It was an effort to talk, but he managed to say, "Did he meet you that night?"

She was still smiling at him, enjoying his discomfiture. "Aaron, you are such a good man. You needn't kiss me at all, for I will kiss you." She leaned in closer to him and tilted her head back so she could look up into his eyes. She grasped his head with her hands and pulled his face to hers. When she placed her cold lips on his, he felt the searing heat through his body. He willed himself not to respond, but his arms crept up, clinging to her, as he pressed his lips on hers. Slowly, softly, she released him.

"You're a witch," he finally said.

She laughed and looked away.

"Ginny." He gazed at her, needing to impress his words on

her. "If you do that . . . things like that . . . I can't come again. I mean this. I won't come unless it's on my terms."

"Why did you come tonight?"

"Because I'm a fool, I guess."

"No, because you want my help." She looked surprised as soon as she said it. "Is it true, Aaron? Is there something you want me to do?"

He fought for control, stepped back. Her arms hung limply at her sides.

"Tell me about her, then, so I can help you," she said simply. She stood before him looking like an innocent child. "Your wife and your little girl. It's about them, isn't it?"

"Yes, it's about them. They aren't here with me. They wouldn't come."

"They should have come," she whispered.

"No, they were right. I need to change some things. I . . . ." It was hard to go on, and the thickness in his throat made it difficult to talk. Ginny searched his eyes, her compassion and sympathy terribly evident on her young face. He felt his eyes beginning to smart. "Can't you see it, Ginny? Can't you tell me what I need to do?" The words twisted from him painfully. "Why am I like this? What am I supposed to do now?"

"Tell me everything," she said. "I'll help you."

His answer was a muffled sob.

"It will be all right," she said and rushed to him, catching his crumpling form. Then she repeated it, holding him gently, supporting him. "It will be all right," she soothed, as his tears washed over his face and soaked into the soft cotton shoulder of her gown.

Chapter 34

IT FELT RIGHT to drive the SUV. He wondered if Foster Wolf's frank questions and Connie's gentle teasing could be right on the mark. Were the canoe, the packbasket, even the clothes he wore just props he used to prove himself? He admitted that it was a possibility. Connie had told him a week into their blossoming romance that he had a pretentious edge. He had laughed and dismissed the criticism, but now the memory humbled him. Why wasn't he content to be plain old Aaron Latimer?

He pulled into the parking lot of the small local library and locked the car, then strolled into the red brick building and asked the clerk at the desk to direct him.

The local history room was packed with old newspapers and programs, boxes and cartons full of tattered articles that had been clipped and stored according to date, and entire newspapers bundled chronologically.

"You're on your own," the tired librarian told him. "All we have is paper copies. I hope you can find what you need."

Ginny's death had been big news in the area, so the articles had likely spanned several weeks. He knew the approximate year of her death and it would have been summer news; he would begin with the July newspapers, and then move to August. It was a time-consuming process, but he had plenty of time.

By the end of the second hour, he had uncovered the information he wanted. Her picture, a likeness that he might have taken yesterday, smiled from several different issues of the local paper. She was an art student at a small, private college, a good student. She left behind two younger brothers, her parents, assorted aunts, uncles, and cousins. Her mother had given the most detailed interview, and it made Aaron cringe to read her remarks. Why did the media do this to grieving parents who didn't even know what they were saying?

She had talked about quitting school to marry her boyfriend, Eddie Safford. Of course her parents were against it. She had talked about eloping, had threatened suicide if her parents didn't give in and allow her to leave school, had sneaked out of the house when everyone thought she was asleep. Virginia Dunn, for all her talent and beauty, sounded very much like a self-absorbed, immature adolescent, which was exactly what she had been, Aaron was sure.

Eddie had been questioned, of course. He was distraught, beside himself with grief. He hadn't seen her the night she disappeared. He knew nothing. It seemed clear that Eddie had cared for her. Aaron examined the head and shoulders shot of the clean cut young man who had wanted to marry Virginia Dunn.

Then Aaron read a detail that made him grimace. Her shoes were found in the woods, neatly together as if she had purposely left them there; they were bagged as evidence. Had she removed her shoes and left them in so organized a way, or was there more to it than that?

When her body washed up later in Big Trout Lake, foul play seemed out of the question. There were surface abrasions; she had been banged up by rocks, but that was all. No one had assaulted her in any way. Virginia Dunn was simply one more foolish young person believing she could solve her problems by taking her own life.

Aaron sat and digested the information he had just read. Regardless of the conclusions drawn ten years ago, he knew Ginny had not taken her own life, so why had it ended so abruptly? Did Eddie Safford know more than he admitted? Was he somehow responsible?

Why was Ginny haunting Spruce Lake? What was she waiting for? Looking for?

Aaron sat back in the hard wooden chair, feeling a flicker of shame. He had returned to Ginny hopeful that she would prove useful to him. Aaron Latimer at his controlling best. Well, maybe it was possible that he could do something for Ginny, as well.

He intended to find out more. Somehow he would uncover the truth and give Ginny back to the eternity that waited to claim her.

Chapter 35

EGAN SEEMED HAPPY enough, Connie noted with relief, and she could thank Justin Rime for at least a bit of that. He had read her stories several nights running, and both Egan and Connie were highly entertained by his quirky humor.

Right now Egan was in her rented Saratoga room, dolls and doll clothes spread out on the bed. Her Barbie was dressed as an Egyptian queen, and Egan was busily attaching all of her own hair ornaments to the mysterious queen's long, blonde hair.

Justin Rime was sprawled on the sofa in the living room, leafing through *Heart of the River*, examining the photographs, arrested now and then by a paragraph or caption. "He's good," he called to Connie in the kitchen. "I'll say that much."

Connie's head appeared, a broad grin on her face. "I know he's good. I bought that the day I met him. That was *how* I met him." She brought the bouquet of fresh wildflowers into the living room and placed them on the fireplace mantel. "These are so pretty," she said. "It was sweet of you to bring them for Egan. She loved it."

He grinned. "I thought she would."

Connie came to the sofa, sat down near Justin, and peered over his arm at the familiar book. He edged nearer to her, holding the volume between them.

"He's incredibly talented," Connie said. "If we were at my house, I could show you a stack of magazines that have his work in them. He's done everything, articles on the Colorado Rockies, things on Boston Harbor and the Maine coast. He did an amazing spread on the Badlands and one on the prairies out west. It's always something to do with nature."

"He must be pretty sought after with that kind of resume."

She grinned and nodded. "Absolutely. He's made a good name for himself already, and his career is just beginning. He has his pick of assignments."

Justin was looking at her somberly. "Then why isn't he here?"

"What?"

"I've been wondering about it, Connie. Why isn't he here with you and Egan? If you wanted to spend a summer in Saratoga enjoying the ballet and the races, why didn't he come along, too?"

"Well, I told you before, it's his work . . . ."

Justin stood up and paced to the fireplace. He toyed with the vase of wildflowers, pulled a daisy from the vase and repositioned it, then turned back to Connie. "If he has his pick, if he's so important that he can choose which assignments to accept and which to reject, then why didn't he choose to come?" He looked frankly at her, straightened the vase, and came to sit beside her. "He should be looking out for you, shouldn't he?" His voice was husky, and she felt her breath coming shallowly.

It had been creeping around the edges of her consciousness for the last few days, and now it broke upon her like an unexpected rain shower, unwelcome but warmly comforting, spilling softly, enfolding her. Justin was interested in her, not as a convenient friend, a sympathetic adult to talk to and have fun with, but with another kind of interest, the kind a man felt for a woman.

Their night at the coffee house had been a pleasure. She'd had fun, yes, a lot of fun, and so had Egan. After the initial awkwardness, it had seemed so natural to spend the evening with Justin. He was attentive and funny and had spent as much time talking with Egan as he had with her. She had appreciated that and told him so. They'd eaten a delicious dinner and talked animatedly all the way back to their building. He had come in with her, read a story to Egan, and said no to Connie's offer of coffee.

"Coffee, no thanks," he said. "I had enough at dinner. I've got a bottle of wine, though. I'll only be a minute." By the time she had tucked Egan into bed, he was back, opening the wine, scrambling through her cupboards for wine glasses, and pouring a glass of merlot for each of them.

"To a really great evening," he said with a grin, and he clinked his glass to hers, laughing.

Smiling, she agreed.

He had come over the next day, hanging around her

apartment, staying for lunch when she invited him, sitting on the floor with Egan and Oboe and a length of red yarn that Egan had pulled from a ball of yarn she'd found in the spare bedroom. Oboe had chased the string, tying himself in knots and making all of them laugh.

Justin had suggested a pizza, had taken notes on everyone's favorite toppings, and had gone to his own apartment before he picked it up, returning with a green salad. Connie had insisted he take the leftovers home with him.

The next day they had run into him leaving the building. It was a silly coincidence; they were headed to the same diner for lunch. It would have been ridiculous not to go together.

He had stopped by to see if she had any letters that needed mailing; he was on his way to the Post Office. He had called her cell to see if there was anything she needed at the pharmacy or the grocery store; he was on his way to do a couple of quick errands. He had invited Egan to bake real New Orleans baguettes with him, and Connie had enjoyed a delicious hour of shopping on her own, knowing that Egan was fine and safe and happy with Justin and Oboe right across the hall from her own apartment.

She had grown fond of him, and he knew it.

She knew she had absolutely nothing to feel guilty about, but guilt crept within her every time she opened her door to Justin or heard her daughter chatter on about him or considered whether or not to include him in their plans.

The frank, interested look Justin was giving her now made panic rise in Connie's throat, and she rose abruptly from the sofa, aware that his gaze followed her across the room. She turned her back to him to hide the flush rising in her cheeks.

"I'm sorry," he said. "I don't mean to criticize him, but I can't help wondering. It takes a couple of hours to drive here from the Adirondacks. He could be here any evening, any day. He could practically commute from here. Where is he, this man who loves you more than his own life?"

Connie felt anger replacing confusion and wheeled back to face him. "He does love me, Justin; he's my husband. And I love him, too. There's nothing that will ever change that."

"Which is what every victim of divorce probably says at some point near the beginning of the end."

She laughed scornfully. "There's not going to be any divorce. That's never been an option. Never."

"No, Connie?" He was beside her now, and she was very

aware of his nearness. "When he's content to leave a beautiful woman like you alone often enough that it bothers you?"

"I never said it bothered me."

"You don't have to say so. Why are you here? If you're not hiding out, if there aren't any problems, then why are you here?" His voice was soft and fluid, caressing her bruised heart. "I'm sorry, but I do care about you. If you didn't want that, you should have stopped me a long time ago."

He remained chastely apart from her, but his arm swept the room. "If he cares so much, why has that little girl in there gone to sleep every night for the last five weeks without her dad tucking her in or kissing her goodnight? I'm a good storyteller, but I'm not her father. Doesn't he care that another man is doing the things he should-"

"It's his work, Justin," she barked, interrupting him. "I've told you that. This," she indicated the glossy-covered, hard-backed book he had cast aside, "doesn't come from sitting around doing nothing. It comes from hard work, and his kind of work requires travel and dedication. A man like Aaron-"

"A man like Aaron is a big fool," he interrupted, "if he thinks *that*," he indicated the book scornfully, "can possibly be more important than you are."

"I think you should leave," Connie said tightly. She stared into his eyes, anger blazing in her own.

He placed a hand on her arm and drew her closer to him. There was no misunderstanding the look he gave her. "I know I don't have any right," he said, "but Connie, it drives me crazy to see you here alone like this. You talk about your husband as if he's some paragon who tosses you a crumb now and then. You haven't even seen him in over a month, have you?"

"That's not your-"

"You don't have to answer. I know, and it's wrong."

She wrenched from him and marched to her front door, flinging it open. She didn't even bother to speak; her eyes screamed her message.

Justin looked down at the floor, then back at her. His face was ashen. "I'm sorry," he said. "Don't throw me out, Connie. I'm sorry if I was out of line. I said too much. Sometimes I don't think first."

From the hallway, they could hear an upstairs tenant clattering down the stairs. He walked by, peering into the open doorway with interest. Connie shut the door.

"My marriage is a good one," she said calmly. "I love Aaron and he loves me. What's between you and me is just a very nice friendship. If you thought otherwise, then you misunderstood me. If that was my fault, I apologize."

He shook his head somberly. "No, you didn't do anything. I imagined there might be something between us. My fault completely."

"Maybe it would be best if you left," she said gently.

His head came up and he stared into her eyes with great sadness. He saw something there that made him approach her where she stood by the door and grip her shoulders tightly. "And sometimes I act without thinking, too," he said quietly.

She didn't shrink away. "Justin," she said, but she didn't fight him. There was no shock or rage or fury, just her quiet grief that this man saw in her a value that Aaron had once seen. Their last telephone conversation still hurt her. Aaron had begged her to come to Spruce Lake. She was on the verge, missing him, wanting him. And then his reason: he couldn't seem to get the article written and maybe her presence would help. Was that all she was to him now?

Justin's hands slid up her neck, gently pushing her hair aside. His thumb caressed her ear, and he cradled her head, tipping it back. His mouth was inches from her own.

He bent his head to kiss her and she sighed sadly. "No, please, you shouldn't," she whispered. She turned her head away.

"I should," he said, and turned her head back, kissing her very gently, letting her feel the pressure of his lips before he lifted them from hers and released her. "What kind of marriage is it," he asked softly, "when I can kiss you like that and it feels so right?"

She stood numbly, not sure of the answer.

"If you think about this and want to see me, I'm easy to find," he said. "I'll leave it up to you."

She stood silently, sadly, holding the door open for him.

"Good night, Connie. I'll be right across the hall."

He was in the corridor, reaching into his pocket for his key, when she found her voice, stopping him with a word. "Justin?"

He turned.

"He never abandoned us. You've read it all wrong. It was me. I abandoned him."

He swallowed, but said nothing, and opened his own door. He went in, the door clicking shut behind him. She retreated to her living room and closed her own door, leaning against it, allowing silent tears to drop from her eyelashes and course down her face.

The truth, now that she saw it, had hit her very hard.

Chapter 36

AARON HAD BROUGHT HIS CAMERA to take pictures of his friend, the ghost of Virginia Dunn. He was willing to see her, wanted to, but walked as if on shattered glass now, careful with each word he spoke to her, conscious of every touch between them.

The idea of the pictures excited him. He was curious to see how they would come out, *if* they would come out. Would he get fuzzy, vague shapes hardly discernible as a human being? Would the shots show background only? Whatever the results, he would show Connie. He needed to have Connie understand his weird behavior lately; he wanted proof that he was not going mad.

For the first time, he regretted his impulse to do everything the old-fashioned way and missed his laptop and digital camera. But he had prepaid mailers which he would ask Cathleen Parnell to mail for him. After that, he'd just have to wait.

He had insisted that Ginny meet him in daylight, and she was so pleased at the thought of having her picture taken that she agreed. "I haven't had my picture taken in years, Aaron!" she told him with a grin.

He vowed to himself that this would not be a repeat of the last time they had met in sunlight.

He placed her in the shadows behind her cottage, in front of a stand of birch trees. The light was good, and he asked her not to pose; rather, he wanted to catch her as she was. Some of the pictures should show her smiling, some serious; in one, she impetuously hugged a birch tree, a young girl hamming it up for the camera. He snapped another unexpectedly, as she threw her head back and laughed at something he said, and one when she was growing tired and asked him if they might stop. The sun had been full on her face then, her expression wistful, and he hoped he had taken it before she cringed from the sun's rays.

For the last picture, he posed her formally, her hands touching the tree's surface gently; she looked over her shoulder at him and gave a small, trusting smile.

"That's the end of the roll," he said. The last six shots on a roll he'd begun weeks before when his article had seemed important to him. He pressed the camera's release button and rewound the film, opened the back of the camera and dropped the canister into his palm, pocketing it. "When I get them back I'll show them to you if they're good."

"Well, even if they're not, Aaron," she said, "I want to see them anyway."

Unless I end up with half a dozen pictures of a birch tree, he thought. The idea seemed impossible to him. She was so obviously concrete matter, a palpable and very genuine young woman. She was not an angel, but a girl, complex and mystifying.

He stowed his camera in a drybag in his canoe and settled down, leaning against a tree, to eat the sandwiches he had brought. He offered her one, but she gave him such a look of confusion that he took it away again. "I don't know how to eat that," she said. "I think I used to know."

"Never mind. You don't need it anyway." But he did, so he ate them all. He was famished, and he devoured his lunch in big bites while she watched him in fascination.

"Ginny," he said when he was finished, "I have come to realize that I detest my camp, I hate Spruce Lake, and I despise my brother, and I'm going to tell you why." It all came out matter-of-factly, and he wondered if she could tell how much effort it had cost him even to say the words. He couldn't wait to hear what kind of advice she might have for him now that he was ready to face the ugly truth.

She was sitting, leaning against a rock, looking at him sadly. "That's a lot of hate, Aaron. Are you sure?"

"Okay," he sighed, "you don't think I hate them. Tell me why." She knew, he was convinced. She always knew.

"Tell me what *you* think," she said.

He tossed the remaining crusts of bread from his lunch into the woods and sprawled out near her, making himself comfortable. The sky was azure, and a few puffy clouds floated over Spruce Lake and lingered high above the mountains. He shielded his eyes from the sun briefly, then turned on his side to look at Ginny.

"I don't see why, but somehow I think it has something to do with Connie, too," he said.

"But she hardly comes here, you said." Ginny giggled and reached a hand to him, letting her fingers play in his hair for a moment. "Poor mixed-up Aaron. Tell me about Chris," she said, "Let's start with that. You promised to tell me what happened."

He took her hand and set it down gently on the warm rock. "Don't do that, Ginny," he said.

She pulled her knees in their cotton gown up to her chest, encircled them with her arms, and rested her chin on them. Her toes peeked out, small and white. She smiled at him demurely. "I'm waiting, Aaron, and I've got all the time in the world."

He heaved in a breath, looked up into the sky above them again, and then glanced at the girl beside him. Then he told her his story.

Chapter 37

AT TWELVE, AARON WAS TALLER, stronger, faster, and more coordinated than his older brother, and they both suffered for it. Chris, just thirteen, refused the games and sports that he might have enjoyed because he knew he could never beat this hulking younger brother who played to win every single time. And Aaron grew to resent his weak sibling who wouldn't even try.

It had been a Saturday, and the family had driven to the lake for a three day holiday. The weather was fine, and the food was good. His mother had spent hours preparing and packing enough for an army, and now that dinner was over, the four of them - mother, father, Chris, and Aaron - talked, stretching lazily in the rockers on the front porch.

How had the conversation turned to athletics? His father must have brought it up. He was a sports fan, and Aaron had inherited not only his burly good looks, but his passion for the major league games. Aaron had all kinds of opinions about sports, and his father never ignored an opportunity to razz him.

"It's too bad we can't watch the Yanks today," his dad said lazily, looking sideways at Aaron. "If we had brought the television up like I suggested, we'd all be in there right now."

"Yeah, like *you* suggested," Aaron said bitterly. He had begged to cart the TV along. "They're playing Boston, too."

"Yep," his father drawled. "The Sox are likely to trounce us this time."

Aaron gave a disgusted snort.

His mother rocked slowly. "Oh, you can take a break from the TV for one day. You have a whole lake to swim in."

"I'd rather see that game, though," Aaron said. "It's pretty obvious who's gonna win." He glared at his father.

The big man laughed, a huge, hearty sound. "They'll be on again tomorrow," he said. He glanced at his older son. "Right,

Chris?"

Chris raised his eyebrows and said nothing. He stood up from his rocker, pulling his towel from the back of the chair. The boys were dressed for swimming. Aaron's beach towel was flung over his shoulders, and Chris was wrapping his around his slender waist, tucking it in at the side.

"Chris, for God's sake, you look like you're wearing a skirt," his father chided.

"Oh, leave him alone," their mother said with a disinterested shrug. "You boys have a good swim, and be careful out there." She looked at her watch. "Has it been an hour already? Lord, the time goes so fast up here."

"Because we aren't doing anything," her husband said.

"I thought the time went slow," said Aaron. "I've been waiting to swim all day."

"Well, you don't want to get a cramp," his mother said.

"I don't even care about going in," Chris muttered. "It's probably freezing."

George Latimer groaned and gestured toward the sky, as if asking some greater being how to handle this most delicate of sons. "Stop being a wimp, Chris," he said. "You used to love swimming and you could have been great at it, even better than Aaron."

Aaron guffawed. Not likely.

"It's true," his father insisted. "When you guys were at the Y taking lessons, Chris was a fish. He couldn't get in the pool fast enough."

It *was* true, although Aaron hated to admit it. They had both been excellent swimmers and Aaron had loved having a built-in rival to compete with. Who had the stamina to swim more laps? Aaron. Who loved diving to the bottom, eyes open, to retrieve a tossed object? Aaron again. Who could hold his breath for sixty seconds? Well, that had been Chris. They'd had contests for that, the two of them, in and out of the water, and Aaron, as determined as he'd been to best his brother, had always given in first, retching and gulping air while Chris smirked in victory.

"Better watch out, Chris," their father had warned. "Or Aaron'll be beating you at that, too."

When Chris dropped out of the YMCA lessons, George Latimer had had a fit. "You're a quitter!" he'd roared. "The one thing, the *one* thing you're good at. Why quit? What's wrong with you?"

Even then, Aaron had known. Obviously Chris had quit while he was ahead. He'd begun to avoid all contests with his younger brother and had never again accepted Aaron's challenges in anything, even those breath-holding competitions. So the record still held: Chris Latimer: seventy-eight seconds at his best. Aaron: always less.

"You boys go ahead down," their mother said now. "Just don't get a cramp. And be careful, Chris. You haven't been in the sun that much. Don't get burned."

Chris unwrapped his towel from around his waist and carried it down, a sullen look on his face. Aaron raced ahead of him down the bank, and, always eager, thundered out to the end of the wooden dock and jumped in, feet first. Chris stepped off the stone step that curved and led into the water near their grainy beach. He stood there with his feet barely wet. "Brrr. It's cold again. Just like I said."

Aaron splashed him with a fistful of water, laughing as Chris grimaced and shivered and backed away.

"Come on in, the water's great!" Aaron yelled. He did a quick dive underwater, opened his eyes and reached down to bring up a broken diving mask that had been hibernating in the water since the summer before. He tossed the mask to the bank and swam out to deeper water with a firm breaststroke. Chris still hovered near shore. Aaron did a couple of back flips underwater, sped further out into the lake, and then darted back toward shore, a streamlined fish in the water.

Suddenly, Aaron felt a tug at his left foot. He tried to shake his foot loose, but found that whatever had him would not let go. He swallowed a mouthful of water as his head went under and felt a moment of excruciating panic. His foot was caught; something had a tight hold on his ankle. But what? An old fishing line? Some lake creature hungry for a meal? He couldn't tell, but he was being dragged under, further and further. His lungs threatened to burst. He could feel himself getting lightheaded, and fought the panic engulfing him. Moving by instinct, he raised his hands above his head and pushed them down to his sides, the slow motion movement of a jumping jack, slicing through water, making himself a bullet that would shoot through the deep lake waters and rocket him to the surface.

Nothing happened. Something held him underwater and he couldn't breathe in. He allowed a gurgle of air to escape his lips.

Again, he pushed down, feeling the heavy water over him,

cupping his hands to give the maximum lift. His brain was fogging, and he thought he heard birds chirping crazily over him. That couldn't be, he was underwater, underwater, and his head was about to explode. He needed to . . . He raised his hands again and thrust downward with all the strength he could muster.

His ankle shot free and he pummeled toward the surface, kicking out. His foot, flailing in the thick, green water, made hard, brutal contact with something. He reached the surface and his head shot through. He gulped in the sudden fresh air, gasping and panting. He coughed and then breathed in again, as slowly as he could, waiting for his head to clear, treading water, using as little energy as possible.

There was no sign of Chris on the shore or in the shallow water near the beach, and he wondered where his brother was, then caught sight of him, doubled over on the surface a few yards away, holding his side, grimacing in pain.

"Chris!" he panted. He swam closer to his brother. "Something had me; I'm not kidding. Something had me underwater."

Chris wasn't listening. His eyes were closed tightly in terror and pain, and he was holding his side, trying to swim toward shore.

"My God, it got you, too." Aaron reached him quickly, hooked a gentle arm around his brother's chest, and glided toward shore, holding Chris safely in the crook of his arm. Chris moaned in pain.

"Dad! Mom!" Aaron shrieked. He pulled Chris onto the shore, grabbed the nearest towel and wrapped it carefully around his brother. Chris held his side, gasping and moaning.

It took the doctor almost forty minutes to get there, and by then they had carried Chris up the bank and into the camp, where he was stretched out on the living room couch, clutching his side in agony.

"I don't know what it was. It had us both," Aaron said. His excited explanation was garbled, lost among the frenzied panic of his mother and the doctor's soothing tones.

Chris's eyes fluttered open. He gazed at Aaron's face briefly. Then, "Aaron kicked me," he suddenly complained.

Aaron blinked and backed away, shocked.

"He kicked me really hard." Tears filled Chris's eyes now and he couldn't look at his younger, stronger brother. "He probably didn't mean to hurt me," he added.

The doctor gave Aaron a quick glance, probed gently at Chris's side, and suggested an x-ray. Chris was bundled off to the nearest hospital, while Aaron waited alone at camp, nervously hurling a tennis ball against the painted clapboard, catching it, hurling it again.

He was relieved to learn that Chris's injuries would not be permanent. He would hobble about in great pain for a day or two, but he would, ultimately, be fine.

Aaron saw the discouraged looks his parents gave him and cowered in shadows while they bustled about, fixing Chris's blankets, massaging his injured side, bringing him food. He watched his brother limp upstairs to bed on their father's arm and listened in humble confusion to the lecture his father gave him later that evening. When one had the gift of strength, it was important not to misuse it, he said. Aaron was bigger than Chris and had the physical stamina that Chris would probably always lack. He must be very careful to understand his own power. Most were far weaker than he.

When he allowed himself to guess the truth, Aaron seethed inside and waited for Chris to say something. He waited for three weeks before it dawned on him that Chris had no intention of confessing his sin. He began to look at his brother in a new way then. Chris was not someone to be pitied; Chris was someone to be despised. He was cowardly, and he was deceitful. And he had tried to injure his own brother. Maybe he had even tried to kill him.

"Didn't he ever tell them what he had done?" Ginny asked. She frowned, looking at her hands in her lap.

"No, at least not that I know of. And all these years, I've resented him, and I've never really admitted to anyone why I hate him so much. No one knows but the two of us, and now you. I used to pray that I could forgive him, but all that happened was that I'd get more agitated."

"Did he ask you to forgive him?"

"No, he's never said anything about it. He's weak, but he's my brother, the only one I've got, and I'm not proud of the fact that I hate him."

"It's hard to love the person who tries to destroy you."

"But he's my brother. He was a child. He was probably fed up with me."

"If you had been the weaker one, you would have drowned," Ginny said. She looked vague for a moment. Her eyes held a faraway cast. "That must be a terrible way to die."

Aaron stared at her. Finally he said calmly, "If I had been the weaker one, he wouldn't have been jealous of me and it never would have happened. Anyway, it ruined things between us."

"But that doesn't mean you hate him."

"Don't I? Should I?"

She looked at him quizzically. "Why are you asking me? He's your brother. How do you feel about him?"

Aaron thought carefully. She was the first human soul he had told that story to. Even Connie knew nothing of the terrible hurt he had suffered, the physical and emotional pain that his own brother had inflicted upon him. "Well, I *want* to care about him because he's my brother. And I do in a way, very privately. But I don't like his kids."

"That's not true," Ginny said easily. "You don't even know them."

She was right, of course. He had never bothered. "I don't know his wife either."

"But you think she's probably a good sort, maybe?"

"Maybe he's a good sort, too, Ginny." He glanced at her cautiously. "I have to admit something. He has asked me to talk about the past with him, but I won't."

"So you think maybe you're still punishing him?"

"Is that what I'm doing?"

She looked at him in exasperation. "Aaron, I'm twenty years old. I'm not a psychiatrist. I'm just reflecting what I see inside you."

"You make a very fine mirror," he said ruefully. "And am I punishing Connie, too? That doesn't even make sense. She has nothing to do with this. She's never done one thing that I could fault her for."

Ginny shrugged. "Then you should rejoice. Why do you want to convince her that you don't deserve her?"

He looked surprised. "I never said that. Why would I do that? Is that what I'm doing?"

Ginny smiled sweetly. "It's more like you're punishing yourself, sounds like."

Chapter 38

LATER, CANOEING HOME in the twilight, he thought over the things she had said.

Refusing to let Chris ask for forgiveness.

Trying to show Connie how little he deserved her, how unworthy he felt.

Was he really doing those things?

The ideas had pounced upon Ginny suddenly, surprising her and glimmering like wet sunshine, obvious as soon as she said them.

How was it possible that a girl like Ginny, with all her best years snatched away so suddenly, had attained a wisdom that even she didn't understand?

Aaron hauled the boat up onto the sand, his mind full as he secured the canoe on the usual post with the usual ropes. He was bent over his task, snugging the line to the dock as he always did, when he heard the sound on the water. Her light song came tripping along the surface, a breezy, lilting tune, making him smile, filling his heart.

However the truths had come to her, he knew she was right.

Chapter 39

WHEN HE VISITED HER NOW, Aaron would brace himself for her touch and accept the whisper of her hands in his, ignoring stoically the ice that seared through him.

He had taken to walking to her camp sometimes, following the path that darted in and out of the woods along the waterfront. Occasionally, he would come upon a deer lapping at the edge of the lake; he would watch unmoving until it finished drinking and loped away. If it were alerted to him suddenly, he would watch in silence as it pricked up its ears and dashed briskly up the mountain, canting gracefully from side to side.

Sometimes in the late night, he would hear Ginny's shimmering voice sailing across the lake, the lilting melody she had sung for him, her happy tune. Her moaning, whimpering cry was a rarity now, a sound he heard only when days passed and he forced himself to stay on his own side of the lake. When she cried in anguish, he would go to her, ashamed that he had given in, guilty if he stayed away.

She made a halfhearted effort not to beguile him, but when she grasped his hands or touched his arm, it sent burning cold pulsing through him, forcing him to clench his fists and look away, which caused her to laugh in victory. He realized that in life Ginny had been very much a flirt.

It was even harder when she was despondent. Her aloneness fired a sympathy even more difficult to control.

"Why have you come?" she would sometimes ask him. On her low days, the question meant, What is the point? Why are you here to torment me when I can never have your world and you refuse mine?

When she was happy, giddy, she posed the question impishly because she loved to hear him answer.

"Because I need you," he would say. "I need you to help me

save my marriage, witch. And help me figure out who this screwed-up stranger is who's living in Aaron Latimer's familiar old body."

He could have driven to Syracuse to develop pictures at home in his darkroom, and he knew he probably should have. He had several rolls ready to go, pictures he had taken in his earlier productive days at the lake. But now he disliked the thought of being away from the lake and Ginny. So he had taken just one roll of film to Cathleen Parnell to be mailed and developed commercially, and he awaited the pictures with a kind of nervous reluctance. When he was with her, Ginny was very real; he wasn't sure he wanted proof that she was simply a vapor.

He had brought her a drawing tablet and pencils, and now he sat in the sunshine watching her draw. Earlier, she had sketched him in his canoe, drifting on the calm lake while the sun set behind him, flashing bursting rays over the water. He held that sketch now, unbelieving, a picture drawn by talented hands that did not exist. He decided to take it back to his own camp, frame it, and display it beside her painting.

He enjoyed watching her work, serious and relaxed under a shady tree, her brow knitted in concentration, and he tried not to interrupt her, but when questions and ideas popped into his mind now and then, he felt compelled to verbalize them lest they escape him.

"So you were twenty that night?" he asked her.

"When I fell from the boat?" She was engrossed in her art.

"I didn't know there was a boat, Ginny."

She looked up, startled. "Oh, there was. I was twenty, yes."

"You still look twenty. Sometimes you look younger. You act a lot younger sometimes."

She shrugged and continued drawing. "I was immature."

"Tell me about the boat," he said.

"If I can remember." She cocked her head on one side, thinking, a gesture that had become very familiar and dear to him. "Eddie said to meet him that night, but I didn't tell anybody. He left a note on the kitchen windowsill." She grinned. "He did that sometimes. It was so romantic. So at midnight, I left the cottage. I had been sick; I had a cold or a touch of flu, so I didn't get dressed. I was just going to tell him I couldn't meet him and then go right back inside."

He could feel his heart hammering. She was telling him about the night she had died. Had anyone else in the world ever experienced such insanity? He encouraged her. "Then what?"

"Eddie wasn't there yet, so I walked through the woods and found him near the channel."

"Through the woods? You wore shoes, right?"

"I threw a pair on, but I took them off. They were pinching, and I don't mind going barefoot, even in the woods. Eddie was in his little motorboat, but he had cut the engine. He wanted to talk, so I got in the boat. He rowed us down through the channel into Sentry Pond to the beginning of Little Trout Lake."

"I thought it was a motorboat."

"Well it had oars, too, Aaron."

"He didn't want your parents to hear the motor?"

"Right, I guess that was it. In Little Trout, he started the motor and we went into Eastern Bog. That's when I told him we ought to turn around."

"Why?"

She looked up from her sketch, exasperated. "Well, I was in my nightgown, Aaron. Plus, I didn't feel well." She caught him smiling and tucked her bare feet under the hem of her gown, the very same gown. "Anyway, he didn't have life jackets and I was afraid. There weren't any lights; it was real dark."

"There are only three cottages on that lake, aren't there?" he asked.

"There weren't any then. It was dead quiet, no lights. I was scared, a little."

"Why were you scared?" Had Eddie done something he had never admitted?

"Oh, I don't know," Ginny answered. "It was dark . . . ." She stopped speaking and concentrated on the sketch before her. Her pencil moved in smooth arcs.

Aaron watched for a moment, but the nagging questions wouldn't leave him. "What did you talk about?"

"I can't remember. Oh, wait, I told him that my parents were right and that I had to go back to school in the fall." Her pretty mouth broke into a happy grin. "I *did* want to go back to school. You see, Aaron? I knew I was going to become an artist. Anyway, he was angry, but you know, I really don't think I was ready for marriage."

"No, you probably weren't. Twenty is pretty young."

She sighed as if the pressures of the world weighted her shoulders. "Eddie tried to talk me into it." A girlish smile stole onto her face, lighting up her eyes. "He was really in love with me, I could tell. But I told him we'd have to wait. I did want Eddie, but I wanted to finish school, too. I'm so glad about that."

A feeling of dread was sneaking over Aaron. What was she leading up to? Was it possible that Ginny had been murdered? Eddie Safford must know far more about Virginia Dunn's death than he had ever let on at the time. Fear curling in his stomach, Aaron waited for her to continue.

"There are a lot of rocks in Eastern Bog," Ginny continued, "and when he tried to turn the boat around, I think we got hung up. I'm not sure. It was dark and I felt kind of dizzy, you know, from the flu, and . . . somehow I fell over the side. I couldn't grip the rocks; they were slimy under the water, and I can remember that Eddie kept whispering my name, calling for me."

"So he tried, at least . . . ."

"His voice was harsh and raspy; he sounded really scared of what he'd done. Or wait," she paused. "I don't think he meant to. He couldn't have." She thought briefly. "His boat cut loose or somehow he got it loose, and it was drifting farther away, and so was I. My hair kept floating into my face and getting caught in my mouth. I couldn't answer him. I was so cold, too, at first."

Cold and terrified, Aaron thought. Scared out of her wits, as he had been years ago, trying to force through the heavy water to save himself. His lungs overfull, his mind blurry . . . .

"I couldn't grab anything," Ginny was saying. "I kept reaching out, I kept trying. My hair kept tangling around my neck, in my mouth. And I couldn't make a sound . . . ." She stopped. He realized she was gasping for breath, reliving her fear.

"But what about Eddie?" he said. "What did he do next?"

A glazed look had come over Ginny's face and she turned her eyes to Aaron. "The bottom was very sandy there. With big boulders and little stones all over and tall, spindly reeds."

She gave her attention back to the sketch pad in her hands. "Do you want to see what I've been working on?" she asked.

The sketch was finished, and she moved over next to Aaron to show him. He let out the breath he hadn't even known he was holding and took the paper from her smooth white hands into his shaking ones. He glanced down to see a good likeness of the Eddie Safford whose picture he had seen in the newspapers in the local public library.

"That's what he looks like," she said. Then she saw his hands. "Why, Aaron, you're trembling." Her voice was full of concern as she took his hands in hers. He saw her eyes fill with tears. "Don't be sad, Aaron, dear. Eddie didn't mean to leave me. He couldn't have meant to. He loved me."

Aaron swallowed. "You couldn't swim," he said. "He must have known you couldn't swim."

"But he couldn't find me in the dark. I'm sure he tried to."

"Most of Eastern Bog is barely five feet deep. It's only deep through the very central part of the lake."

"That's where we were. I don't know why, but we were there by those big rocks near the island, in the deep part. And I'm barely five feet tall. A baby can drown in two inches of bathwater, they say."

"He let you die. Are you sure he didn't push you?"

She put her hands over her ears to block out his words. Gently he removed them and held her, cradling her. "I'm so sorry, Ginny," he murmured. "I wish I could do something."

"Love me, then." She lifted her face and kissed him softly on the mouth.

He held her more firmly, then a thought occurred to him. "The first time you kissed me, you gave me your flu. Did you know that?" Stumbling around his camp on the edge of sleep, dizzy, congested, feverish, and shaking. That was the gift he had taken from Ginny. He realized suddenly that although time had passed for him, and he was over the debilitating symptoms, for her it was still that night. She didn't act sick, but somehow, inside . . . .

"Ginny, Eddie told the authorities that he didn't know anything about your . . . ." He couldn't bring himself to say the word. Sometimes she seemed so completely unaware that she had died; at other times the mention of it sent her fleeing. He felt his head spinning. "Eddie lied to the police. He should be made to tell the truth."

"It doesn't matter, I guess."

"I think it does matter, though. There may be more to it than you remember. Look at you. You cry every night, searching for him."

"Not so much anymore," she said. "You make it better for me."

He ignored the compliment. "What are you waiting for, Ginny? Are you looking for him to come back and rescue you? To change the past somehow?"

"I don't think so." She whimpered the words.

"I'm going to find him and make him tell the truth about this," Aaron said abruptly. "He should be responsible."

She was up and out of his arms. "No, no!" she cried. "Don't you understand? His only crime was weakness! His only sin was not telling what he knew!"

Aaron was shocked at the fervor of her words. "How do you know that? You said yourself you can't remember. And anyway, he should have told!" He felt a strong compulsion to punish the man who had done this to her. Had Eddie Safford searched for her? Had he called her name as loudly as he dared, groped about in the water with his hands or an oar, and eventually, terrified and panic-stricken, rowed his little boat home? Or had he meant for it to happen, enraged at their argument? Had he cleaned off his boat, gone to bed, and been legitimately terrified when the sun came up and the questions began? Aaron set his teeth firmly. "I am going to find him, Ginny. I'm going to confront him and make him tell the truth."

"Please don't do that, Aaron." She sounded suddenly like a mature woman. The little girl posturing was gone and she was begging him, with all the authority she held over him, to spare the man who had ended her life.

Aaron stared at her.

"He loved me, Aaron. I loved him. That's all that matters now."

Chapter 40

ENRAGED, AARON RIPPED GINNY'S SKETCH of Eddie Safford into small shreds and threw them into the fireplace. Obviously, he would not be contacting Ginny's fiancé. Anyway, it was likely that Safford had already punished himself more than any court could have. If he had killed Ginny intentionally, had shoved her to her murky death, it had been a crime of passion, one he must have relived and regretted countless times. If he hadn't, his grief and guilt must have been nearly impossible to bear.

Besides, just how public did Aaron choose to make his relationship with Virginia Dunn? He would surely be laughed at and maybe jailed to give him a chance to sober up. Not to mention the humiliation Connie would endure. And how would he prove Eddie's involvement? Would he tell the police that a ghost had informed him? Maybe bring Ginny to testify? Or, better yet, he could bring the authorities to Spruce Lake and suggest they hide out at the Dunn cottage just in case their star witness might appear by lantern light at quarter past midnight on any given evening.

No, Ginny would have her way. He would let it rest. But it infuriated him that she spent each night mourning her ruined life and waiting for the one man who might have set it right for her, who may have stolen her very best years.

When Aaron had first gone to her it had been idle curiosity, and then an attraction so powerful he still couldn't explain it. But now it was something else, sympathy perhaps, or compassion. Maybe it was even love.

The thought left him reeling. He loved Connie, his wife, the woman he had vowed to stay with for the rest of his life. That was a given, the focus that made his life worthwhile.

Did he love Virginia Dunn? He couldn't answer that and it

frightened him to think about it. He hoped fervently that the events of this summer were not simply some weird overextension of his own imagination. What if they were? What if he had gone slowly and completely nuts up here in the lonely Adirondack wilderness? What if he had made Ginny up?

His roll of prints had been shipped back to the lake store, and he went there feeling an unaccustomed nervousness. Cathleen Parnell seemed genuinely happy to see him and asked if he'd been having a nice stay over at Spruce Lake.

"Yes, pretty nice," he answered.

"It's been a lovely summer," she agreed. "Hard to believe we only have a few more weeks."

"It's always a surprise when summer ends," he said.

He had come here to write an article and enjoy his fury over Connie's selfishness, and he had done neither. What would Cathleen say if he told her, right now, exactly what he had been up to this summer? He smiled at Cathleen, thanked her for the package, and forced himself to carry the sealed folder to the SUV unopened.

Back at his camp, he set the envelope down on the kitchen counter. The remaining bracken shoots he had long ago intended to cook had turned dry and brittle on the table, abandoned and forgotten. He swept them hastily aside and then clattered together a pile of dirty plates and silverware and dumped them into the already overloaded sink. He spread his hand over the tabletop, felt the stickiness, and found a clean dishcloth in a drawer. Dampening the cloth, he scrubbed at a section of the tabletop, making it smooth and clean, then drying it thoroughly.

He picked up the envelope of photographs and slid out the prints of Solomon's-Seal and Indian cucumber root, useless pictures he had taken early in the summer. He noted quickly that the colors weren't true. If he had used his digital camera, he could adjust those colors and tweak the contrast a bit. Well, he thought with impatience, he hadn't. The pictures would have to do just as they were.

It didn't matter anyway. Those were not the prints he wanted to see right now. He found the half dozen shots he was looking for and spread them over the kitchen table with shaking hands, trying to make sense of what he was seeing. The form of a girl leaned back against a glittering birch tree, her face a little hazy, her expression somber. The background was sharp and clear, the girl a vague image, but not because he had adjusted the lens for that; in fact, he had done the opposite and deliberately set the camera for a narrow depth of field.

This didn't make sense. It looked like a blurred photograph, the type a beginning photographer might throw away, but Aaron knew better. He was a pro; he didn't take blurry shots.

The second picture showed her looking full into the camera. A little smile parted her lips; her eyes were laughing. Again, the background of the tree, the woods, a rock nearby were in sharp focus, crystal clear; tiny veins stood out on the leaves behind her, but the features of the girl were mottled and diffused. In this one, the sun had crept onto her left cheek and her gauzy hand paused there, as if caught pushing away the bright intrusion.

The posed picture turned out to be his favorite. It was an idyllic shot, a beautiful young woman with a wistful smile on the verge of asking a question. She was captured in cloudy uncertainty in a crisp natural surrounding of great peace. Her long gown looked white in the picture, as it did in the dark; her hair showed the blonde tint he had first noticed by day; her eyes were hazy. She looked like the bride she would never be.

He packaged up the other five photographs of Ginny, along with the poor images of Solomon's-Seal and Indian cucumber root, and resealed them in their folder, then gazed at the posed shot again. He had found some picture frames in an old trunk in one of the bedrooms and had confiscated one of them for Ginny's sketch of him in his boat. He searched again and was rewarded with an antique frame of the right size for the print, the dusty glass still intact. Carefully, he cleaned the frame and glass and positioned the picture of Ginny, sealing it in and attaching a wire to the back. He looked through the trunk again, hoping to find a glass panel to replace the one he had cracked on Ginny's painting. There were none the right size, all either too big or far too small.

In the living room, he hung her photograph over his writing table, between her watercolor and her drawing of him, and sat looking at it. She was a beautiful girl, alluring and mysterious, but only because she was a spirit. He knew very well that Virginia Dunn in life had been a perfectly normal, sometimes childish young lady who had never been given the grace to grow up.

He reminded himself of this daily. It was Connie he loved, his wife of nine years, the mother of his child, the woman he had vowed to cherish and honor. When he thought of Connie, his breath came quicker; he still wished, numerous times a day, that she were here to carry this burden with him. Connie would see it all rationally. He knew she was his salvation.

He sat back in the straight chair before his typewriter and stared, first at the machine keys, then at Ginny's painting, then at her photograph. Another man's bride, smiling wistfully, beckoning with her eyes. It was no wonder he couldn't keep his mind on business.

Chapter 41

THE ARTICLE was a disgrace - incomplete and badly written - and his illustrations were practically non-existent. Aaron needed to control the situation, get back to work, and make a success of it. He threw his camera strap around his neck, grabbed his tripod where it stood getting dusty behind a bedroom door, and put a few things into a small pack, then headed for the swampy roadside stream where a narrow mountain spring emptied into Spruce Lake.

It wasn't long before he found the stand of spotted touch-me-nots that had always grown there, at least as far back as his early childhood. He'd wondered if the fragile plant might have been overtaken by now with some bigger, stronger variety. But, if anything, there were more now, rather than fewer.

Carrying a notebook and pen tucked into the pocket of his jeans and his tripod over his shoulder like a militiaman's rifle, Aaron stepped gingerly into the midst of the tall, fragile plants. Their jewel-like orange blossoms dangled like pendants from thin stalks, and their slimness caught every slight breeze, swaying them delicately. The ground was marshy, and water oozed up around his boots, but he ignored it. These would be among his best shots if he could control the environment correctly.

He touched one finger to a delicate, ripe seedpod and smiled in satisfaction when the pod burst and the tiny seeds jumped. He heard a quick ding as a seed ricocheted off his camera.

He knew that touch-me-nots bruised easily and gave some thought to the best way to arrange his tripod. The waist-high flowers surrounded him, and, try as he might, it was almost impossible to set up for the shots without trampling a few. Finally, he simply slung the tripod down and set it up in the dense sea of plants, crushing several of the slender stalks. It was inevitable.

The tripod steady, he adjusted his camera for focus, light, and speed. He could hear the marshy water sucking around his boots and stepped sideways, trampling a few more plants. He grimaced, sorry that it could not be helped.

The look through the viewfinder pleased him. Perfect. He snapped four or five frames in quick succession, changed the f-stop slightly, and took several more pictures.

These would be terrific photographs; he was sure of it. Satisfied and pleased with his work, he replaced his lens in the pack and slung the pack over his shoulder. He snapped the legs of his tripod together and pulled it hastily from the earth, then groaned as he felt the tug of three or four of the lush plants twining around the tripod's legs and saw the drooping orange flowers tangled in aluminum, uprooted by his carelessness.

Well, that had been unnecessary. He began picking bruised greenery out of his tripod and felt the daypack slip from his shoulder. Righting it, he moved the tripod, slashing several more of the fragile touch-me-nots.

"Damn!" He was trying hard not to destroy this stand of flowers, and with every turn, he did more damage. He stepped out of the sea of orange blossoms and felt the muck squishing around his boots and perspiration beading inside his shirt. He was irritated with himself and with the weak, thin plants that couldn't survive a simple photographic shoot. How could such a delicate plant survive the harsh Adirondack winters and resurface every year?

Later, he decided, he would look for Labrador-tea, a hardier plant that he could photograph without feeling like a butcher.

Frowning, Aaron removed his camera strap from his neck, placed the camera in the pack, and strode away from the dense patch of touch-me-nots. He hated weakness in all forms, and the little orange blossoms, by giving up so easily, evoked in him an annoyance with all things so simple to crush. Plants - and people - needed to be tougher than that.

The feeling itself irritated him, and he glanced back. Hundreds of orange blossoms waved as if in forgiveness. What difference, he realized, did half a dozen casualties make in a stand that size?

But the satisfying afternoon had turned sour. Feeling sullen and angry, he shrugged his pack to the ground, fell beside it, and leaned against an oak tree. He dug in the pack's side pocket for his water bottle and jerked the cap off, letting the cool water flow down his throat. It helped a little.

The real problem was Chris, of course. Chris coming shyly up the camp steps, Chris averting his eyes, trying to talk with Aaron. His glasses, his smallness. Chris getting exasperated when Aaron refused to play the game. He admitted that Chris's weakness bothered him most of all.

It always had.

He and Chris had been very young, perhaps eight and nine, when Aaron had discovered the pair of snakes living under the dock at Spruce Lake. Aaron stood on the dock jamming his wet feet into sneakers, while Chris sat in a lawnchair nearby, fastidiously drying between his toes before donning his own shoes.

Unexpectedly, a snake had slithered out from the dark, moist earth where the dock met the bank. "Cool!" Aaron exclaimed, bending low over the creature, examining its long yellowish stripes. He was fascinated. "Chris, come and see this!"

Chris glanced over and was held mesmerized by the undulating creature moving slowly along the dock, down the sandy shore and under an overhanging bush at the water's edge.

"Did you see that?" Aaron crowed. His attention was riveted as a second snake appeared from the same hole, following along the same path. He ran closer and squatted near the reptile. The alarmed snake flattened its body, making its markings appear even more pronounced.

Aaron was fascinated. "Cool," he said again. "He's gotta be a foot and a half long."

"I'll get Dad," Chris announced. He stood up from his lawn chair carefully. His feet were planted firmly, but his gaze wavered from the snake to its hole, then moved suspiciously to the bush under which the first snake coiled, then back again to the hole and the second snake. He was riveted to the spot, unable to move.

"Well, get Dad," Aaron said, "before they're gone." He glanced up at his brother and made a disgusted noise, then looked back to the hole, hoping more snakes might appear there. "They'll be gone by the time you get him."

It was too late. The second snake, by this time, had slunk around the side of the dock and back into the moist haven below. No third snake appeared.

"That was cool," Aaron said for the third time. "I wonder

what kind they were. Do you think they live there?" He knelt on the dock and stuck his head over the side and underneath, peering around, hoping for another glimpse. Chris watched, still and frightened.

When they asked their father about it later, he assured them they had seen a couple of innocent garter snakes. "They're very docile," he said. "They don't bite, and they won't hurt you if you leave them alone."

The snakes made their second appearance several days later. This time it was Chris who spotted them first. He had come down from the camp and removed his sturdy shoes, but stood looking at the hole, not quite believing snakes weren't about to attack him, not quite daring to go for a swim in water that might suddenly be infested with the squirming reptiles. In fact, Chris was so busy staring at the hole that he nearly missed the snake slithering behind him through the underbrush. He heard the slight swishing and turned suddenly, just in time to catch a glimpse as it slunk by.

It was Chris's sudden squeal that alerted Aaron, who had just arrived at the bottom of the path. Aaron darted into the bushes and managed to hook the creature with a maple twig. "I have him!" he sang. "Chris, look! Go get Dad!"

Chris recoiled from the snake that danced on the end of the twig, doubled over and jerking its sinewy body first this way, then that. Aaron controlled the stick, moving it in a gentle twisting motion, back and forth, displaying the dangling snake. In a flash, Chris was off, his eyes terrified. He was back in a moment, safe behind the bulky figure of his father. Their mother followed, last of all.

"Yep, a garter snake," their father pronounced. "Good for you, Aaron. You got yourself a pet."

Aaron laughed and laid the stick on the ground, then watched the snake hurry off up the wooded bank. Chris's startled eyes glanced around worriedly and, sure enough, spotted the second garter snake lying coiled on a cluster of rocks some fifteen feet up the bank.

"There's the other one." Chris's voice was a frightened whisper.

Aaron picked up a pebble and gently tossed it toward the sunning snake. It uncoiled slowly and slithered off.

Their father grinned at Aaron, his broad-shouldered son, bursting into adolescence even at this young age, then turned to

Chris, cowering behind him. "To hear you tell about it, I thought they were at least three feet long and six inches around."

"Oh, leave him alone," said their mother. "Chris doesn't have to catch snakes if he's afraid. I'd be afraid myself." She tousled her older son's hair gently and smiled down at him, a conspiracy of the faint-hearted.

Aaron felt himself clapped on the back by his father's big, heavy hand, a hand that had always applauded his heroic bravado and didn't seem to have much use for his quieter brother.

Chris had seemed content to mirror their mother's retiring ways, but now, in retrospect, Aaron wondered. Maybe Chris had spent his childhood refusing to compete with a brother who already had the contest all sewn up.

Aaron had cultivated his strength and physical prowess throughout middle and high school, made the teams, played college sports, collected the shiny trophies, and watched the nodding gleam in his father's eye throughout it all. He would have done anything to keep that approval.

And Chris plodded along, apparently resigned to being second string, second best. Aaron shuddered to think that the accident of birth had made him the bigger, stronger son. What if their roles had been reversed?

The memory of the snakes left him feeling uncomfortable.

Was it any wonder that Chris, after a while, chose not to make much eye contact with his arrogant younger brother? Chris's life would have been better if Aaron didn't exist.

The realization made Aaron groan in sadness.

When Veronica came along, Chris drifted into marriage because she had hung on like a tenacious dog, following him everywhere until everyone naturally assumed they would marry. His two sons were conceived and born in short order, and he had fallen into his job at the hardware store without much fanfare. He continued to work at it, stodgily keeping the company books, doing the taxes, bringing home the same old paycheck to his plodding wife.

In almost every way, Chris had played out the small, unassuming life his father and mother had mapped out for him, just as Aaron had lived strongly and surely, gone after the things he wanted and attained them all. His parents had expected no less. The work he did was because he had chosen it; he had married Connie because he had chosen her - a strong, warm, capable woman who was his intellectual equal and would always fulfill him.

Which did not explain why he left her so frequently and insisted on controlling their relationship. Or why he worked so hard to prove himself unworthy of her.

A truth came to him suddenly and he sat still letting it take fierce root in him. He knew that Connie's love did not depend on book deals and hefty paychecks, but what if she suspected that inside, he, Aaron Latimer, was no one, nothing? Did she see that the falsely important nature writer had blossomed from the terrified boy garnering trophies and existing on the nourishment of his father's approval? Aaron shuddered and admitted the thing that had always worried him: If Connie knew the real Aaron, she would surely scorn him. And leave him.

So he had done everything but leave her first.

Aaron twisted the cap back on his water bottle and restored it to his pack, then inhaled deeply and let his breath out slowly. What a fool he was, playing this dangerous game with his wife, and taking such chances with their marriage.

He glanced back at the slaughtered touch-me-nots and heaved a sigh of relief that the patch of flowers had spread and grown since he'd last been here. Next year it would grow again. And the year after that, and after that.

He might return with his great, careless boots, but the delicate plants were not that easy to eradicate.

He stood up, chastened, and trudged toward the camp.

Chapter 42

WITH THE PHOTOGRAPHS under his arm, Aaron followed the path along the shore to the Dunn cottage. Rain threatened the noon sky, so he had wrapped the pictures well and cushioned them in a plastic bag which he secured flat in an inside pocket of his jacket. He strolled along Ginny's waterfront for a few moments, not sure if she would appear; they hadn't made an arrangement. His shoes squished in the jungle of growth beside the water's edge, and he could hear the first drops of rain hit the leaves of trees above and behind him. Rings appeared on the lake, a few at first, then more and more until the surface was a glassy palette of concentric circles.

He hadn't brought an umbrella; whether she came or not, he would be walking home drenched.

Suddenly she was there, barefoot and standing before him in the chill, damp air, her gown whipped by the wind that was picking up, her hair blowing around her head. She reached up a hand and gathered her long hair into a makeshift ponytail, and he smiled at how young and girlish it made her look. He was reminded again of Katrina Jeffers, and his sympathy for Ginny's plight mingled with a sense of guilt over selfishness long past.

"I brought the pictures," he said. He indicated the protected inner pocket of the windbreaker he'd worn. "But we'll need to hold something over them so they don't get wet."

"Does the rain bother you?" she asked. Drops were spotting her nightgown and making her face damp. She dropped the misty clump of her hair and it sat on her shoulders. Little drips ran down her neck.

"No, but it will ruin the photographs."

She smiled benignly. "Come inside, then, and we'll look at them there."

The idea did not please him, and she saw his hesitation. "It's daytime. You said you would go inside in the daytime. You've never seen my drawings."

He nodded vaguely, and she smiled. "Maybe you can meet my family. We have fun, Aaron. We get up family card games and bet nickels. Royce cheats, but we all know that, so I guess it doesn't matter." She chattered on. "My mother has been teaching me to cook. Mostly we just make a big mess in the kitchen."

A peculiar lethargy was taking hold inside him. He knew that the mess he was likely to see inside her cottage had nothing to do with cooking, and it worried him that she seemed oblivious to the current state of the once trim building.

When they reached the top step to the camp and the small overhanging roof, he stopped her, just outside the door. He detected the stale, acrid odor of dying and nesting animals and wondered- Was it only at night that her presence overpowered even the smells of nature?

"This is good, Ginny," he said. "The roof will keep them dry."

By now rain was beating steadily and dripping down inside his shirt collar as it leaked through the shingles of the rotting roof and coursed down the outside wall he leaned against. He unwrapped the parcel and took out the cardboard folder of pictures. He held them under a dry section of the roof, low enough that Ginny could see them, too. She was thrilled with the results and made lively comments about each one as they stood squeezed together trying to keep the pictures dry.

He had brought along the five in the folder, as well as his favorite one, framed under glass, and they amused themselves making comments about his photographic eye and her photogenic beauty.

"I still say it's the expensive camera," she teased, "or maybe the subject."

"No, Ginny, it's the talent behind the lens."

She laughed easily, huddling next to him. "Thank you for taking them," she said. "What will you do with them now?"

That was a good question, and he knew the answer: absolutely nothing. How many photographs of supposed ghosts had he seen published? Quite a few, and none of them matched the quality or clarity of these, yet he knew he would never share these pictures or exploit the young girl who had had them taken with such innocent delight. "I'll just keep them, Ginny," he said. "I'll be glad to have some pictures of you."

"I'm like your little sister, right?"

He reached out and touched her damp hair.

He could feel the cold rain soaking down his back, and he shivered, very aware of her young body pressed close. He rewrapped the prints and placed them in the plastic bag and back inside his jacket.

Ginny clasped his hand and smiled up at him. "I want you to see my work now," she said softly. He closed his eyes briefly, then nodded.

Ginny grinned mischievously at him and glided through the rotting wall, leaving him standing alone and stupefied on the little porch. He breathed in sharply, lurching suddenly, feeling utterly desolate. Unexpectedly, it terrified him. He put his hand out to the door and grimaced when his fingers came away green with slime. He regained his balance, forcing his eyes shut.

He must retain his nerve and his sense of reality. Yes, she had just gone through the wall. Why did that stun him? And yes, he was on the verge of following her, a ghost, into the dilapidated Dunn cottage. But the fact that filled him with dread was the simplest; he had rarely felt such panic as when she had disappeared from his side. Was that what it felt like to be deserted?

He opened his eyes and she was standing there, smiling.

"Don't abandon me again," he said. His voice was raspy, and she laughed. He smiled thinly, covering the sudden, irrational fear that had overtaken him on the stoop.

The wooden door was rotten, its paint peeling. It opened easily when she took his hand and led him through. He was immediately assailed by the powerful stink of rodents and the sour stench of mold. He swallowed in disgust and tried to breathe through his mouth.

As they entered, mice flitted away over gnawed tabletops and scurried into ruined upholstery. Chair cushions had been torn apart by tiny teeth and claws, and stuffing lay about in damp clumps. The beech tree that had smashed the roof years before still barricaded one corner of the main room, its mossy limbs stripped of leaves, bark chewed off uncleanly, its trunk black with slime. Wet leaves, sticks, stones, moss, and debris brought in by the wind and forest animals created a viscous carpet under their feet. Over it all, slick puddles glistened and rain dripped, soaking into already moldy walls and floor and furnishings.

"It's hard to walk in here, Ginny," he said. He felt somewhat dazed and determined to see it through for her sake. "Are you sure we should stay?"

She laughed a pretty, lilting laugh. "You want to see my pictures, don't you?" They were hanging on a far wall, and he stepped through piles of black muck to reach them. He heard a skittish noise as he moved too close to a wet mound on the floor. Ginny moved effortlessly before him.

Squinting, he saw, high on a mossy shelf, Ginny's familiar lantern, a square box of metal strips, corroded and green with age and weather. The glass was cracked in one panel and missing in another; the other two were dingy with dirt and grime. It sat among a few other decorative items - a nautical clock, run down years ago and a china sea captain winking mischievously from one dirt-encrusted eye.

Her parents had probably placed the lantern there, in among other whimsical treasures. How could they have known that their daughter's dead hands would choose that item to illuminate her search for the man who knew the secret of her death?

Swallowing with difficulty, Aaron picked his way over the floor and stopped where Ginny had, before a series of curling papers on the far wall.

"This is Little Trout Lake, the north shore," she said, indicating a tattered fragment hanging by a rusty thumbtack. The paper might as well have been blank. The sun damage from the collapsed roof, and the water, wind, and animals had all done their bit to destroy the picture. "I like watercolors best, so I do them most often." She gestured to another picture and grinned at him. "Do you recognize it?" she asked. It was blank, utterly blank, and curled on the edges. Long rips created tatters where some creature had gripped the paper with sharp claws and finally dropped to the floor.

He found his voice. "You'd better tell me, I guess."

"The lake store!" she said, disappointed. "Don't you think it looks like it?" She peered at the painting again and then nodded. "Oh, they added the third dock after I did this. It does look different."

She glanced around the room, looked through a far doorway, and shrugged her shoulders. "No one's here. I guess they've gone somewhere. This is the kitchen." Destroyed. The table legs had been gnawed to thin sticks, the cupboard latches were rusty, rotten doors sagged on broken hinges. A chorus of tiny mammals somewhere inside squeaked hungrily.

Some of the window panes were still intact, but foggy with

dirt and grime and thick with mold. Paint peeled from the walls in long, wet strips; big, faded stains gave evidence that year after year of rainstorms had drenched the inside walls, then dried, leaving telling brown rings.

And over all of it was the stale air, permeated with the smells of mildew and death.

"Would you like to sit down, Aaron?" she asked in her innocence. She indicated the couch. Its center cushion undulated sickeningly; tufts of foamy filling squirmed up from the hole in the fabric. He fought the bile that was creeping up his throat and looked around for another place to sit. A chair whose seat was clotted with damp leaves. Another with the gelid, bloody remains of some recently dead small animal.

His disgusted glance traveled back to the sickening movement inside the sofa cushions, and then to the fresh, youthful face of the beautiful girl beside him. She was still holding his hand, smiling sweetly, inviting him.

When the sudden horror struck him, he emitted a groan and turned his face from her. Virginia Dunn, whose battered body had washed up in Big Trout Lake, did not really look like this lovely vision. Virginia Dunn was in a grave somewhere and had been decomposing there, perhaps not very peacefully, for more than ten years. His feverish nightmare returned, hideous, paralyzing, Ginny's face a grinning mask of death.

Shock finally overwhelmed him and he pulled his hand away in revulsion, ignoring the injured look that passed across Ginny's guileless features. He pushed her aside, choosing not to hear her baffled, hurt cry, and ran from the ghastly truth of the cabin.

He could feel tears of regret and dismay stinging his eyes while fear and disgust fought for his emotions and drained him. The rain pelted him with cold fingers as he collapsed on the forest floor. How could it be that she could not see it? What was death if it robbed a person of the right to see clearly?

Sobbing, his tears mixing with the rain on his face, he lay there for some time. Finally he sat up and rubbed the back of his hand across his eyes and nose, trying to wipe away the wet mucus along with the horror he had experienced. A shudder swept him. His clothes were soaked and dirty. The folder of photographs was bent, but safe and dry inside his jacket. He was sure the pictures must be creased. He felt the carefully wrapped, framed picture and could tell the glass was cracked. He stood up slowly, and that was when he saw her.

She approached him tentatively, dripping in the rain, and he could see the terrible hurt of Katrina in Ginny's wide eyes. "It wasn't my pictures, was it," she said. "You saw something else in there." She pleaded with him. "What was it, Aaron? What is in my cottage?"

He gripped his emotions tightly. He would not run away from her or hurt her again. "Your pictures are beautiful, Ginny," he said. "You would have been a hell of an artist."

She stared sadly at him. "You're going to leave me now, aren't you, Aaron? You'll never come back, will you?" She lowered her eyes. The loose tendrils of her hair dripped rainwater over her soaking gown, plastering it to her slim body. He looked away.

"Everyone has left me," she wailed. "Every single person. I have no one. I never will." Tears began to fall unguarded.

His hands clenched at his sides. He had nothing to say.

Tentatively, she extended one ice cold hand and touched his wrist. The familiar cool, burning fire raged up his arm, throughout his body, thrumming within his bloodstream, jolting him and drawing from him a promise he could not possibly keep. He grabbed her close and held her.

He would not repeat his usual folly; he would see it through to its natural end. "I'm not leaving you," he said. "I won't do that. No one is going to leave you anymore."

Chapter 43

AARON SAT HUNCHED on a painted stool in his camp kitchen, blindly seeing the aged wooden walls burnished to a dark shine with years of careful scrubbing and oiling. The wainscot cupboards were latched, his meager food stowed inside. They had always kept tins on the counter to keep things safe from mice, and the salt in the shaker was laced with bits of macaroni to keep the grains from sticking together in the lake air. Generations of Latimers had handed down camp traditions and preserved the structure to maintain its pristine charm.

He knew now why he disliked this beautiful place, and it was Ginny who had shown him. The memory of his brother's attempt to murder, yes, *murder* him had molded his responses to almost everything he did in life, every attitude he possessed, every decision he made. If he hated Spruce Lake, it was because of that memory.

Aaron realized it was not the attempt itself, not his brother's actions, that had formed him into the man he was, but his own sick reaction to that day. He held a grudge because Chris had lashed out in a fury of childhood rage. He'd coveted that grudge and rejoiced smugly in the sadness and pain that it brought to him and his brother both. By embracing vindictiveness, he had ruined his relationship with Chris and nearly destroyed himself and his marriage.

Connie deserved better; Egan certainly deserved better. Even Chris deserved better. He intended to tell them so and make it up to them. If they would let him.

But there was Ginny, and he rocked forward holding his hurting stomach as he thought of her. Katrina's face appeared in his mind, the young girl he had hurt and cast aside, and then Ginny's, her nightmare face, shocking in its horror, and then the lovely face he had come to know. He had not cast Ginny aside, oh no. The heroic stance he had taken made him cry out helplessly, the vow made in a moment of foolish passion.

How could he have made such a promise? Was he losing his mind? She had such a hold on him that he had promised to remain faithful to her, take care of her. Did she even exist? Would a sane man make such a promise to a ghost?

"Bastard," Katrina had spat at him. And she had been right. Aaron Latimer had been raised to get the best of other people; he had to emerge the winner, a boy who took what he could, and thwarted responsibility afterwards.

He wanted desperately to prove to himself that Aaron Latimer the man could be different.

So he had vowed everlasting love and protection- to a ghost.

The whole thing was chilling, and his heart broke as he recalled with irony that he had made Connie the very same promise on the day he had married her.

He rose from the stool and shoved it back against the wall where it belonged, stumbled to the living room, and stared at the three frames hanging side by side over his typewriter - the pretty watercolor of his own camp, the new pencil sketch, and the photo of the artist who had created them. The plates of glass covering the painting and photograph were cracked, and the sketch showed a flawed person, himself, canoeing on the peaceful lake he claimed to hate. It was an art gallery of defects.

He reached out and removed the sketch from its nail, staring at the posture of Aaron Latimer as seen through Virginia Dunn's eyes. A straight figure of a man, strong and powerful. What her sketch didn't reveal was the turmoil of the man inside.

Why did he want Ginny when he knew she was nothing but a vapor, young, immature, and in love with someone else? How exactly was he thinking he would live with her while all this heroic loyalty was going on? Would he take up residence on her beach? In her cottage?

Did he really think he could make things right with Connie when he had already done so much damage to their relationship? And he was still doing it, running across the lake to carry on with a young girl. What the hell was he thinking?

He was about to lose Connie; that threat had been hanging over him all summer, and it hit him now, sudden and solid, that he had been kidding himself when he thought he heard love or affection in her voice. Why, *why* would she want anything to do with someone like him?

And wasn't it poetic justice that he was about to lose her just as he finally recognized why he had neglected her in the first place.

The shrilling of the telephone startled him, and he dropped the framed sketch to the hard wood floor and heard the quick burst. He stared stupidly at the newly made crack, a lightning zigzag dividing the glass into two uneven halves.

The phone shrieked again and he stumbled to a chair and grabbed the receiver off its hook. "Connie?"

"It's not working, Aaron." Her tone was businesslike, and it terrified him. "It isn't working, and it was a dumb idea. I miss you." He heard certainty in her voice. "The longer we're apart, the worse it is."

He could hardly come up with a response. His words were raspy when he finally said, "I'm really glad to hear you say that."

"One of us has to be mature enough to give in, and this time, it's going to be me," she said. "*This* time, Aaron, and we really have to talk. I want to give us another chance, but it's going to be up to you whether we make it or not. Anyway, we're coming to the lake." He heard the controlled excitement in her voice and allowed himself a flicker of hope. Ginny's face came into his mind and he banished it, clutching his stomach, willing the gnawing pain to go away. "We'll commune with nature and fry eggs on sunny rocks and whatever else you want," Connie said, "but it has to be a two-way thing, Aaron. Anyway, we should be there Saturday night around nine. Egan's last class is at four, so we'll leave right after that."

He was silent, unable to answer, until finally, hesitantly, she spoke again. "Aaron? Is that okay? You haven't changed your mind, have you?" Now he heard panic and felt something that was almost a choked laugh traveling up his throat. She had no way of knowing that tears were coursing down his face.

"Well, I'm all choked up, here," he tried to say lightly. It came out a raspy breath. He set the phone down and blew his nose.

"Aaron? Are you crying? You're kidding, right?"

"No," he laughed quietly, in great relief, "that's the odd part. I was pretty sure you were going to tell me you'd had enough and were going to shop around for someone worthy of you."

"I never said you weren't," she said slowly.

"You never would. I came to the conclusion myself. I figured that's why you got interested in your new friend Justin."

She hesitated slightly. "Interested? No, I wasn't. I'm not. We did a few things together- as friends. Egan and I went with him once to see a friend of his play at a coffee house." She said the words in a rush. "It was just an evening out with a friend."

"You took Egan?"

"Of course I did. There was no reason not to."

"Out with this guy you met?"

"He lives across the hall. It meant nothing."

"Except that my wife and my daughter went around to social events with some man you met this summer." The relieved tears were drying on his face, but the clenching he had felt earlier was nothing compared to the gripping pain ravaging his stomach now.

"Aaron, please don't overreact. We became friends; Egan likes his cat and he's a decent guy. And I don't talk to him anymore anyway."

"Why? Did something happen?"

"Yes," she said bluntly. "Aaron, listen to me, okay? It turned out he thought there was more to our friendship than there was. He kissed me one night. That was the end. I told him to leave, and he did, and I haven't seen him since."

The familiar old clenching in his stomach burst, a slow, painful throb, as if he had been punched ruthlessly. "He kissed you?"

"I'm sorry, Aaron. It was unexpected and unwanted."

"Did he do anything else?"

"You need to ask me that?" She sounded shocked. "No! He left. Aaron, how could you think . . . . Not even close."

He couldn't respond, remembering Ginny's face, Ginny's laugh, the days and nights he had gone running to her cottage, taking her picture, confiding in her, holding her and kissing her, completely unable to work and totally bewitched by her. What had they done to their marriage, he and Connie?

"Aaron," Connie sounded scared now. "Do you still want us to come?"

"There's nothing I want more. I really need you here." And now it was his turn to tell about Ginny, to let her interrogate him, and give her the opportunity to forgive if she could. But the thought of her suspicion, her anger, cold and justified, or worse, her laughter, were more than he could bear. He said nothing.

Her voice lost its uncertain quality. "I love you, Aaron, and you love me. Whatever differences we have, I know we can work them out."

"Can you come before Saturday? Can you leave now?"

"No, we need to let Egan finish her classes. I'll have the car all packed and we'll leave right after. I love you. I'm sorry I insisted on this separation. It didn't solve anything." Her voice broke. "Maybe it just made everything worse."

"Don't say that, Connie. Please don't say that." Yes, everything was worse, but maybe he could still salvage something. Maybe he could make things better for all of them.

Today was Sunday. She would arrive on Saturday night. Would one week give him enough time to begin to repair the damage he had taken twenty-five years to create? He could only pray that this Justin was out of the picture for good, that Connie meant what she said about him. He forced himself to breathe easier, grateful and humbled that she had chosen to stick with him. He rubbed his clenching stomach. The pain would leave when everything was resolved.

She had changed the subject and was telling him about Egan's classes. For her age, Egan was doing well in the beginning stages of horseback riding, no surprise, and she loved the dancing. In fact, Connie was considering letting her sign up for dance lessons at home. "What do you think of that idea, Aaron?" she asked. "Do you have an opinion?"

He had a lot of opinions, about this man she had befriended, about his own folly and stupidity, but he thought he would save them for when she came in person. He tried to relax in the chair and allowed himself the luxury of listening to her voice, the voice he had fallen in love with years before. She put Egan on and he chatted with her, too.

The news of their coming filled him with hope and a calm desire for this absent wife who loved him still. He replaced the telephone receiver and slumped down in the chair. He had things to put right, and he needed to plan. He would try to make amends with Chris. And Ginny. He needed to commit himself to the changes he had sworn to make for Connie, and, as an afterthought, maybe even finish his article. He couldn't wait to see his wife, and the thought filled him with excitement.

But a dread heaviness was seeping through his body, too. He realized that the other thing he felt, on top of relief and love and gratitude to Connie, was a deep and numbing despair.

Chapter 44

HE TAPPED VAGUELY at the typewriter keys, wondering if he would ever land another assignment when the editors saw the mess he was making of this one. He had barely written half the article; he had stopped taking photographs in the woods; he had absolutely no interest right now in Adirondack foliage or edible wild plants. The photo essay was a dismal failure, Latimer's first, as far as publishing went.

Only one in a long, long line if you considered his personal failures.

But, he admitted, it was possible his weeks spent at Spruce Lake had been the most insightful of his life. Finally, by admitting he had screwed up everything good in his life, he was beginning to know himself.

"Why now?" Ginny had asked him. "Why this summer? All this time, I've been so alone. You've never stayed at the lake before or you would have come sooner."

He shrugged. "I was here as a kid."

"But I didn't need you then."

"I hardly ever come here now," he admitted. "It haunts me."

"But not because of your brother."

No, because of himself. The lake beckoned with its shimmering calm, its fragrant, tender quietness. But there was another Spruce Lake, too, mocking him with the terrible thing his brother had done to him, the thing he had done to his brother.

"You do love the lake," she said matter-of-factly.

"Yes, I guess so." Before he had finished the sentence, he was looking at her in surprise. "I do, don't I?" He did, and he had allowed the memory of Chris's jealousy to distort that, too, and color his views of this magnificent place. He had let Connie believe that the lake was an evil cancer that poisoned him, making him tense and angry, that it would also poison her. But it was his own fear of inadequacy that infected them both.

Aaron realized he had stopped typing and found himself gazing at the three little pictures above his desk. He would leave them where they hung and would explain them to Connie, every detail, and beg her to forgive him.

And what if she didn't?

People didn't always.

But if Ginny Dunn could forgive and love the man who had, at the very least, let her drown, wouldn't Connie find a way? And he could do the same for a brother who had committed the sin of envy. *His only crime was weakness. His only sin was not telling what he knew.*

Aaron turned his focus back to the article and forced himself to thumb through pages in the guidebooks, to examine his own mediocre photographs of coltsfoot and Solomon's-Seal. He typed sporadically, a sentence, two sentences. His gaze traveled, as if by a puppeteer's string, back to the three pictures hanging before him. He rested his elbows on the writing table and covered his face with his hands. His breathing was quick and shallow and sounded to his own ears strangely like gasping.

His vision blurred by tears, he stood up. The sheet of paper in the typewriter was two-thirds blank. He would never be able to get it right, would never finish it.

Suddenly, without thinking, he grasped the old typing machine with both arms. Reaching the porch, he hurled the typewriter as far as he could. It sailed through the air and landed on the bank, crushing a stand of wildflowers and ferns. The broken stems stuck up around it; leaves and torn blooms scattered to the ground.

He breathed out heavily and stared at the symbol of his work, the thing he had made his whole life, then looked at the pink sky turning gray over Spruce Mountain. It was dusk. The first stars flickered dimly overhead; the filtered pink glow sifted down behind the mountain and cast long shadows onto the lake. The Dunn cabin was barely visible at the water's edge. He could just make it out, looking deceptively innocent in the dusk. From here one would never guess that the roof was battered, the walls spongy, that its coziness was chaos, its solitude anguish.

Connie had given him five days to right wrongs and prove himself worthy of a second chance. He might not get a third.

In the morning he needed to drive to the lake store to look up an address in one of the telephone books that Cathleen kept handy for summer residents. He would help Ginny if he could. After that, he could concentrate on fixing his floundering marriage. He had reached the bottom. There was nothing but to climb up and out of his pain. He felt a weak tug of hope that maybe he could right things.

Maybe.

Chapter 45

AARON BEACHED THE CANOE in among the reeds on the Dunn shoreline and strolled to Ginny's camp, hopeful that she would appear. He suspected she would try to reject his idea, a plan that stemmed from the night he had made that utterly ridiculous promise. A mortal man, a married man and responsible father, had no business making such a vow to the ghost of a beautiful young girl. But he had made it, and it was proof of the power she still held over him.

For the first time that summer, he felt sure he was doing the right thing. He would not shirk the responsibility he had taken for Ginny Dunn.

He spotted her coming toward him from the end of her beach, shimmering in the sun's morning rays, gliding effortlessly through the weeds and rocks. She hadn't been there moments before. A chill swept him.

"You love the sunlight, don't you, Aaron?" She grimaced, shielding her eyes from the powerful light of day.

He grinned at her. "I do. I wish it weren't so painful for you, but I don't think you'll need to worry about that for much longer, Ginny."

She looked surprised. "What are you talking about?"

"Come with me," he said. "I have something serious to talk with you about." She followed him to the rocks on the side of Spruce Mountain and took her favorite spot in the shadows. This time, he joined her there.

She gave him a shy smile. "I'm glad you came back. I knew you wouldn't let me go on alone. It's been so lonely for me." She looked around contentedly. "It's so lovely here, Aaron. Don't you think we'll be happy here?"

He caught in a breath and answered her honestly. "I'm glad we're here in daylight. To me, everything is better in the light."

She pouted. "You never said if you liked my cabin," she said. "Didn't you like the wallpaper my mother chose for the kitchen? And the new dishes?" Her tone became wistful. "I wish I could decorate a kitchen of my own. I would paint the walls with murals."

Images from his fevered nightmare took hold in Aaron's mind, and he looked at her serenely, making his face a careful mask while he tried to decide what to say. He recalled his vision of her as the truly dead Virginia Dunn, his horror at the damage in her cottage, the rustlings in the furniture. He squelched the memories. They seemed unreal here in the sun-dappled woods. It was easy to force the images away from him.

"It was enchanting," he told her. When she smiled at him, he added, "Ginny, I've realized you can't read my mind as much as I once thought you could."

"I never said I could. Sometimes I just have a feeling; I reflect back to you what's been there all along."

"I know, I know. It was me using you to figure out things I've known for years. I just wasn't smart enough to face them."

"You're very smart," she corrected him.

"You helped me figure out what to do about Chris. And my wife. Do you know how grateful I am for that?"

"I'm glad." A tiny smile played at the corners of her mouth and she looked at him shyly. "I love you, Aaron."

He put a quick finger to her lips. "No, you don't, Ginny. You love Eddie, and you always have. I love my wife and I always will."

"You can love two people," she shrugged.

He shook his head, negating her opinion. "Ginny, I'm going to Albany to talk to Eddie. I'm going to bring him here."

She gasped, then stood up, agitated. "Oh, don't do that, Aaron."

"I'm going to. Something happened that night. Maybe he can help you remember."

"No, I don't want to remember." She turned away from him.

"Well, whatever it was, he needs to take responsibility for what happened to you, so that you, all of us, can get beyond it."

"But he won't want to come. He could have told the truth right away, but he didn't."

"And that bothers me. Or maybe he was just a scared kid. Don't you suppose he's grown up by now? That he might have regrets? But if he . . . if he meant for you to die, Ginny, shouldn't he own up to that?"

Her hands were over her ears. "No. No."

"All right." Defeated, Aaron moved her hands gently with his own.

"What if you ask him and he won't come?" Ginny said dully. "What if he no longer loves me?"

Aaron felt a glimmer of hope. She was considering. He tried not to push too hard. "I think no matter what he did, he loved you very much and he'll come here to tell you that. Not to stay with you, Ginny; you can't ask him for that."

"I would never ask him for that," she said indignantly.

"But you asked me."

A guilty look crossed her face, and Aaron knew. Ginny was perfectly aware of the sacrifice she had suggested Aaron make. She would never ask it of Eddie Safford. She sank down next to him again and looked at him sadly. "But I can't . . . I don't see people . . . ." she stuttered.

"Ginny, come on. You do; you see me. You spend your nights haunting a deserted beach, crying, and looking for Eddie to make it okay." She turned her face away, but he turned it back again. "Listen. When you look down toward the channel with your lantern, do you realize what you're doing? You're waiting, not for him to rescue you; it's too late for that. But for him to take responsibility, to ask for your forgiveness."

Tears ran down her cheeks. "There's nothing to forgive him for," she insisted.

"Yes, there is. Even if it was an accident, he let you drown. He didn't scream or call for help or get everyone out on the lake to try to save you that night. He just let you go."

"But I've already forgiven him for that."

"Does he know that?"

"How could he know, Aaron?" She turned away, irritated.

"Then let him know. Let him ask to be forgiven. Let it be a partnership, something that's important to both of you, that you agree on."

"I don't understand."

"I think you do, Ginny. For twenty-five years, I've been unable to forgive my brother and he's been too afraid to ask me. He hedges around the subject, hoping I'll encourage him and make it easier. It makes me crazy that he's so weak, and I haven't had the compassion to help him. If I could, we'd both be better off. And do you know what else? Chris has forgiven *me*- over and over again. But I've rejected it."

He turned her to face him again. "I think Eddie will come. He'll ask you to forgive whatever he did, and you will, and it will free you from this terrible trap you're in. You won't be doomed to these awful rituals every night. It will give you peace."

Her eyes were dry now and she looked longingly at the man who had become her only friend. "What will happen to you?"

"I'll stay with my wife. That's where I belong. It will set me free, too."

"Free of me, you mean."

"Yes, because you are beautiful and appealing, and when I'm with you, I forget what's right. I forget who I am." He stared deep into her eyes. "You won't need me anymore."

"And you won't want me." Her sadness was deep and plaintive.

"But you won't care." He felt brutal and callous, but for Connie and Egan and himself and Ginny, and maybe even for Eddie Safford, he suspected this was the only way.

"I still think we could be together," she murmured. "I think we could be." Her face was buried in the crook of his arm, and he felt her soft tears sliding down his flesh, soft, glittering tears that burned him and left jabs of ice on his skin.

He exhaled deeply, begging her. "It isn't easy for me either, but it's the only thing that can save us."

"But Aaron," she said, and her words were a still, soft breath on the air, "Eddie was so long ago. If I had to choose, I think I would want it to be you."

Emotion welled up in him, strong and potent. He envisioned a possibility, a future with her, an end to all his difficulties. He breathed in deeply and forced out words. "It can't be either of us. You know that. I am in love with my wife. And Eddie . . . ." He braced himself and felt her react, sitting up straighter beside him. "It can't be any living man."

"Stay with me," she whimpered. "You know you could if you only-"

He placed a finger under her chin and tilted her head up, forcing her to look at him. "Is that what you really want? For me to end my own life?"

Her answer was in the look of guilt and sadness on her face.

"Life is so good," he said, reminding them both. "Don't you remember? It isn't something you just throw away. Don't ask it, Ginny. Not of either of us."

191

She leaned away from him, and he saw her tears coming fast and wet. Her arms came up to cover her face; her shoulders shook with pain.

Aaron held her away from him. "My God, Ginny, what did he do to you?"

There was no answer, just the wind whispering in the ferns nearby and rustling the treetops above them. A pileated woodpecker's rat-a-tat-tat startled them both. The insistent drilling continued for a moment, then echoed and died away.

"I think he was angry and he lost control," Aaron murmured finally. "I think he killed you."

"He wouldn't have done that," Ginny said. Her voice was quiet, unsure, laced with her tears. "Why would he have done that?"

Aaron didn't speak for a moment, but his resolve was firm. "Promise me that you'll meet us here, Ginny," he said. "I'm going to go to Eddie."

Chapter 46

WHETHER GINNY AGREED or not, he was going to Eddie Safford. If the man was a murderer, he should pay the price. But how could he convince Eddie to come to Ginny, a girl ten years dead? Safford would probably throw him out and bolt the door against the madman from Spruce Lake. There had to be a way to persuade him . . . .

Aaron was pulled from the path his thoughts were taking when Ginny suddenly stood, a glowing, radiant figure, and stretched both hands toward him, trusting, beseeching. Her tears were gone. "Aaron," she said, "come with me to my cottage. I want to show you one last thing."

He groaned. "Ginny, no."

"Please. This one last time."

"No."

"I'll see Eddie," she said, "if you will come with me now."

Resigned, drained, he followed her to her cabin and up the rotten steps. He was weak and very flawed, and he hated himself with every step. He feared that she might abandon him to the stoop again, and breathed in relief when she opened the door. The same smells and sights assaulted him, and he followed her wearily, picking his way over the damp, mucky floor.

She glided over the mess, and Aaron stared in fascination as a bit of decomposing matter stuck to her bare foot as she moved. She seemed unaware of the sticky substance and moved ahead of him.

"What are you waiting for?" Ginny asked softly. She had turned back to him and held out her hand, her eyes locking with his. "Come."

He hung back. "Ginny, no, please." She took his hand and led him up the stairs to her ruined bedroom. He followed numbly.

The fallen beech tree had opened part of her ceiling to the sky. Her bed linens were tattered and stained, soggy with stagnant rainwater, and on her dresser a growth of moss had overtaken the top two drawers. Her artwork, curling and blank, decorated the dank walls. He stood still with grief and shock, wondering if she intended to seduce him here and now. How would he resist her if she did?

She turned slightly and faced him, a coquettish look in her eyes. Her profile was delicate, rare porcelain washed with rain. "Aaron," she said softly, "will you kiss me?"

He stared at her, one hand still held in hers, the other clenched into a fist at his side. He barely felt his head move, a slight twitch. No, no. He shook his hand free from her and stepped back. His throat constricted.

She smiled suddenly. "That's what I thought. Eddie never would have refused me." She went to a spot in the wall and removed a board that was already hanging loose. "I always hid his notes in here," she said. "He'd leave them on the kitchen windowsill and I'd bring them up here and put them behind the wall. I knew no one would ever find them." She gestured to a tiny metal case jammed between the wooden slats. "Open it, Aaron."

He took the box in trembling hands and lifted the lid, flicking away rust that had accumulated on the hinges. Inside were dozens of scraps of paper, carefully preserved from the elements, readable and clear.

"It's in there," she said. "The one he left me that night. They're all dated- he always did that. You can take it. You were wondering how to convince him . . . ."

He sifted through, his breath coming hard, and found the note dated the night of Ginny's death. He read it quickly, then stared at the dazzling figure before him. She replaced the box in the wall. "Maybe it will help him remember," she said. "Maybe it will help him finish what we started."

She flung her arms around Aaron's neck and pressed her lips to his. He hugged her back furiously, oblivious to the indecent smell in his nostrils.

"Ah, Ginny," he breathed. How easy it would have been to live in her world and see it the way she saw it. He broke from her and hastened down the damp steps, picked his way through the living room, and left by the rotten screen door hanging askew on its broken hinges.

In the open air, he paused and breathed in deeply. His hands were shaking as he held the little note firmly and read it over again.

It had to work. It was the only thing he had, and his entire future, their entire futures, depended on it.

Chapter 47

THE RED SPORTS CAR pulled in next to his blue SUV, and Aaron rose from the rocker on the porch with trepidation in his heart.

Chris emerged, gave a slight, embarrassed wave, and jaunted up the twisting path to greet his brother. He glanced sideways at the old typewriter nestled in among broken ferns but said nothing about it. When he reached the porch, he stood silently for a brief moment, then spoke, glancing off down the bank. "Hi."

"Hi. I got mad at the writing the other day." Aaron gave a brief, awkward laugh, realizing the situation wasn't exactly funny. He felt foolish explaining himself further.

Chris waited.

Aaron looked at his brother, the self-deprecating pose, hands thrust into his pockets, lips twisted as he bit the inside of his mouth. This was his big brother, the person who should have been his mentor and friend. Instead Chris Latimer looked out of place and awkward, afraid of what Aaron might say next.

Aaron swallowed the old animosity, and vowed to make this as easy for Chris, and also for himself, as he possibly could. "I'm ready to talk," he said. "And I apologize for making it so hard all these years."

Chris let out a held breath. "Well, okay, so you said on the phone. That sounds good."

They stood staring at each other, neither knowing how to begin.

"I made dinner," Aaron said. "I thought that might make it less awkward. At least we can pretend we're chewing when we can't think of what to say."

Chris sputtered a nervous laugh and followed his brother into the camp. Spaghetti was boiling on the stove, and Aaron turned the burner down and lifted a strand onto a fork, testing it by slurping it into his mouth. "It needs a few more minutes. Do you want a beer?"

"Sure."

He handed Chris a can from the refrigerator, and Chris politely thanked him. They stood in silence until Aaron said, "How are your sons?"

"Great, great," Chris said with forced enthusiasm. "Rory's showing a real interest in the computer."

"What grade?"

"He's in fourth. He seems to have a knack for it, you know, besides just playing games and searching the web. And Jeff made it to the school spelling bee. We went to see him compete."

"How did he do?"

"Uh, not bad. He made it through the first couple rounds."

Aaron nodded and stirred the spaghetti.

"I'm proud of them," Chris said, "even if they aren't really scholars. Veronica does a great job with them."

"She seems like a good mother, Chris. I'm glad for you."

Chris showed a slight animation. "Yeah, it's funny how we just kind of drifted together. We went out for a while, then all of a sudden we were engaged, then married. Then, suddenly, kids. It's funny when you look around and see where you are, without any planning or anything."

It was obvious to Aaron how different they were. He had trouble recalling a single decision of his life that hadn't been made with great, deliberate plotting. He wondered briefly which method was really the right one, and decided it was his way, definitely. He wouldn't have Connie if he had left it to chance. He wouldn't be a writer or have achieved success so quickly if he hadn't planned and researched every career move. Even Egan had been planned for, anticipated, and solidly rejoiced over.

"Of course, I realize she isn't very educated or anything," Chris said humbly of his wife. "Not like Connie."

Aaron stopped stirring and looked at his brother. "I didn't marry Connie because she's educated."

"Oh, I know, I know."

"She's not some investment," Aaron muttered.

"No, of course not," Chris gestured forcefully, "but you wouldn't have picked someone like Veronica."

It was true. Aaron never would have settled for the simple, good-hearted redhead and her silly, kindly nature. For some reason, the admission filled him with shame.

"How is work?" he asked, changing the subject.

"Good." Chris nodded to emphasize his answer. "Rob has asked me to update the website for the store, so I'm learning how to program now. So far it's fun."

"Really? That's good, Chris. You'll be good at that."

His brother smiled slightly. "Yeah, I think I will be. Veronica's proud. She keeps telling everybody." He was still holding his unopened beer can, and he twisted it in his hands now, agitated and uncomfortable. "Of course, all this isn't really why you asked me here."

"No," Aaron said. Another silence descended.

"Look, Aaron," Chris said finally, "I appreciate you making the gesture to have me here, I really do. I just don't know what to say to you."

"Yeah, we've been hating each other for so long. Old habits die hard."

There was a pause while Chris popped the top of his beer can and took a swallow. Then he said very quietly, "I never hated you." Aaron didn't answer. Chris added, "But I was jealous of you."

"I know." Aaron tested the spaghetti again and dumped it into a plastic colander, shaking it slightly to remove the excess water. "I thought we ought to talk about that."

He had taken plates from a cupboard and placed them on the table. He gestured to them. "Help yourself."

Chris busied himself spooning spaghetti onto his plate, ladled some canned sauce from the saucepan on the hot stove burner, and sprinkled it liberally with grated cheese. He took a seat at the table. Aaron had set out bread and butter and a lettuce and tomato salad and had moved his latest accumulation of crusted cans and dirty dishes and silverware to the counter. The tabletop was clean; the rest of the kitchen was cluttered with five weeks' worth of debris.

"This looks good," Chris said, studiously avoiding the messy counter and eyeing the food on the table. "Thanks for making it." He sipped his beer.

"So, you were saying you were jealous," Aaron prompted.

"Yes, you were always better at everything," Chris said hesitantly. "Not that that's a good excuse for jealousy. But you were pretty hard to live with at times."

Aaron remained quiet, picking up forkfuls of food and chewing silently.

"Especially since I was older," Chris said. "It was embarrassing to have a little brother who could beat me up. Who beat me at everything."

"I'm still bigger than you," Aaron said. "Are you still jealous?"

Chris smiled weakly. "No, I guess not. I have a pretty good life. I guess there isn't too much I'd trade."

Chapter 48

THEY ATE IN SILENCE for a few more minutes. "So, you do know why I haven't been the devoted younger brother all these years," Aaron finally said. It was hard to keep the sarcasm out of his voice.

"Would you like to tell me?" Chris answered politely.

"Don't you know?" Aaron was becoming irritated. He was willing to forgive, but for God's sake, was Chris going to sit there and pretend he didn't know what had gone wrong between them?

Chris lifted another forkful of spaghetti into his mouth, chewed, and swallowed. "I know you always treat me like a leper. I guess it's up to you to explain it."

Aaron jumped up from the table with such ferocity that his chair tipped over backward and crashed to the floor. "Great, Chris. I'll do that. I've been really irritated all these years because you tried to kill me one day. Does that clarify it for you?"

"Kill you?" Chris lowered his fork to his plate and cowered back in his chair.

"Kill me! Drown me! And then went on to live your life as if the incident never happened."

Chris was silent, watching his brother with terrified eyes.

Aaron righted his chair and sat down heavily. "I see," he muttered, "that you're still afraid of me." He helped himself to bread, began mopping up sauce with it, and took a big bite. "Would you care to comment on what I just said?" he asked Chris with exaggerated politeness.

Chris put his elbows on the table and hid his face.

Aaron groped for words, and when they came, he tried, harder than he had ever tried in his life before, to say them calmly. "Chris, I believe that when we were young teenagers, twelve and thirteen, to be exact, you tried to drown me here at

Spruce Lake. I had to fight you to get lose, and I kicked you and hurt you, and you let everyone believe that I started it. Does that sound familiar to you?"

The muffled sound coming from Chris Latimer might have been a yes; Aaron couldn't be sure.

In an even gentler tone, he said, "Chris, take your hands away from your eyes. You never look at me. Talk to me, would you?"

He heard Chris make a snuffling sound, and closed his eyes against the emotion that was welling up inside his own throat. When he felt composed, he opened his eyes and saw Chris looking at him. Chris had removed his glasses. His eyes were damp, and he was holding a soggy handkerchief to his nose. "Yes, it's familiar," he said.

"And I have never been able to forgive you for that," Aaron finished.

"Why should you?" Chris asked. "Why on earth should you forgive something so unforgivable?" The words ended in a moan of self-contempt.

"Nothing's unforgivable," Aaron muttered.

Chris was overcome with emotion. A small sob escaped him. "You saved me that day. After what I did, you brought me to shore-"

"I didn't realize you had done it," Aaron said. "I don't know what I thought, that there was some kind of sea monster in the lake, I guess." He gestured meaninglessly.

"If you had realized, would you have saved me? Maybe if you had known, you would have let me drown."

Aaron couldn't answer, for he didn't know. Would he have allowed his own brother to die? Would he have stayed there, treading water, watching Chris doubled over in agony, fighting for breaths, until Spruce Lake claimed him as Eastern Bog had claimed Virginia Dunn?

Aaron turned away in shame. He was no better than the brother he had despised all these years. No better than Eddie Safford.

"Forgive me, Aaron," Chris said. The catch in his voice made Aaron look at him. There was real pain on Chris's face, anguish in his eyes. "I'd like to say it was a kid's prank, and that I never would have let it go on, but I'm not sure. I really don't know. I know I was furious with you. I thought it would serve you right if I scared you a little, made you fight for your life. When you couldn't get loose, I was shocked, just . . . shocked that I could actually beat you, and I held on tighter. It was the first time I ever really had the best of you." He looked down and muttered at the table, "Who knows how it would have ended if you hadn't been strong enough to fight your way loose."

"God, Chris," Aaron said.

"I've tried and tried to talk to you. I've hated myself all these years."

"Yeah, that's what I wanted you to do." Aaron rose from the table and walked to the porch door where he could look out at the gray dusk over Spruce Lake. "And you never took another risk in your whole life."

"I know you've always despised me," Chris said. "And I don't blame you for that."

"I've always hated your weakness in never holding your own against me."

"I never tried to after that. It scared me that I had come so close to drowning you. That kind of power is the last thing I'd want."

Aaron turned back to look at his brother's distressed face. "And it crossed my mind that you might try it again someday," he said. As he spoke the words, he admitted to himself the other feeling he had harbored all these years: fear of his own weak brother. He exhaled painfully. "I don't want this animosity between us anymore, Chris. I don't want it any more than you do."

Chris was nodding. "I'm glad. I'm sorry. I used to worry that it would ruin your life."

"It didn't," Aaron said shortly.

Chris smiled thinly. "No, you have Connie. Boy, she's beautiful. And that little Egan is smart as a whip."

A lump formed in Aaron's throat. His family, the people he had left for weeks at a time just to prove his own inadequacy. "I guess it will help us both that we're talking," he said to Chris.

"I hope so. I never saw you look so bleak as when Dad was lecturing you that day."

"You were in your room upstairs, weren't you?"

"I was watching from the stairs. I kept wanting to interrupt, but I was scared to death. I've never been very brave, you know. It would have been one more screw-up for me, one more righteous act for you. I couldn't tell him. He would have held it over me from then on. I've been wishing all these years that I had."

"How did it start, Chris?" Aaron asked his brother. "What ever happened that made you hate me that much?"

Chris shrugged. "It was no one thing, and I was wrong, anyway. I was jealous. The way Dad was always proud of you, and Mom would make excuses for me."

"Like the day we found the snakes."

"Oh, the snakes," Chris said. His eyes met Aaron's. "That was one. I did hate you for that, I guess."

"For . . . ? What do you mean?"

"Jabbing it in my face, trying to taunt me with it." Chris said the words softly, hesitating.

Aaron stared at him. "Taunt you? I didn't do that. I picked up the snake on a stick so it wouldn't get away and told you to run for Dad."

"You jabbed it right in my face, Aaron," Chris said with certainty. "You enjoyed seeing how it terrified me."

The snake had hung on the stick, yes. And Aaron recalled twirling the stick, watching the reptile twist in the air. He closed his eyes. *Had* it been like that? Had he intentionally thrust it close to his frightened brother's face to torment him? It seemed familiar. And Chris had stepped back in fear, getting a . . . .

Aaron's eyes flew open. "A sliver." His words were hushed, a revelation. "You got a sliver in your foot, trying to get away."

Chris nodded and said more boldly, "And you laughed."

And Chris had cried. Not just then, but other times, too, a sad, weak cry, longing for a brother who might be a pal instead of a torturer. No wonder Virginia Dunn's sad, mournful cries had seemed so familiar.

A groan escaped Aaron's throat. Shame flooded him as the memory crystallized. "Chris, I . . . I had actually forgotten that. I'm sorry. I was a jerk."

Chris shrugged. "You were a kid and so was I. I can accept it now. I had a hard time with it then." He glanced at Aaron, his eyes clear and steady. "It doesn't matter anymore," he said. "It was a long time ago. And I'm not jealous of your life or your job or anything. I just want to get along."

Aaron cleared his throat and picked up his dirty plate from the table, piling it on the counter with a month's worth of accumulated garbage. "I think we have more to talk about than I realized," he said quietly to his brother. "Did you bring your things to stay over? It's a long drive back."

"Yeah, I did," Chris said. "They're in the car. I didn't know if I would end up staying."

"Do you want to? I think you should. We can keep talking."

Chris nodded and excused himself and went to his car to get his bag. Aaron leaned over the kitchen sink and exhaled a large breath. He had taunted his brother. He had ridiculed and teased him and then took offense when Chris felt the world might be a better place without him.

Aaron went to the living room and gazed up at the row of high school and college trophies that meant so much to his father. Reaching up, he removed one, then another. *AARON LATIMER – Most Valuable Player, AARON LATIMER – Coach's Award For Dedication.* Fun for Chris to vacation at Spruce Lake and have these monstrosities glaring down on him the whole time. No wonder he made reservations for his family in Speculator.

Aaron picked up a third trophy: *Sportsmanship Award.*

Grimacing, Aaron found the cardboard carton he had used to transport his groceries and lifted in as many trophies as would fit, then closed the box and shoved it under a table, out of sight. He would need another carton for the rest and would take them home to Syracuse and store the lot in his attic.

Someday maybe Egan's kids would be proud to brag about their grandpa. But for right now, Aaron knew, it was time to grow up.

Chapter 49

THE GOLD LETTERS on the glass door panel read *Edward R. Safford, Attorney*. Aaron hesitated and drew a big breath, then pushed the door open and entered. A receptionist took his name and returned moments later to tell him that Mr. Safford was ready for him. He had set aside the usual half hour for an initial consultation. Aaron glanced again at the gold embossed business card he had just picked up from the receptionist's desk. *Estate Planning: Wills, Trusts, and Probate*. He pocketed the card and went through to the inner office of Eddie Safford.

Aaron looked around the office curiously. Leather bound volumes lined one wall, a big map of the county was posted on another. Two computers and an array of papers and cardboard files crowded the desk, and filing cabinets were jammed in a row against the window. There were no personal effects, no mementoes, no family photos. There was one stained coffee mug on top of a file cabinet and a jacket hung on a hook on the door.

Eddie Safford stood to greet him, removing a pair of black rimmed eyeglasses and motioning him into a chair. "Ed Safford," he said, extending his hand. "What can I do to help you?"

So this was the man, the boy, who had been so anxious to marry Virginia Dunn. Aaron wondered if he would have become a lawyer if Ginny had married him when they were both so young. He doubted it, but then again, Ginny was a strong force. She might have been the kind of wife who pushed and prodded and supported her man fiercely. He wondered if Eddie Safford was married now. He suspected not.

"My name is Aaron Latimer," he said. They shook hands, and Aaron sat down. "I'm here because of something rather unusual." He paused and considered the carefully worded explanation he had planned. "I'm a photo journalist, and I've become interested in the case of a girl's death at Big Trout Lake a number of years ago."

Ed Safford's face drained of color and his lips went slack.

"You know who I mean, of course, Virginia Dunn."

"Yes?"

"You knew her well, didn't you?"

"Yes, I knew her."

"You loved her, right?"

Safford had regained some composure and settled himself in his leather chair. "Where is this leading, Mr., um, Latimer?"

"I understand Ginny didn't really die in Big Trout Lake," Aaron said bluntly. "She actually drowned in Eastern Bog and her body was carried into Big Trout by the current. Isn't that correct?"

"I don't believe I've heard that theory before."

"Well, it's based on new evidence that has just come to light."

"New evidence?" Safford's eyes never left Aaron's face.

"Mr. Safford, to be perfectly honest with you, I know a lot about that night. I don't intend to write an article about it; it doesn't need to become public. But I do need your complete cooperation."

Ed Safford passed his tongue across suddenly dry lips and rose from his chair. "I'm sorry, Mr. Latimer, but I'm not sure how I can help you. The police did a thorough investigation of Ginny's death at the time. I knew her well, and it was tragic, but I can't see how going through it all again-"

"Sit down," Aaron said.

"I beg your pardon?"

"I have something I think you should see." As Eddie Safford lowered himself into his chair again, Aaron pulled out the copy he had made of the lined scrap of notebook paper. He had placed it inside a clear plastic sleeve and now handed it over to the man who had written it ten years before.

"See how it's dated there?" He pointed to it, helping Eddie Safford to see the date. "And that's your signature down below. It says you wanted Ginny to meet you the night she died." He watched Safford read the words scribbled in his own handwriting: *Ginny, midnight tonight, down at our rocks. Keep it just between us! I love you! Eddie.*

Eddie was breathing shallowly. He looked, indeed, as if he had seen a ghost. "Where did you get this?" he asked hoarsely.

"Where I got it is immaterial. I have the original elsewhere and access to all your other notes, too. The important thing right now is that I know you never told the truth about that night."

"What is it that you want? I really don't understand-"

"I want you to tell the truth. Was it intentional? Did you *mean* to kill her?"

"Who are you?" Ed Safford rasped. "Is this some dirty plan for an exposé of some kind? Do you think that just because you have a note that could have been written by anyone, you can come in here and make accusations?"

"You know how Ginny died, Mr. Safford."

"Mr. Latimer, I think you need to leave right now." Safford's voice became suddenly quiet, as if he had just recalled the receptionist on the other side of the door. "For God's sake, let Ginny Dunn rest in peace."

"How can she rest, Mr. Safford? Everyone thinks she took her own life. You and I know that isn't true. Somehow, she fell off your boat. She drowned. Was it because you couldn't save her? Or did you push her under?"

Ed Safford gasped. "I don't think-"

"No, you didn't think. You were a terrified young kid. You probably couldn't believe what was happening. You lost control and killed her, or maybe it was an accident, and it never occurred to you that trying to cover up the details of her death would come back to haunt you ten years later. But you've been living with it all this time." His voice softened. "It's been hell, hasn't it?"

"Where did you find this note?" Ed Safford asked. The belligerence had faded from his voice, replaced by quiet fear.

"You left it on Ginny's windowsill, didn't you?" Aaron said. "Just as you always did? Maybe you even went to her cottage to retrieve it and couldn't find it. Believe me, I don't necessarily want to make your life more uncomfortable, Mr. Safford, but I want to know the truth."

"Who are you?" Safford asked. He was clenching the plastic sleeve in his hand, clearly wishing Aaron Latimer far, far away.

"Mr. Safford, my motive isn't publicity. I don't even intend to write about this. But for Ginny's sake, I want you to meet me at her cabin at Spruce Lake."

"For Ginny's sake? Ginny's dead."

"Mr. Safford. You don't have much choice in this. If you don't meet me there this Saturday, this note of yours will be all over the Internet by Sunday. It won't take long for someone to decide to question you officially, and then you really will have problems." It was a bluff; he would never do that to Connie.

Aaron watched Ed Safford's face, gauging his reaction.

"What is your motive? I don't understand-"

"The truth; that's all I want from you. Meet me there. You don't have a choice.

"I'm sorry," Aaron added, looking at the ashen face of the man sitting before him. "You just have to trust me. As much as Ginny trusted you that night."

Ed Safford was staring at him with terrified eyes.

"Saturday afternoon," Aaron repeated. "One o'clock at the Dunns' cottage. You remember where that is, right?"

Safford nodded mutely, clutching the plastic sleeve with the scrap of paper in it, his innocent little love note to a girl who had been dead ten years. He found his voice as Aaron stood to leave the office. "Why now?" he asked, his words scratchy with fear and distrust. "What do you expect to get out of this?"

"It's not for me," Aaron said. "You need to do this for Ginny."

Chapter 50

IT WAS LATE SATURDAY MORNING. Connie was fitting cartons, bags, and suitcases into the trunk of her car and barely listening to her daughter prattling on about her last horseback riding lesson the day before. Egan had enjoyed learning how to groom and saddle a horse and had loved the excitement of riding Kumquat, the gentle horse she'd been assigned.

"I'm an equestrian, Mom," she said now.

"I know you are, baby," Connie replied.

"Can we get a horse?" Egan asked.

"I don't see where we'd keep it, Egan."

"I'll miss Kumquat," Egan mused. But she was eager to get home to her Syracuse friends and more than willing to take a side trip to Spruce Lake to stay with her dad. Egan had a million exciting things to tell him. This afternoon would be her last dance class, and the children had prepared a special performance for all the moms and dads. "Will Daddy be able to come, Mommy? I want him to see me dance."

"No, honey, not this time, but we'll show him the video." Connie placed another carton into the trunk. There seemed more now than when they had arrived. Well, she could use the space on the front and back seats, too.

"Can Justin come, then?"

"No, Justin's very busy, Egan. He works on Saturdays." She turned her full attention to her little girl. "Would you want Justin to be there?"

"Well, somebody should come to see me dance."

Connie heard the frustration and recognized it. "I'll be there, Egan, like I always am."

"I wish Daddy were here."

"I do, too, sweetie." She did. She missed Aaron, had missed him every day during the last six weeks, and missed him still.

What crazy notion had come over her to insist on a separation that she had not enjoyed one bit?

She hoped he would be welcoming when they arrived at the lake, that he would forgive her indiscretion with Justin. Why had she let the man kiss her? How could she expect Aaron to understand? She knew she should have been more forceful with Justin; she should have been more outraged, more angry.

Well, he had caught her in weakness. His affection for her was genuine and she knew that. And hers for him . . . . If not for Aaron, she admitted to herself, she could have become interested in Justin Rime.

She knelt beside the little girl looking up at her with wide open eyes. "I will be there to see you perform, honey, and we'll leave right after and get dinner along the way so we can tell Daddy all about it tonight. He'll want to know every detail. And we'll show him the movie." She planned to film the whole performance on her camcorder. She'd stand against the back wall, out of everyone's way, and resign herself to looking like a doting stage door mom. Well, so what? There were worse things.

"Do you want me to get my toy suitcase?" Egan asked now.

"That's a good idea," Connie said. Egan began to run inside. "Did you keep a few things out, Egan? For the next few hours and the ride to the lake?"

"Just my bear and some books."

"Okay, let's pack your toys then. The sooner we get this car filled, the sooner we go see Dad."

Egan grinned and ran into the building for her toy sack.

Connie looked across the street at the other Victorian houses there. Sweeping lawns, nicely kept gardens. Saratoga was a pretty town, and she admired its cleanness, its history. Traffic was heavy, but she loved the excitement and feel of city living.

But her choice had been to pay up the rest of the two month lease and skip out early to join her husband at a wooded cabin with no decent shower, no cable television, no museums or cultural centers or theatres within a half hour's drive. Connie grimaced, glad for her decision, hopeful that she would still feel glad after a few days roughing it in the wilderness.

She could picture Spruce Lake in her mind's eye, its black, swirling waters, the gray clouds floating above it.

She shook herself. Where had that image come from? It wasn't like that there. In spite of her own fear of the water, she had been there enough to know that Spruce Lake was pretty, its surrounding trees and woods picturesque. Then why this threatening image of darkness?

It was the dream she'd had the night before, she realized suddenly. She had forgotten it upon awakening, and it tumbled upon her now, surprising her with its vividness.

Egan had been drowning. Connie shuddered as she remembered the desperation on her little girl's face as the water sucked her under, her mouth open in a round ring, calling for help, a mournful peal only Connie could hear. And Connie couldn't swim. She couldn't swim!

Aaron was there, but his back was to the lake; he was trying to show Connie something, a colorful kite lying on the water's edge. He picked up the kite and let the string out carefully. The kite floated in the air at eye level, and Aaron invited Connie to join him.

She tried to get his attention away from the kite, to force him to turn and see their daughter struggling as the black, murky water closed over her head. But he was intent on showing Connie the kite. She could see him laughing while she mouthed her despair, and he wouldn't turn.

What could she do? If she raced into the water to save Egan, it would mean two drowning victims instead of one.

Turn around, she begged him, aware all the while that her mouth made no sound. She was impotent to help their struggling daughter.

We can fly it together, Aaron said patiently, *all of us.*

She needed to get his attention. She turned away suddenly and dashed down the dock. Her feet tripped in rubber flip-flops and she struggled up from her knees, oblivious to the painful scrape on her skin. She forced herself to keep running. The dock was long and splintery, and she could feel the rough boards under her feet as she pounded, pounded down the dock toward the end that was a pinpoint in the distance. Her breath was coming in sour gasps, and the end of the dock loomed. Just before she jumped, she turned her head to see the confusion on Aaron's face turn to fear. She pointed, gestured to Egan's small thrashing form just as she hit the water and felt it close like a shroud over her head.

Aaron dropped the kite and it hovered on the shoreline, pulled in and out by the rippling water. Water puddled in it, sinking it farther and farther below the surface.

Aaron was running after her, his strong feet eating the

endless dock, wondering what had overtaken her, calling her name. And then he glanced in the direction she had pointed and saw Egan.

As Connie plunged, terrified, deep into the dark, roiling waters, Aaron made a clean, perfect dive beside her, and surfaced inches from Egan's disappearing body. In a stroke, he had gathered up his little girl and swum back to his terrified wife, lifting her, too, pulling both of them effortlessly to shore. As soon as his hand touched her, Connie gave herself up to him. His arm was around her; she was safe.

And Egan was safe. Together they had saved her.

Chapter 51

LEANING AGAINST HER CAR, Connie flattened her hands against chrome and breathed out harshly. Reliving the dream had wrenched the breath from her. She recalled that she had awakened, clutching at the blankets and gasping for air, and had quickly put the dream away from her.

She faced it now.

Her terror was not only for Egan, fighting for survival in the deep water, but for herself as well. What if Egan really did fall into the lake or wander out too far? Who would save her?

She knew. Aaron would. Spruce Lake would be safe for them now, while Egan was young enough to be constantly supervised.

Would Aaron always be there for Egan? In twenty or thirty or forty years, would Aaron still be their crutch? Did she want him to be? Was that fair?

Connie's friends believed her capable, competent. Yes, in the jungle of the city, where a wild taxi ride could end your life in a split second. They would be astonished if they could see her paralyzed by woods and water. Some example for Egan to follow. She needed to change that.

She opened the back door of her car and shoved a canvas bag over to make room for Egan's toys. Something, maybe the memory of the dream, made the hair suddenly prick up on the back of her neck. No, it wasn't just the dream. She had the intuitive feeling that she was being watched.

She turned to look back at the apartment building and saw Justin Rime leaning into the shadows of the doorway. She breathed out in relief. He hesitated, then moved toward her. "Are you moving out?"

"Yes, I broke my lease. It wasn't hard right in the middle of track season."

He nodded. "They've probably already rented it. Did you ever get to the races?"

"No, we never did," Connie said. "We'll go some other summer."

From the blacktop, Justin lifted a cardboard carton filled with the books and supplies she had brought and a few she had accumulated during her six week stay. *Heart of the River* peeked out of the top of the box. He fitted the carton into her trunk. "You said you left him, Connie." His eyes questioned her.

Mutely, she nodded.

"What does that mean for you and me?"

"It means that if there's a fool in this scenario, I'm it." She forced a smile, gesturing toward the box of books. "Thanks for helping me."

"Think nothing of it." Still he stood there, waiting.

"We're going to the lake," she told him. "He's expecting us tonight."

Egan was returning with her suitcase of toys, and Connie smiled more naturally as she watched her happy child balancing the heavy case and lifting it to the trunk. Justin stood aside.

"Let me help you," Connie said.

"I can do it," Egan insisted. She thrust the case upward and it toppled into the trunk, needing only a little readjusting by Justin to fit its spot.

"Not bad, Egan," Connie said lightly. "You are quite a capable young lady."

"What time will we see Daddy tonight?"

"Pretty late, honey. You might fall asleep on the way. If you do, we'll wait 'til tomorrow to tell him about your lessons and your show."

Justin squatted to Egan's level. "I'll miss you, little girl," he said. "It will be lonely around here for Oboe and me."

She grinned at him and put her arms around his neck. "But you and Oboe can take care of each other," she said. She nestled her head on his shoulder. "Don't worry. Oboe is a good cat. He won't give you any trouble."

His eyes met Connie's. She turned her back and rearranged some items in her trunk, then slammed the lid down.

If Egan could skip the dance performance later this afternoon, Connie would be happy to leave right now, but she'd never do that to her daughter. She stepped around Justin and touched Egan's hair, then bent down to pick her up. "You're quite a girl, my Egan," she said.

She turned to Justin, her arms safely busy holding her wiggling child. "Good bye, Justin," she said.

Egan squirmed loose and ran back into the apartment.

"Just because he wants you to?" Justin asked. His voice was almost accusatory.

"No," Connie smiled a little. "It may look like acquiescence to you, but I had to gather all my courage to make this decision."

"You didn't decide anything," he insisted. "You're letting him do all the deciding."

"Justin," she said, "returning to Aaron is the best and wisest thing I can do. It's the only sensible thing." Aaron had been wrong, she knew, to change their summer plans, and they had plenty of things to work out, but distancing herself had only added to the tension. "Two wrongs never make a right," she added. It came out sounding flippant.

"He's getting it all his own way," Justin said. "He tosses a crumb and you respond. Your own happiness matters, too, Connie."

She laughed and turned away from him. "Yes, it does," she said, "Lots."

She entered the apartment and found Egan in the kitchen that was theirs for just a few more hours. Thankfully, for just a few more hours.

Egan was rummaging in a drawer. She removed a set of measuring cups, then opened the cupboard for the box of macaroni and cheese she had requested as their last Saratoga lunch. Something easy, Connie had told her. Something we can make quickly so we can eat and pack and finish up our errands, and then get to your performance, and leave for the lake right after to see your dad.

Egan lined up the box of macaroni, the measuring cups, two plates, two forks, and a wooden stirring spoon, and grinned at her mother. "Come on, Mom," she said. "Get the big pot and fill it with water so we can make lunch."

Connie smiled. "Looks to me like you have it almost ready yourself." She picked up the box and started to tear it open.

Egan grabbed it. "I'll do that part. I like to open it. Will you get the big pot, please?" It was in a high cupboard which Egan couldn't reach.

"All right," Connie said, "Miss Take Charge."

Egan laughed and pulled back the tab on the box of prepared food. A capable, confident child, Connie thought, the product of two people who loved each other enough to create not only this beautiful little girl, but the warm, loving home that nurtured her. Two people who would work out whatever their differences were, not just for the sake of the child, but for the sake of all that was good and right in the world.

Connie filled the pot with water and set it on the stove burner, then opened the refrigerator. "Here's the milk we saved," she said. "Go ahead and measure it. You need one fourth cup. The rest you can drink."

Tonight she would see Aaron again and they would make a new start on the vows they had made nine years before. A thrill chased down her spine at the thought of Aaron's arms around her, Aaron's eyes looking into hers. But tonight was hours away. For right now, it was Egan she needed to embrace.

She smiled at the look of concentration on Egan's face as she selected a measuring cup, poured out the milk, and set it aside on the counter.

Eight more hours, Connie said to herself. She laughed aloud and Egan gave her a questioning look.

She grinned down at her little girl. "I think I'm going to start teaching you to cook, Egan," she said. "There are all kinds of things it's useful to know when you're grown up. That would be a good place to start. And when we get to the lake, Daddy is going to teach us both how to swim. Wouldn't you like that?" She smiled broadly at Egan. Eight more hours and she would be at the lake, playing the part of the woodsman's wife, Aaron's wife.

"Swimming will be fun," Egan said. "I'm glad we're going to the lake. I think Daddy must really miss us." She checked in a drawer for two paper napkins.

"He does miss us," Connie said. She bent down and kissed the top of Egan's head. Her little sage. It was a simplistic view, but it was true. Aaron missed them, and they missed him. It all boiled down to that.

Chapter 52

THIS WAS THE LAST TIME Aaron would stand on the rocky ledge of Spruce Lake's eastern shore and wait for Ginny. Ed Safford stood beside him.

Safford had arrived in a small, rented outboard motorboat, pulling into the shoreline of the state land and cutting his motor. He anchored the boat and climbed out, stalking toward the Dunn camp. Aaron could see the agitation in his step and the glint of the pistol he carried before the two men were twenty-five feet apart. "I hope you're not planning on using that thing," he called.

"Do you think I'm a complete fool?" said Safford. "I wouldn't meet you here unarmed. It's up to you whether I use it or not." His eyes were black, his glance darting about the forest. It was obvious that Eddie Safford felt nervous. Why wouldn't he? Living with such knowledge for ten years. Aaron wondered if Ed still loved Ginny, if he had ever grieved for her.

"You won't need it," Aaron said. He told Ed Safford a little of what had gone on that summer and ignored the suspicion and distrust on Safford's face. "You need to take care of this," he told the lawyer. "When you see her, you'll know why you had to come. She's been waiting for you; you need to finish it."

"Finish it?" Eddie fingered the gun, staring at Aaron. Aaron felt cold sweat prickle on his back.

"You're a screwball," Eddie said.

Aaron had expected Eddie to show skepticism, even incredulity, so Safford's cynical look didn't surprise him. Hadn't he had his own doubts six weeks ago? There were still moments when he wondered if he might have imagined the whole thing. But no, he had her photograph; he had her sketch. Her touch was burned into his skin.

What Aaron hadn't expected was his own agitation over this meeting, that he would be so filled with confusion and, if he were honest, a weird kind of jealousy. He needed to be free of Ginny, but he wasn't sure he really wanted to lose her.

He glanced again at the young man facing him. This was the man that Virginia Dunn had loved and wanted to marry. Barely thirty years old, he was good-looking, intelligent, and successful, and he had come today, maybe out of fear of that innocent little note going viral on the Internet, but also, Aaron suspected, out of curiosity, and, he hoped, out of a not-quite-dead love for Ginny.

"So where is she?" Ed Safford asked cynically. He gestured around the woods.

"She'll be here. She knows I went to find you," Aaron said. "I told her I thought you'd come because you've suffered as much as she has. I hope that's been the case."

Ed said nothing. Agitation convulsed his face. He clutched the pistol tightly.

"She needs to forgive you," Aaron said.

"I didn't kill her," Eddie said. His voice trembled.

"Well, how did it happen then?"

Ed Safford did not answer, of course. Why would he admit anything to the stranger who had forced his hand?

Aaron looked at him with pity. "Anyway, you're responsible, one way or another. You have to own up to that."

Eddie's fingers tapped the pistol nervously. "No, I'm not."

"Are you telling me you didn't ask her to meet you that night?"

"I didn't say that. I'm just saying that it's a little hard to believe what you've been telling me. A ghost? I don't believe in ghosts." He peered into Aaron's face. "I hope you're just a harmless crackpot, Mr. Latimer, because I'd hate to-"

Aaron interrupted him angrily. "Ginny has been suffering for ten years because of you. At least have the decency-"

"Do you think I haven't suffered?" Safford bit the words off, furious and agitated. "I loved Ginny." He ran a wild hand through his hair. "I didn't kill her. I don't know where you got that note or what your plan is, but *I didn't kill her.*"

"All right," Aaron muttered. What was the point in fighting Ed Safford? Aaron made his tone resemble sympathy. "Are you married?" he asked.

Safford shook his head, clearly attempting to control his flaring temper and raw nerves. "No, I spend most of my time on work. Right now it's enough to be a damn great lawyer, and I am one."

Aaron gave him a quizzical look. "Don't count on that being enough."

Ed shrugged. "Get to the point. What is this? A hoax or trap of some kind?" He glanced around the woods. "Whatever you-"

He never finished his sentence. Aaron heard his sudden intake of breath, a loud rasping. He felt the familiar cold stillness in the air and glanced at Ed Safford, and then in the direction Ed was looking.

Through the woods, advancing easily over the sharp stones, pine needles, and brittle dead leaves, and staying very cautiously in the shade, came the ethereal figure of Virginia Dunn, dainty, delicate, and pulsing with life. Her gown was pale blue, her hair golden, her feet bare, her eyes wide with anticipation.

Eddie was breathing heavily now, nearly collapsed by Aaron's side, his hand gripping the low limb of a nearby tree for support. Aaron thought with a pang of jealousy that Ginny had never looked more lovely.

She spotted them and stopped. Her fingers came up to cover her lips, and her mouth broke into a wide smile. She looked at Aaron and then at Eddie and came forward again, faster, as sure-footed as a deer on the leafy forest floor.

"Ginny," Eddie breathed. "My God, Ginny." He peered at Aaron, his face pale. "She is exactly as I saw her last." The gun was forgotten; it fell to the forest floor with a muffled thud. "How did you do this? What-" He turned back to Ginny and took a hesitant step forward. Aaron Latimer, too, was forgotten.

Ginny ran to Eddie, and he embraced her. Aaron saw the shock on Eddie's face as he touched her cold, burning skin and then gripped her more fiercely. He threw his arms around her and whirled her, and she threw back her head and laughed.

Aaron thought of the photograph he had taken of her with just that expression. The laughter then had been because of him, the smile for him.

Eddie stopped twirling her and held her away from him. "Ginny," he stammered, "my own sweet Ginny, how can this be?"

She raised a radiant hand and touched his cheek softly. Ed Safford grasped Ginny's hand. "I never stopped loving you," he said. "It's been terrible. How can I . . . I want to be with you, Ginny." He looked around him, at the steep ledge of rock, the cool, seductive waters. His gaze caught the pistol, the sun's rays glancing off it, sparks darting from it as it lay invitingly on the ground.

He bent to the pistol, eager in his need, clutching Ginny with one hand, reaching for the gun with the other. His hand scrabbled impatiently over leaves and twigs. Aaron had seen the change wash over Eddie's face, knew how Ginny could affect a man, could make him contemplate things he'd never consider – except under her spell. Aaron stepped forward to grab the gun before Eddie could take hold of it.

But it was Ginny who stopped him. "Not that way," she said. They were the first words Eddie had heard her speak and he reeled backward at the hollow, musical quality of her voice. "Life is too good," she said. Her brilliant eyes pierced him. "I loved you, Eddie. You loved me. That's enough. You never meant for it to happen."

"But right now-" Eddie started.

She covered his lips with her hand. "Someday," she said, "when it's the right time."

Eddie glanced again at the pistol lying undisturbed on the earth, then took Ginny in his arms and kissed her. Years of guilt and pain sloughed from his face as he stared at the ghost of Virginia Dunn. Finally, with effort, he turned to Aaron, who was hidden in shadow, watching the girl long dead and the man who had never stopped loving her.

"How can such a thing be?" Eddie Safford asked.

"She's been waiting for you," Aaron said simply. He saw the love in Ginny's eyes, and devastation coursed through him, followed quickly by shame at his feelings. He had heard her song and felt the cold heat of her skin, had felt her tears dropping onto his face and running into his mouth, tasting of salt. He had consoled her and made her laugh and cried over her. He had loved her, too.

Aaron picked up the pistol, turned away, and started down the bank to the canoe that would take him back to his own camp. He understood the impulse overpowering Ed Safford, the need to be with Ginny, the way his mind would be spinning.

He could throw the gun far into the lake. It would break the surface and sink, sending rippling circles that would bubble, spread, and disappear. He could control Ed Safford's actions with that one small gesture. He hesitated and glanced down at the gun in his hand, feeling its smooth cold metal against his skin.

He turned back once and saw Eddie down on the earth, beseeching, gripping Ginny's hands in his, gazing into her eyes.

"I should have tried harder," he said. "I should have screamed for help, jumped in after you. When you fell, when you hit your head on those rocks . . . ."

"It wasn't your fault," Ginny said, her unearthly voice calm and sure.

Aaron heard the admission and felt a burden lift. Eddie Safford hadn't murdered Ginny; he'd been living a life of despair.

"I've relived it a thousand times," Eddie moaned. "I've never forgiven myself."

Ginny looked down at him, a world of peace reflected in her eyes.

"Forgive me," he begged. "Forgive me, Ginny."

It was seconds later that the wail rent the stillness of the sultry afternoon. "No!" screamed Eddie Safford. "No, Ginny!"

Just yards from his canoe, Aaron halted, arrested by the heartbreak in Eddie's cry.

Eddie came lurching through the woods, staggering toward Aaron. "She's gone. I just found her, and she's gone."

"I didn't-" Aaron said.

"You had her all summer, and you set me up . . . ." Eddie's wild eyes rested on the pistol Aaron held. "Give me my gun."

Cold fear crept over Aaron. He made no move. "I didn't set you up. I didn't realize she would . . . ."

Safford lunged at him, swiping for the gun.

Aaron backed away, holding the weapon firmly.

"I should shoot you," Eddie sobbed. "I should use it on you for doing this to me." He sank onto the dirt and pine needles of the forest floor. "She's gone," he whimpered. "She's gone again."

"Shooting me - shooting anyone - isn't going to solve anything," Aaron muttered. "Don't be a fool." He stood over Eddie, holding the pistol well out of reach.

When Eddie lunged suddenly and grabbed at Aaron's ankles, Aaron's knees buckled with the unexpected force. Eddie snatched at the gun, wresting it from Aaron's grip.

"Don't be a fool," Aaron repeated, but this time his words came quickly, a rasped breath. He backed away from Eddie Safford.

Eddie still crouched on the forest floor, doubled over in shock and pain. He held the pistol as if he'd never seen it before, then aimed it up at Aaron. His hand shook.

Aaron inhaled, motionless.

"What do I do?" Eddie moaned. "Use this on you? On

myself?" His eyes met Aaron's and held them. He let his hand drop; the pistol scraped the dirt floor of the forest. Then he flung the gun sideways. It skittered over a rock and lay still. He sought Aaron's face again and looked at him, breathing in ragged gasps. "Now what?"

"I guess we go on," Aaron said tiredly. He would burn Eddie's note when he returned to camp; Safford had suffered enough. He stepped into his canoe and untied the mooring ropes. He breathed deeply, waiting for his wildly beating heart to slow. Ed still sat in the pine needles; an occasional low moan was his only sound.

Exhausted, Aaron picked up his paddle and started to move slowly across the lake. Eddie Safford's low cries evened out, and Aaron watched him rake the underbrush for the gun. He found it, stood erect, and became very still.

Aaron stiffened, waiting in shock for an explosion that never came, then watched Eddie Safford walk to his small craft and drop the gun in. He climbed numbly into the boat and started the motor. The boat cruised slowly toward Sentry Pond, then dwindled to a speck near the channel. Its soft buzz disappeared and the lake was quiet.

Chapter 53

WHEN HIS FAMILY ARRIVED, dark had fallen and Aaron had turned on the porch lights. He heard the car before he saw it and was already in the parking area waiting when Connie rolled to a stop.

"Aaron," Connie said, as she tumbled out of the driver's seat. She threw her arms around his neck and pressed in close to him. "Dumb, dumb, dumb. I will never do that again. I didn't realize how stupid it was until, by my own foolish choice, I didn't have you around for a while. I was such an idiot. Six weeks wasted when I should have been with you."

Aaron felt physically and emotionally drained. Connie loved him and was willing to blame herself for their separation. Aaron knew with certainty that he was to blame, not Connie.

He held his wife, clinging to her, gripping her tightly as if she might evaporate into smoke at any minute. "I needed those weeks, though," he said, "to help me know what I want."

In the darkness, he felt her stiffen and sensed rather than heard the concern in her voice. She backed up a little and said, "What do you want then?"

"Well, you first of all. Hell, Connie, just you. The rest will fall into place. I've been going nuts thinking about this guy you met. I blame myself for that."

She pulled in close to him. "He was just a friend, Aaron."

He hugged her fiercely. "You've always told me the truth about everything, Connie. That's the one thing I've always counted on." He held her away from him and peered at her achingly familiar face. Even in the dark, he knew that her steady blue eyes gazed back at him.

"He was a nice person," she said gently. "A friend. He did kiss me, Aaron, but not because I wanted him to. I'm sorry it happened. Are you going to think about that every time you kiss me for the rest of our lives? Or are you going to let it go so that we can love each other the way we promised we would?"

She was very serious, staring at him, awaiting his response. It was his call to determine the tone of their entire future together.

"Did he know about me? That you're married to me?"

She smiled slightly. "Yes, he could tell by the fact that you were my favorite topic of conversation."

He pulled her to him and kissed her, thankful that he would have another chance with her. Judging her would have been ludicrous.

"I'm glad you didn't change your mind about our coming," Connie said. Her words were muffled, her face pressed against his shirt front.

"Nothing could make me change my mind," he said. He found her mouth again and kissed her fervently.

Connie stepped back finally and gestured toward the back seat of her car. "It's amazing she can sleep that way."

Aaron unstrapped Egan from the back seat, where she was surrounded by cartons and bags. She had slumped over in an impossible position; her mouth was slightly open and she breathed softly. Aaron hoisted his little girl gently into his arms while Connie grabbed a couple of bags from the trunk. She pressed close to his side, walking beside him up the path.

"We hit so much traffic on Route twenty-nine," she said. "It was slow." She glanced at Egan's soft cheek, nestling against her father's shoulder. "Poor baby. She slept the whole last hour." Her eye was caught by the gleam of metal glinting from the bank of ferns before the camp. "What's that?" she asked, peering into the darkness.

"My typewriter."

"Your typewriter."

"The writing didn't go that well."

"I guess not." They entered the camp, and she looked around in dismay. Dirty dishes were piled in the sink; his clothes and towels were strewn around. Empty cans made a grimy pyramid on the kitchen counter. The floor was littered with crumpled papers and dried bits of forest plants, pine needles, and dirt. He hadn't swept in weeks. "Have you been taking care of yourself, Aaron?"

"Good enough, I guess."

"What is this?" Her glance had landed on a pile of dried

vegetation, brittle and brown.

"Bracken shoots. I was going to eat them. I did eat a couple-They were fresher then."

She grimaced. "Are they safe to eat?"

"Supposedly."

She poked one finger at them curiously, picked up a bit of bracken and crumbled it in her fingertips, and then gazed at Aaron's face. "You look tired," she said.

He glanced into the rippled mirror that hung by the kitchen door. His reflection stared back at him, dark circles under his eyes, an unexpected thinness to his face. He looked as if he'd been on the verge of joining the dead. "It was hard to sleep," he said.

"Is this what you've been eating?" she asked, gesturing to the empty cans and dirty can opener.

He shrugged. "I had kind of a hard time this summer."

She swallowed guiltily. "Aaron, I'm so sorry. I was wrong to take such a silly, dramatic pose when we should have just talked to each other."

"Talking was never very productive," he said, shrugging. "I wasn't a great listener. You were right to make me see that." She was looking around the dirty kitchen with distaste and turned in surprise when emotion gripped his voice. "I'm glad you're here, Connie. It was pretty terrible without you."

She reached up to kiss him and gave Egan, still sleeping on his shoulder, a loving pat.

"I got a room ready for her," Aaron said huskily. "Come on up." Connie carried Egan's bags, placing her toy case within easy sight of her bed. She deposited a few things into Egan's dresser while Aaron changed his little girl into pajamas and tucked her into bed. She awakened just long enough to say, "Hi, Daddy," and kiss him with soft, warm lips.

"She won't know where she is when she wakes up," he said in concern.

"She'll be all right. I told her she'd be waking up at camp and to try all the bedroom doors until she found us." She leaned over to kiss her sleeping child. "Come downstairs," she said to Aaron. "I want to show you what I brought. Before the dance performance today, we did some shopping." They turned out Egan's lamp, but left the stairway light burning and descended hand in hand.

The evening was cool and he had lit a fire before their arrival.

225

He poked at it now, stirring the dying embers back to life, then stood before the hearth, watching his wife. Connie sat on the couch and opened a canvas bag she had carried from the car. She dug in it for a moment and held up a cookbook with a glossy cover. "*Woods Cooking*," she read. "It has all kinds of recipes for cooking peculiar things you find in the forest, like wild parsnip and skunk cabbage."

Aaron laughed. "That's not really necessary, Connie. There's a refrigerator and electricity, and a store right down the road."

"Wait," she said. "There's more." She dug in the canvas bag again and came up with a shoebox, pulling out a pair of hiking boots. She looked at them distastefully, but shrugged her shoulders and gave Aaron a wan smile. "My size. The outfitter's store said they'd be just the thing." She held up another pair, tiny orangey boots with rawhide laces.

"Well, I like the cut," Aaron drawled, "but my feet have grown since you saw me last."

Connie laughed. "I figure we'll try them out tomorrow maybe. Or maybe with luck we can put that off indefinitely. Maybe we should take a drive to the store first for groceries," she mused.

He smiled and tossed a thin maple stick onto the fire, watched the flame catch, and came to sit next to Connie. Gently he took the boots out of her hand, and removed the cookbook from her lap. He put his arms around her, tilted her head up with one finger, and kissed her, a long, lingering kiss. "I love you," he said. "None of these things matter, Connie. I love you exactly as you are. I don't care if you hike or swim or even if we vacation here. None of that means anything, as long as I'm with you."

"Ooh," she said, teasing, wiggling away from him. "Swimming; that reminds me." She rummaged in her bag and pulled out the skimpiest black bikini he had ever seen, with the outlandish price tag still on it. It was far more daring than anything he had ever seen on her. She held it up in front of her. "You like?"

He gave her an appreciative look. "I do. Not your usual style, is it?"

"New image," she said dryly.

"So you're telling me you're going to *swim* while you're here?"

Connie grimaced. "I'm considering it. I need a good teacher." She looked deeply into his eyes. "A really good teacher. I'm terrified, but I'll try. Egan, too."

He couldn't help smiling. "I volunteer. It's been years since I've had a swim in this lake."

"This whole summer . . . ?"

Aaron shrugged. "I have a lot to tell you."

Chapter 54

WELL," CONNIE SAID, shrugging off his words, "if we all swim together, it will be a family baptism of sorts." She peered at the swimsuit critically. "And then I figured it would look good for the dock. Now that summer is nearly over, I've decided to work on a tan." She glanced at him coyly. "This is the only occupied cottage on the lake, right? I'd never wear this in public, only for you."

She rumpled up the suit and threw it back in the bag, following it with the cookbook and hiking boots.

"Now where were we?" she said. She grabbed his face and pulled it close to her own, kissing him again and again. She was leaning back against the sofa cushions, pulling him almost on top of her.

"I screwed up, Connie," he murmured. "I'm going to fix it."

"We'll fix it together." Her familiar voice soothed him. "You sounded a little crazy when I called sometimes, Aaron. Maybe that was my fault."

He sat up, pulling her with him, holding her by the hand. "I have to tell you what's been going on this summer," he said. "It's been a very strange six weeks. I found out a few things about myself while I was up here, and they weren't all great. I've been very unfair to you and Egan."

She put a finger on his lips, avoiding his words. "It was me, too," she said.

"Well, I was stupid. I've always taken from you and not given much in return. I'm changing that."

She looked at him, surprised. "I think you're being too hard on yourself. It certainly hasn't all been bad. I just want you around a little more."

He swallowed. "I've already decided not to take any more travel assignments unless you can come with me," he said. "If you can't come, I won't go unless we agree on it. I don't want you to be alone anymore."

Connie leaned back, relaxing against the couch cushions, smiling. "That sounds really good," she said. "Maybe we can travel together a little. We could probably leave Egan once in a while. I guess I don't have to be mother-of-the-year. At least not every year." She became thoughtful. "I'm sorry we put her through this, though. It can't have made much sense to her. In a way, I wish we'd left well enough alone."

"And there's more," Aaron said doggedly. "My brother Chris. I asked him to come up again and we talked. He's bringing his family for a cook-out next week."

"Really?" Connie was surprised, but rushed to agreement. "That's great, Aaron. Whatever will help." She got up from the couch and wandered to Aaron's writing desk. Two or three wrinkled, finished pages sat among the pencils and overturned reference books. "How is the article? Did you finish it?"

"No."

She was standing before his desk, the typewriter obviously missing, several mugs with tea stains dried inside their rims standing where a completed manuscript should have sat. She gazed at the three little frames hanging above the desk. "What are these, Aaron? All the glass is cracked. This is a nice painting of the camp." She removed it from the wall and peered at it, carefully fingering the zigzag crack in the glass. "Who did it?"

He swallowed a lump in his throat. "A local artist. I bought it from a guy with a place over on Big Trout Lake. Foster Wolf, remember? I told you about him. The others . . . ." He paused. He wanted to tell her; he was willing to explain it all, but he hadn't yet figured out how to do it. "The others, well, there's a story behind them."

"A story?" She glanced at him briefly, then back at the framed display, ready to accept whatever 'story' it was he needed to tell her. He came to join her, putting his hands on her shoulders and nuzzling the back of her neck. She still held the painting. He could see in it the hazy shades of green and purple in the mountain behind his Spruce Lake camp and Virginia Dunn's small, compact signature.

"I love you, Connie," he breathed. "So much."

She turned her back to the pictures and snuggled into his arms, smiling encouragement at him. "I know. It will be fine, Aaron. We'll be okay."

Over her shoulder, Aaron glanced at the pictures on the wall.

They captured the light and reflected back his own taut image. Suddenly his breath caught in his throat and he squinted to see better. There was no Ginny gently touching the bark of a birch tree, looking as if she might smile at any moment, although the birch tree was there. There was no sketch of Aaron in his canoe, drifting on Spruce Lake while the sun set behind Colson Mountain. The drawing was glaringly blank. A photo of a tree and a blank sheet of white paper, both nicely framed behind cracked glass, hanging together above his desk, the manic art gallery of an obsessed madman.

He set Connie aside gently and moved toward the frames, peering closely, searching for a hint, however small, of what had been there before. There was none.

She was really gone then, and he was truly free from her. It was what he had wanted, but he couldn't shake the little sadness inside. She hadn't even said good-bye. She was so caught up in Eddie Safford's return that she had forgotten about Aaron Latimer and all he had endured, and almost thrown away, for her.

Connie reached up to kiss him. "You look so intense, Aaron. Let's go to bed. It's going on twelve."

"Wait, let me tell you first." He gestured toward the framed papers, toward the little watercolor Connie still held. "I told you there was a girl who drowned, not this summer," he stammered, "ten years ago. She painted this."

Connie glanced at the picture and nodded. "It's pretty."

"But she did a sketch, too," Aaron gestured toward the empty frame. "It was . . . ." He stopped, resting his hands on the tabletop, taking in a rasping breath.

"Aaron?" Connie set the watercolor down and went to him.

"It was of me. She sketched me in the canoe."

"Years ago, you mean."

"This summer."

There was a pause before Connie said, "Honey, you said she died years ago."

He ran an agitated hand through his hair. "She did." He stared at his wife. His eyes pleaded with her. "I know what you're thinking. It sounds insane. But I sat right there in those woods and watched her draw her . . . ." He wouldn't mention Ed Safford. There was no need to involve him. ". . . draw other things, other people."

"Aaron-"

"And this one," he pointed to the photo of the birch tree, its leaves crisply defined, "it was a picture of her. I took it. I photographed her."

The look in Connie's eyes disturbed him. He saw confusion there, pity, maybe fear.

"She's not there now, I see that," Aaron said. "I don't . . . There are others, though. Maybe . . . ." He rushed from the room, picked up the cardboard envelope of prints, and shook free the other photographs he had taken of Ginny. There were birch trees, rocks, ferns. There was a forest floor shimmering in sunlight, a sky as soft as a summer kiss. But no Ginny caught in time, sensual and eager, looking back at the camera. No Ginny with blonde hair cascading down her back, no wistful smile or laughing eyes. The five prints were scenery. Just that.

Connie had followed him and stood staring down at the phantom photos as they fell from Aaron's hands.

"They were good shots of her before," he said lamely. "I think they faded because she's gone now." Something else occurred to him. "But I can show you what she looked like. He found the photo album and turned to the picture of Virginia Dunn on her dock, smiling for the camera, the wind playing with her long hair.

Connie examined the photo and looked at Aaron. "It's just a photo of a girl, Aaron," she said quietly.

"Of Ginny," he said. "Virginia Dunn. And wait." Eddie's business card. Connie couldn't very well argue with something as tangible as that. He patted his pockets, thrust his hands in deep and came away empty. He knew which shirt he'd worn that day; he grabbed it from a kitchen hook and rummaged in the pocket. "On the mantle?" he muttered. His eyes searched there and the rest of the room. He lifted stacks of magazines and shoved cushions aside.

"Aaron," Connie said, "we need to get some sleep." Her voice was soft, caressing, the voice she might use to soothe an ailing child.

"But I know I had it," Aaron insisted. And there's more," he pleaded. "I want, I *need* to tell you so much more. I want you to believe me, Connie. I need that."

She put her arms around him and kissed him. "It will wait," she whispered. "You can tell me the rest tomorrow. Come up to bed. You're exhausted."

He allowed her to lead him to the stairs, but stopped at the bottom. "You're right," he said contritely. "I know it all sounds ridiculous to you. I'll tell you all the rest tomorrow. Let me just close up down here and I'll be up in a minute."

"Promise?" she asked with a smile. "I've been waiting six weeks for you."

He smiled back, reassuring her, and headed for the kitchen. His heart was breaking.

Chapter 55

SHE DIDN'T BELIEVE HIM, he knew. She was worried about his sanity; she even pitied him. With a heavy heart, he checked the stove burners and locked the living room door. Then he stared again at the two absurd papers under cracked glass in their little frames- the insane gallery he'd created above the space where his typewriter belonged.

He rehung Ginny's painting, relieved that it was as it had always been. He'd been in too much of a hurry when he had burned Eddie's note, too anxious to absolve him. But it had all happened, hadn't it? He had been in her cottage; he'd spoken to Eddie, had seen them reunited. He recalled the days staggering around the camp with the illness he had caught from Ginny's kiss. He was sure he hadn't imagined any of it.

He wandered back to the kitchen, where the clock said twelve fifteen. It was a quarter past midnight, the start of a new day.

Today, he thought, he would take his family out on the lake for some fishing and maybe pack some sandwiches for a lunch. The loons might appear, floating companionably, and maybe they'd watch them dive silently for rock bass or bluegills. He would instruct his wife on baiting a hook and kiss her soundly when she refused, as he knew she would. Then he would bait it for her. Or maybe she'd forego the fishing altogether and just read a magazine. He couldn't care less if she really learned such skills.

And he would show his daughter a beautiful rocky outcropping across the lake where he believed deer sometimes came to graze. Egan would like that and would probably develop an interest in animals. They would go to the library in Syracuse together and check out some books . . . .

He put on his jacket and stepped out onto the long porch that overlooked Spruce Lake and the abandoned cottage across the way.

The air was still, and no wailing or moaning assaulted him; there was no flickering light that traveled up the dark beach and stopped, while a sad young girl searched vainly for the man who had abandoned her to a watery grave.

So, it was over.

Chris would be visiting next week, bringing his family for a barbecue, exchanging awkward conversation, and helping Aaron close up the camp for the winter. Their relationship would find surer footing, he knew, because they both wanted that. Connie was here of her own accord and still in love with him. He knew there would be no more running from her. Their daughter was sleeping peacefully and would grow to womanhood with two devoted parents to love her.

And his infatuation with Virginia Dunn had passed. She was apparently resting peacefully now. He was grateful.

It was a fair trade. Connie was back.

He still needed to confess the rest of his transgressions. He dreaded seeing the hurt on Connie's face and he worried she would think he had fabricated the whole tale – For what purpose? To make her jealous? To prove himself even more deranged than she already thought him?

Perhaps Connie was right to be concerned, he thought glumly. Maybe he'd been sick, feverish, had imagined the whole thing, created a living ghost to help him sort out the tattered pieces of his wretched life.

He knew that couldn't be so.

Aaron sighed, turned, and opened the porch door to enter the kitchen. When he became aware of the sound, he stopped, arrested. He sensed a slight hush on the air, and then a melody reached him, trilled trippingly like birdsong, a little minuet on the wind. It came over the water, trilling up a light octave, joyous and free.

He listened in perfect stillness until the tune reached its end, then grinned suddenly at the message that he knew was meant for him. She was happy. He had pleased her. He could rest.

Connie had not gone upstairs, but had returned to the kitchen, worried about him, checking on him. She stood waiting in the kitchen doorway, her arms crossed over her chest to ward off the evening chill. She gazed at her husband, her eyes wide with unabashed love.

"Are you coming?" she asked.

"Did you hear it, Connie?" She must have heard it; it was so clear, and she had stood right here. He was breathless, awaiting her response.

"Hear it?" She nodded and gave him a little smile.

"The song? It's what I need to tell you about."

"Song?" Connie said. "The wind, you mean. I hope it doesn't awaken Egan."

Aaron returned to the living room and checked the dying fire, then turned out the lights and took Connie's hand in his. Together they went up the stairs, and while Connie went ahead to their bedroom, he looked in on Egan and adjusted the blankets around her. He stood for a moment, gazing down on his daughter, making his silent vow.

"Connie?" He found her in bed, pretending to look through *Woods Cooking* , but her eyes darted around the room, searching suspiciously for mice or bats that might be lurking in the curtains or snickering in the sleeve of the jacket she would wear tomorrow.

"What, Aaron?"

He looked at his wife with such love and devotion that she put the book aside and stared at him. "Aaron, honey?"

He sat on the bed and pulled off his shoes, then lay down beside her. How would he tell her? He stretched out and smiled at her. He felt freer, younger, and lighter in spirit than he'd felt since he was twelve years old. "It wasn't wind, Connie," he said, "that noise downstairs." She might think it was a fiction he had concocted or his imagination at its most vivid, but he would know, he would always know.

Tomorrow he would tell her the rest, confide the drama of how he came to finally find himself. Virginia Dunn, he would tell her, had drowned here at Spruce Lake. It was a sad story. They believe it was a suicide, he'd say. He'd explain that she had some artistic ability, that she was pretty and a little headstrong. Aaron thought about these facts. Well, he knew she was pretty; he'd seen her picture in the old album. And he knew she was artistic, too. Foster had sold him that nice little painting of his camp.

He tried to remember more, but parts of the story seemed hazy now. Was she really a suicide? Aaron didn't think so. He thought maybe she loved life too much for that. But then again, how could he know for certain?

What had she been like, he wondered. Was she quiet? Fun-loving? Was she smart? How did she feel about her family? Had she ever been in love?

He thought he'd known those things, but he couldn't recall and it disturbed him. He felt compelled to share the tale with Connie, but how could he if he couldn't remember it himself? He felt sure there was more to Virginia Dunn's story.

But it could wait until tomorrow, he knew. Tomorrow was a new day.

He turned to his wife and touched her behind her perfect, small ear, feeling the warmth and life in her that always stirred him. She reached a hand to his face and let it linger on his cheek. He was shocked at the sudden burning desire that raced through him, a searing passion that touched his very soul.

A pretty young girl had drowned in the lake, and he wondered why that should seem so important to him. Her hair was long and she made beautiful pictures. But as for the details, well, only the wind really knew them.

A NOTE FROM THE AUTHOR

Are ghosts real? Is Ginny? Or is she just a figment of Aaron's imagination? Does she help him resolve issues within his life, or does he simply help himself?

I started *Quarter Past Midnight* one October, three days before Halloween, and had completed a 161 page double spaced first draft within four days. That's how excited I was about my ghost story! The text has undergone revisions and additions since then, but the basic story has stayed the same.

My family's Adirondack camp, built by my great grandfather and his four sons just after the turn of the century, does sit high on a mountainside overlooking a beautiful lake much like Spruce Lake. With a few changes, it became the setting for this book. Even if you don't know that camp specifically, the rustic beauty of the area and the tranquility and peace emanating from those deep waters will be familiar to anyone who has spent time in the Adirondack Mountains, one of the most beautiful places on earth.

Thank you for taking the time to read *Quarter Past Midnight*. If you enjoyed the book, I would urge you to tell your friends and leave a review on Amazon to guide other readers, and if you notice things in the book that you feel merit my attention, I invite you to contact me at janpresto@gmail.com. I love to hear from readers!

Happy reading!
Jan Prestopnik

THANK YOU

. . . to Amy Sponenberg, Rosemarie Sheperd, and Nathan Prestopnik, who read the 'almost final' draft of *Quarter Past Midnight* and shared many helpful and insightful remarks.

Also, thank you to Nate for creating the perfect cover design. You may see further examples of Nate's talent and professional expertise on his website, *imperialsolutions.com*.

Thank you to my husband Rich, once again, for helping with the technical aspects of preparing this book for publication. Without him, the manuscript would still be sitting unread in a file drawer. I do love to write, but technology has been known to baffle me.

Last, thanks to those who contacted me after reading my first novel, *Captive*. It was gratifying and humbling to receive phone calls and emails about the book, some from people I had never even met, and to sit with friends over a cup of coffee or a glass of wine discussing writing, reading, and, most surreally, my first published book. I am truly blessed by my large extended family and a slew of wonderful friends, most of whom, fortunately, love to read.

Thank you to all of you.

JAN PRESTOPNIK, a retired teacher of college, high school and middle school English and writing, is married and the mother of three grown children. Camping, traveling, teaching, performing, reading great books, and savoring the atmosphere of her beloved Adirondack Mountains are some of the things that have influenced her writing.

TITLES BY THIS AUTHOR

Available in Paperback, Large Print & Kindle editions

Captive (2014)

Quarter Past Midnight (2015)

Made in the USA
Columbia, SC
31 August 2018